THE SHIMMERING

Trials and Tribulations

ROBIN WITNEY

DEDICATION

Dedicated to my family and friends taken from us so early, especially my schoolfriend George and his sister, Gail, and my brother Brian and his wife Jenny—far too young to leave us so early, and to BP4u Solutions for providing brilliant editing, formatting, and publishing services.

CHAPTER ONE

I LEFT THE CHANCELLOR and Alistair to the tasks, following the arrest of the Prime Minister and his Cabinet. As I walked outside, a vehicle waited to take me to the Grosvenor Hotel. It would not take long to ensure that the Prime Minister's Cabinet would tell the truth about Operation Wipeout. The Prime Minister had a fine mind, and I had entered it to manipulate him into honesty; he was astute enough to know that he would incriminate himself if he spoke, so he remained silent. I entered his mind to compel him to speak. There was a grin on the Commissioner's face as the Prime Minister related the whole story and how the Chancellor was deliberately kept out of the picture.

I took my leave for Media Corporation's headquarters to address the nation about that morning's events, the need for a general election, and the interim steps in the run-up to the election.

Conrad was waiting to take me to make-up; rather unexpected, but I accepted it was necessary. Afterwards, I was taken to the studio, where I sat in a high-backed seat before a large desk. Several people milled around, checking light levels and sound. Someone pointed to the autocue and asked me to read. It was all becoming a pain, so I beckoned to Conrad, and he ushered them all away. "There will be one rehearsal, and then we will go live," I said. "I do not have the time for all this piddling around, and that is final."

Conrad had a word with the director, who said something into his microphone. The lights in the studio dimmed, and the spots illuminated the desk. The autocue started to roll. I looked into the camera and read the script which had been prepared for me. I was happy the rehearsal had gone well. The director gave me the thumbs up, and the whole speech went live to the nation. Conrad would have to later inform me of the nation's reaction to the revelations of the last few hours.

I had to go to the White House and then on to Anders Airfield to get everyone involved in Operation Wipeout into the truth-telling business and assist Rodbridge and Felbrig in the smooth takeover of the presidency.

I left Media Corporation's headquarters and went to pick up a verticular in Hyde Park to take me to Assington, then on to Washington. As I walked towards the subway leading under Park Lane and into the park, my attention was drawn by a motorcyclist who had mounted the pavement and was hurtling towards me. I entered his mind, which was set on killing me, and I had to act quickly. He was reaching for a shotgun, so I disabled his arms. The gun fell to the pavement, and the rider lost control of the bike—the front wheel probably hit something as it turned 90 degrees and came to an abrupt halt. The driver took off, flying like a ski jumper with his useless arms by his sides. He might have survived, had he hit the tailgate of the truck instead of the tail lift. His full-face helmet would have saved him, but it was crushed like a walnut and the noise as his neck snapped would haunt me for some time.

While he was airborne, I had looked into his mind for a clue on why he tried to kill me, but there was nothing; it had been wiped clean. None of my known enemies were capable of that, so it could only be Oblivion...or Dark Seven. I phoned Conrad to tell him what had happened and to find out who the assassin was. I told him, "His mind had been totally wiped clean; someone must be able to identify him using his DNA or fingerprints, or if we are able to reconstruct his head to get a photo of him, and then we might find out for sure if it was Oblivion or Dark Seven".

"I will put my best investigative journalist on it," he replied. I carried on into Hyde Park, and the telltale shimmering was ahead of me. It was so startlingly obvious to me, but no one else in the park would notice it. The portal opened, and I vanished into it; if anyone saw anything, it was all over in the blink of an eye.

I was back at Assington in just over a minute. This time, no alarms sounded as I had kept my tag with me, although instantly appearing to my security guys on the grounds always mystified them. I found Sue eventually—she and Viv were trying to get Lucas out of the lake and hadn't noticed my arrival for all her ranting at Lucas. I could understand why; he looked more like a chocolate Labrador than a Golden Retriever! I called out to him, but what a mistake that was! He came bounding towards me, and there was no escape; my clothes were inevitably covered in the mud from the lake. The laughter emanating from Sue and Viv didn't make me feel any better. They walked over to me with the other dogs, and I marched Lucas to the hosepipe and hosed him down. I told them I would have the edge of the lake paved.

Sue had seen my broadcast and was, like most of the country, still coming to terms with the implications of the Prime Minister's action. I told her about the attempt on my life, which visibly shocked her, and also that I would be going to Washington after I cleaned myself up but would be back home that evening.

CHAPTER TWO

I TOOK THE VERTICULAR to Anders Airfield. Felbrig had acquired all the security clearance I needed to enter the White House without being shot, and the presidential helicopter was waiting to take me there. On arrival, I went straight to the Oval Office. There was quite a lot of turmoil surrounding the office; it had only been a few hours since the President's suicide. Felbrig and I were shown in; Charles Dunedin and the First Principal were already seated. We were both brought up to speed—it appeared that I could not attend the joint Chief of Staff's meeting. I said, "It doesn't matter, but you must insist that all United States troops, in all theatres, are brought back to barracks. All hostile action must cease for 30 days. We will keep to our side of the bargain and will give the Secretary of State a position of strength in brokering a lasting peace so we can get on with the job of saving the planet."

I left the White House and flew back to Anders Airfield for an important meeting with the man who had tried to kill us just a few hours ago. We had saved his life—the recently arrested National Security Advisor wanted him dead and everything to do with Operation Wipeout obliterated as if had never existed, but we had got to Robert Saxham first. He and the two stealth fighter pilots were now my guests at Anders Airfield and would remain there until the trial of all those associated with the cover-up of Wipeout, if necessary.

I disembarked the helicopter on top of the Anders home where my "guests" had been kept, not really understanding what had actually happened to them. The fighter pilots were still coming to terms with having been 11 hours Eastern Standard Time away over Iran and yet back at Anders Airfield in just three hours and there for nearly two hours already. Robert Saxham asked what had happened to the missiles and the stealth fighters, and they were considering explanations, but the dialogue stopped when I walked in, and Colonels Gill and Berry were clearly apprehensive. Gill asked why they were there and when they could leave. I told them they could leave at any time, but I thought it unwise to do so, as the people who would stand trial for the cover-up might have friends keen on keeping them out of jail, even if it meant removing anyone who could incriminate them.

"Robert, you know yourself that had we not rescued you in Washington, you would be on a mortuary slab now for having been the architect of Operation Wipeout. You will remain as a guest of the President-elect until your safety can be guaranteed," I informed him. "Now, I have a problem with which you may be able to help while you are here, and which will give you something to do."

I went over to a computer and opened the folder, recording the sparring between Pat Smith and Sheflin. While whistling over the beauty of Sheflin, I told them that Pat was an Olympic gold medallist in karate but still could not counter any of her attacks, and she could have killed him several times within the first 30 seconds.

"Curiously, she has fallen in love with him and was not prepared to share him with her sisters, which gave us our advantage, but it still took a light gun, two tasers and a couple of darts in the neck to subdue her, and during her capture she hospitalised seven of her would-be captors, injuring them to varying degrees. She is one hell of an adversary and death has no fear for her. Her abilities are stupendous, totally remarkable - but we have been able to turn her around, and she is the first that we have converted to our side. Sheflin has six sisters scattered across all continents and having interrogated her, she believes that her sisters are far stronger and that she is the weakest link outside Messapth. We are trying to get her sisters and take them out of the Dark Seven network; however we need to neutralise their base which is set in a hidden valley between Turkey, Iran, and Iraq which they call Messapth, where there are a further one hundred and twenty females of differing ages, and we must assume that they have the same capabilities as Sheflin. I'm advised that we would need over two thousand special forces to subdue them, but not without incurring a lot of casualties, which I am not prepared to accept. Your job is to find a way to neutralise them without harm to anyone else. These people will continue to fund and perpetrate all the evil that surrounds us, and with them out of the equation, 90% of terrorism should cease since they alone finance it."

I showed them the satellite footage we had taken of Messapth and explained that the cloud cover was always present, as Messapth seemed to create its own weather. The infra-red pictures were helpful as they showed all the heat sources. Robert Saxham was the first to speak: "Are there any other people there?"

"We estimate about a further two hundred people, mostly men who act as servants or studs, but no serious threat to an assault team, unlike the women," I replied.

Robert said, "They all need to be taken out at the same time. Slumberland should do nicely; it's a chemical that prolongs the sleep period for up to 48 hours, causing unconsciousness similar to being under anaesthetic. You could just walk in and gather them up at your convenience." I asked how he could be so certain that it would be effective on all those people, and he continued: "We have tried it out at weekends with volunteers on several large army bases in the US. Those participating remained on camp and were subjected to slumberland. It did not matter where they were

- in billets, cellars, anywhere there was an atmosphere, even in the bunkers without the air conditioning on. They all succumbed to the drug. It only works when your body is naturally asleep; it just prolongs your unconscious state, and when you wake up, you have no idea that you have lost a day or two. The drug itself deteriorates in the bloodstream and so far, there have been no side effects from those exposed to it."

"I will need to see some of the participants so that I can tell from their minds if they have been harmed," I said, "but this sounds promising, although how are we going to deliver it so that it can take effect without Dark Seven knowing? Their martial arts training seems to enable them to block their minds from outside influences. It took two of us to alter Sheflin's mind and correct the inherent evil that was in it; it was a battle of wills, but we did finally succeed."

Robert replied, "I don't understand your abilities with minds, but as I see it, your act towards this woman was a hostile action as she perceived it and she tried to defend herself, which would be a normal reaction, whether mental or physical. If we deployed slumberland surreptitiously, no one would be wise to that fact, and within a twenty-four-hour time frame, they must all sleep at some point. I am sure that these people feel secure in their enclave so providing we can deliver slumberland there, it will take effect naturally during the following 24 hours."

CHAPTER THREE

COLONEL BERRY ADVISED that they had a solar stealth prototype aircraft—silent, invisible to all radar, and capable of operating at night for **three hours from batteries**. "Our aircraft we used for Operation Wipeout were the host aircraft for the prototype. Colonel Gill would fly the solar craft, I would pilot the mother aircraft, it would then be able to detach and complete the mission. Each of us is capable of flying the prototype and it would fit on either of our aircraft, but both seem to have been destroyed in the last mission and it may take two to three months to adapt some other stealth bombers, providing there was sufficient budget to complete the work," he informed me.

I replied, "There is no problem with the money, it's the time frame. I don't have 60 to 90 days. I want Messapth to be nullified within 30 days; we should have Sheflin's sisters under our control within the next week, so I am looking at 14 to 21 days for the assault on Messapth."

Colonel Gill, with Berry nodding in agreement, retorted, "Impossible! We would need that entire time just for training to ensure the mission was a success, and even if the cost wouldn't be a problem, the manpower and materials to adapt these aircraft would be. McDonnell-Douglas, who are contracted for modifications to our stealth fighter force, only have four engineers with the correct accreditations to work on them, and they couldn't work non-stop, they would need sleep and rest, or mistakes would be made. Plus, the material has a lead time of four weeks, which we may be able to shorten by a few days, but that's about all. It's purely a logistical problem."

I had to think this one through. I asked Berry to tell me what actually happened to his aircraft. Did it explode? "No," Berry said, "I just watched it disappear bit by bit, leaving me and my flying suit in mid-air until some sort of beam transported us to your encampment!"

"Your aircraft disappeared and were not destroyed, so they must be somewhere," I concluded. "The transport we used to bring you all here, I must assume it also protects those that travel in it. It's a highly sophisticated piece of kit which I use as a global taxi, but it just does what I ask it and I've no idea how it works."

Colonel Gill suggested, "Go and ask what it has done

with the aircraft!" so I did. I entered the verticular and asked the question. Two beams shone from the floor, and two tiny aircraft were contained within them. I said that the pilots were asking for their aircraft back, as they needed them to assist me, and it was my wish that it should be done, as they were no longer a threat to me. The beams disappeared, and both the stealth aircraft materialised as I exited the verticular and looked towards the engineering hangers. I touched my bracelet; Court and all the others could see what was happening. It was incredible! While we were all connected, I announced that we needed to meet at Assington the next evening. Now that we had the potential to remove Dark Seven, I needed updating on several situations, plus we still had a barrel of beer to finish!

I returned and told the Colonels that their aircraft had been returned, so they ought to check them over. As we approached, the Colonels seemed somewhat perplexed; while these were their aircraft, they were different—similar, but now much sleeker. The changes to the aircraft were more significant when Colonel Gill got into the cockpit, and it occurred to him that everything was so different he might not be able to fly it. Colonel Berry reached the same conclusion as they descended from their cockpits. I could read their thoughts and understood that they believed they would not be able to fly their aircraft as the modifications had been so substantial, and it would take months to retrain on them. Colonel Gill was the first to voice his concerns. I said, "That's a bit negative. Surely all the modifications would have two goals, to make the aircraft more efficient, and easier to fly."

"But most of the instrumentation has disappeared," said Gill, "although perhaps it's not necessary now."

"Why don't we get into flight suits and give it a go?" I suggested. "If what you say is correct, we won't be able to get it off the ground." They nodded in agreement. Colonel Berry was the more confident of the two, so I volunteered him to be the test pilot, plus Colonel Gill was more my size, and his flight suit would fit me better.

We walked to his aircraft and boarded. I took the rear seat and Berry the front seat, and we put on our helmets. He looked round for where to plug it in, but there were no sockets. "Perhaps these helmets do not need plugging in," I said, "and no point trying to do a pre-flight check as we are running blind!" He looked around where the ignition should have been. I had become familiar with how the verticular worked, in as much as I either thought or commanded it into action, so I suggested Colonel Berry simply tell the aircraft what he wanted it to do. "Start engines," he requested. The engines started; our helmet visors illuminated with all the instrumentation that had disappeared from the cockpit. I could sense growing confidence in him, and he asked the aircraft to taxi to the runway. He requested take-off clearance, which was given, then asked the aircraft to take off and climb to eighty thousand feet. In reality, we were both new to Utopian technology, so when that manoeuvre took just under a minute, I felt as if it was only my flight suit keeping me in one piece as it felt as though most of me was still on the ground! Colonel Berry had the same experience but had enjoyed it, and he continued talking to the aircraft, which did exactly what he said. He was hooked, brimming with new confidence. I told him I wanted to get reacquainted with the rest of my body on the ground, so he told the aircraft to land at Anders Airfield with a gradual descent that took the best part of 40 minutes, after which we taxied back to the other aircraft and came to a halt.

Colonel Berry leapt out of the cockpit and related to Gill what had transpired during the flight. Stealth aircraft were designed to be invisible to all known radar. Speed was not as important as remaining undetected. Colonel Berry was enthusing to his colleague how the aircraft had been transformed, "Flying it was a piece of cake, it does what you tell it to do! It's so easy! You have got to try it, it's unbelievable!" I had caught up with them and knew what had been said, and I told them that they should both familiarise themselves with the aircraft, then bring them and the solar stealth craft to Anders Airfield. I also said I would talk to the President to authorise their detachment to Earth Corp for the foreseeable future.

I turned to Robert Saxham, who had witnessed it all. I told him that I needed his skills in logistics to work with Stephen Shefford to neutralise Messapth and all its evil. It would be advisable to work with Stephen directly, and due to the distance, I thought it best that he travels back to England with me.

I turned back to the pilots and told them, "As soon as you have your orders, I want you and the aircraft stationed at RAF Mildenhall in England. Your orders from the President will you give absolute authority to do whatever is needed. I do not want these aircraft visible in Mildenhall, so fly them in at night and hanger them until required. Robert will continue to be your coordinator, and Stephen Shefford will organise the guard around your aircraft. All you have to do is inform the Base Commander that this is a direct request from the President." I told them that I needed to be able to contact them 24/7 and would provide them with the means.

I asked for a verticular, which appeared seconds later, and walked in to find three bracelets waiting for me. I handed the bracelets to them, and they placed them on their wrists. "This bracelet will be your communication device. All you need to do is touch it and think of who you need to talk to, and you will be connected; it also has some side effects which will be beneficial to you," I told them all. To the pilots, I said, "I will see you in England. Robert, you come with me." I touched my bracelet and told Stephen Shefford to meet me at Media Corp headquarters ASAP.

CHAPTER FOUR

ROBERT AND I WALKED OVER to the verticular and, 20 minutes later, arrived at my home, Assington Priory, where all sorts of alarms sounded, and within seconds, we were surrounded by my elite security force. It wasn't so good for Robert because he was on the floor and handcuffed in the blink of an eye, with four guns pointing at his head, and security waiting for the order to fire. I instructed them to back off from Robert, who was as near to white as I had ever seen anyone. He was in shock. While he might have orchestrated many deaths, he had never been so close to his own. Colour slowly came back to him as I helped him from the floor and apologised for the reception, explaining that my safety was their only concern, and they didn't take any chances. I asked one of the unit for a tag for Robert so he would never go through that again.

"I think it will be safer if you stay here," I told Robert, "But you can opt to stay in London if you choose. Your safety here is guaranteed, whereas in London I am not so sure. If you're dead, you can't testify against the former President's Executive. Your written statement could be disputed by a good lawyer, but your appearance in court will undoubtedly ensure their conviction and at least several years in jail."

"Let me think about it," he replied.

Robert and I reached Media Corp headquarters. It was my first visit to the publishing site, but I knew my way around by reading Conrad's mind. We took the lift to the top floor and walked straight into his office, much to the annoyance of his secretary trying to protect her boss from—as she thought—uninvited guests. I had already told Conrad we were on our way, so he was expecting us, and I shut the door in front of her. I introduced Robert Saxham to Conrad, who was cool if not downright cold, as this was the guy who would have had all of us killed had it not been for Utopian technology. I explained to Conrad, "This guy's skills in logistics are needed. He is on our side and your attitude towards him must mellow, as he will be working here where you have all the communication systems that he will need to destroy Messapth and eradicate the evil that is Dark Seven. We must accomplish this while the truce holds, so we have 29 days left." Conrad held out his hand to

Robert, and the pair shook hands.

"I have asked everyone involved to update me tomorrow on the various stages of the tasks I have set them," I announced. "Stephen Shefford is on his way here to discuss and plan the capture of Sheflin's sisters and alter their minds, so they are no longer a threat to us dealing with Messapth. Robert, maybe you can contribute something, so I would like you to be there. Robert is undecided where to stay; I can keep him safe at Assington, but in London, it would be much more difficult, too many variables."

Conrad said, "There is a self-contained flat on this floor which he is welcome to use. Now that our security level has been increased in line with yours at Assington, he should be just as safe here." Robert was already nodding his approval. I could understand that London just had the dynamics my home didn't.

Conrad announced, "I have just received a preliminary report from Scotland Yard about the assassination attempt on your life. Death was caused by severe head injuries. Fingerprints are negative—Interpol and FBI have no trace. His identity is a mystery, but they are rebuilding his face to get a photo record and use it to find where he was prior to the attack. They will be checking all immigration points once the face is restored. They are working round the clock and should have a photo-fit for tomorrow's papers; we have the copy ready to go, just waiting for the photo." I asked to see it, so we went over to his computer where he brought up the paper's front page: £100,000 reward for information on this man, with a toll-free phone number. I thought it a bit over the top for a front page, but I had agreed with Conrad that I would not interfere in his editorial decisions, so I said nothing.

Conrad showed Robert to the flat, which Bruce Kennett had used sometimes as the previous owner of the paper. As befitted a former billionaire, the flat was a little more accommodating than Robert was expecting—it was palatial. Conrad left Robert to explore, telling him to help himself to anything there as the old owner wouldn't ever be back, at which he laughed.

Robert went into the bedroom and sat on a large, comfortable bed, then he got up and went to the wardrobes crammed with casual and formal suits. He tried a jacket on, and it fitted him, providing he did not need to do it up. The shirts were all handmade, new and still in boxes, and looked like they would fit. He found the shoe rack and tried on a pair; a bit tight, but they would do. He was well pleased with his fate and could now live the life of a billionaire but without the money.

The phone rang. He was summoned to the boardroom on the floor below as Stephen Shefford had arrived. Stephen shook hands with Robert, showing no animosity towards him, unlike Conrad had done initially. It was business, and mutual professionalism existed between them.

Stephen reported that a team was in place and ready to take out the remaining six sisters; we would use the same team each time, using the date line to our benefit by starting in the Far East and Australia and working through to the

USA. "Robin has explained how Sheflin was captured, and it does sound a bit brutal," Robert said, "so you may need some replacements to the team. I have told Robin about a new chemical, slumberland, which we are going to use on Messapth. We could put some inside the packages Sheflin will send to her sisters; it could take 24 to 48 hours, but as soon as they do sleep, they will be unconscious for at least 24 hours, so you would be able to walk in and gather them up. We can scan their homes in infra-red via satellite and check for dormant heat sources." There was a pause.

"I really need to be convinced that this will work," said Stephen.

"I can get you all the data we have on the army bases that acted as guinea pigs," replied Robert.

"No, I want to see it work first-hand, and preferably on Sheflin herself, as Dark Seven might have a genetic difference. It took Robin and Monk working simultaneously to control her mind, and we underestimate them at our peril," said Stephen. "We have to neutralise outside influence on Messapth to stand any chance of a successful mission there."

"I am confident that slumberland will work on everybody, but I will get a small quantity and if Sheflin is agreeable—" started Robert.

"No!" Stephen interrupted. "She has to be unaware that she has been exposed to it just as her sisters will be."

I suggested we could ask her permission and then I could remove all knowledge of slumberland from her mind. But once again, Stephen said no, insisting that she had to be totally unaware, whereupon we all conceded and agreed we would target Sheflin and Pat Smith. A member of Stephen's elite force would bring her flowers saturated in slumberland. Both would be affected by it, but a small price to pay to test whether it worked.

Robert then outlined his thinking about the taking of Messapth and the full deployment of slumberland using the stealth aircraft. We waited to hear from the pilots whether the solar aircraft would still fit onto the newly modified aircraft. Assuming that it would, they would fly to Fort Worth, pick up a sufficient quantity of slumberland, proceed to RAF Mildenhall, and arrive under the cover of darkness to await further orders. "USS Mildenhall will be ordered to proceed to the Strait of Hormuz and await further orders; timing is of the utmost importance as the fully charged solar stealth aircraft has a range of three hours once detached from its mother ship. It will have to deploy at a low altitude. Two runs should be sufficient to ensure complete saturation of Messapth. In ten days the moon will be in its last phase so it will be near-total darkness, the solar craft will also make full use of any cloud cover present to deploy inside the cloud, but either way, the pilot will reduce his speed so as not to create air turbulence that could be noticed from the ground and will then deploy the chemical. The mother ship will be following its progress and will green-light the solar craft's successful deployment, as its specially adapted radar can show the coverage. If there are any parts that have been missed, he can give the solar craft the co-ordinates for a third attempt, thus the complete saturation of Messapth is assured. The solar craft will then make its way to rendezvous with USS Mildenhall. Six military satellites will keep a 24/7 reconnaissance of Messapth. This will start from tomorrow; the pictures of Messapth seem to be inadequate and I hope to build up a far better picture using a special computer program my department has developed, that is, if you agree with the plan."

Stephen was the first to speak. "I cannot fault the plan, providing the drug works; my best plan for an assault on Messapth estimated 30-40% casualties. That's a lot of people."

"Which is unacceptable," I said. "So, we will go with this plan. Now tell me, why was this drug developed?"

Robert continued, "In actual fact, it was an accident. Scientists at the University of Georgia were working on a drug to help children with autism minimise the effects of the condition when they found that the side effect was to extend the sleep pattern by between 24 and 48 hours, which did not help the condition but had no adverse effect on the children. It just so happened that a colonel in the local military had a child who suffered from autism and had taken the drug. He was unable to wake his son for 48 hours, and he panicked, but it appeared the boy was just in a deep sleep and all vital signs were good. During this anxious period, he emailed the camp doctor, telling him of his concern. All military email goes through a filter, certain keywords are deemed to be important, and the colonel's email found its way to the top brass, who had been looking for the means to negate casualties in conflicts. A sleeping adversary poses no threat at all, so the drug was developed further by the military to the level it is today although it has not been used other than in the tests which I have told you about, and as we signed the treaty on chemical warfare, its deployment would be illegal in any military conflict, but that's not to say we would not use it, as it's not lethal. It's the army's most secret weapon. Imagine you could put your enemy asleep for up to 48 hours and go in to capture them without any harm to your troops. Your use of the drug will be its first deployment. I know it will work; you will have no problem with the sisters or the inhabitants of Messapth if this drug is deployed correctly."

"The downside is that the sisters will have the top-secret communication device in the interim period before sleep, and we may well lose track of them," I said "but if we tell Sheflin to tell them that the devices will self-destruct unless used properly and that the working instructions are always sent separately for security reasons, then they won't try to use them until the instructions are at hand."

"That should work," Stephen replied.

"How long until the pilots return?" I asked Robert.

"They should be here sometime this afternoon," he answered.

I took my leave and returned home, as there was little I could do on the logistics. I checked my mail and reports and got up to date, although with so much going on, there was an incredible amount of work. Thankfully, my new skills quickly got me through it. I informed everyone concerned that there would be an online conference at 11:00 hours the following day, and then I spent some quality time at home.

CHAPTER FIVE

IT WAS LATE JULY and the turn of the House of Geflin to escort the young daughters to the temple on the border of China and Tibet. The trip would take three weeks from Lhasa but a further three weeks provisioning for a seven-year stay in the temple. Not only that, but they also had to provision for their seven sisters who would be returning with Geflin for their short stay at Messapth before leaving for Switzerland for their seven years "finishing off."

At 14, they would be accomplished in the art of Krurs-Chendo-Da, an ancient martial art designed solely to kill—no self-defence aspect was taught; it was superfluous as the adversary was dead. No martial art system had counters for this because no one had survived an attack; it was certain death for all who were confronted by it, although, of course, the practitioner could employ levels to incapacitate the victim first if information was required.

Krurs-Chendo-Da was thousands of years old. The emperor of what is now China had fought many wars and concluded that it was the people in power who caused the wars, not the peasantry. Therefore, if the peasantry had no leaders, they would have no one to follow and fight for, so that would bring peace to his borders and beyond. He created a sect of his finest soldiers to infiltrate and kill all the hierarchy of civilisations with which they came into contact, and to get the peasantry to just look after themselves, as they could always seek help from the emperor. Instead of a hierarchy, they would have merchants who would trade and provide the emperor with news from his "new lands" while creating enormous wealth for him.

The sect travelled thousands of miles and encountered vast civilisations, which, by the sheer size of them, the sect could not subdue. They tried it with the Assyrians, a well-organised civilisation, failed and were hounded out of the country, while many of the sect were killed by the sheer weight of numbers put against them. They had reached the end of the emperor's plan and returned home. It took them two years to get back and report what they had found and why they had failed. The emperor was concerned that a civilisation equal to or even greater than his own was just two years away but reconciled himself that there was no threat to his empire as any advancing army would perish in the weather or on the mountains and even if they survived, they would be so weakened that his army would polish them off.

His next problem was what to do with his sect; they had accomplished all that he had asked of them, and the failure was understandable; he now knew that other civilisations existed far beyond his borders, so he rewarded them well and asked them to hone their skills and become the teachers of his army elite. The sect decided that isolation would be the key and built the temple on what is now the Tibet-China border. After some time, the sect became devoted to attributes of death and fanatical in the pursuit of it. Wealthy by normal standards from the emperor's largesse, they needed to try out their skills but had to go vast distances, out of the sphere of influence of the emperor, and this is where they made first contact with what we know now as Dark Seven.

Some of the sect had come across the trap Dark Seven set for caravans heading west to east on trading missions and back again. Who could resist the sight and comfort of beautiful women when you have been on the trail for months? That was the hook to catch the lustful men of trade. Although they had to let some live to ensure that trade continued, the price was worth it. The trade routes were dangerous and the merchants who put the caravans together expected only half to return. However, this time, Dark Seven came unstuck with the sect Krurs-Chendo-Da, because the sleeping draught they gave their victims did not work on them, as they could isolate their minds from the effects of the drug. So, in slitting their throats, they got more than they had bargained for. Although the drug made the sect less effective, they still easily overcame the assault on them. With the tables turned on Dark Seven, Sheflin cried out, "Please don't kill us!"

which they didn't, and so a pact was formed whereby only Dark Seven would have the skills of Krurs-Chendo-Da, lasting to the present day.

The best part for the young daughters was the provisioning, as this was their first time out of Messapth. Paris, Rome and Zurich enchanted them all. They were children now but would be young women when their schooling finished. All their shopping was shipped to Lhasa and after the best three weeks of their lives so far, the girls were on the last leg of their journey and hardest time of their lives—the long trek to the temple of Krurs-Chendo-Da.

Over a hundred and fifty porters, yaks and donkeys were assembled for the trek; the porters were required for the last week as the temple could only be reached by foot. Porters had been doing this trek for aeons and knew exactly what was required. The legacy of the trek is handed down through the same families. As soon as the first goods started to arrive, they were on guard 24/7 as if their lives depended on it, which in fact they did, should something go missing. Another duty they had was to procure several fit young men who would stay at the temple and be trained to become part of the sect if selected. Their families would be paid handsomely. Others would work in the temple and the rest would be victims. The families of those who never returned would be paid and told that the recruits perished on the trek to the temple.

The time scale for this had to be at the height of the Tibetan summer, as the path to the temple was only open for 12 weeks before the winter closed in, and it became impassable because of ice, wind and snow. It would be downright stupidity to attempt it at any other time. The trek had been hard as always; it repeatedly amazed the porters that the young initiates managed the whole trek without help, didn't moan or cry and just got on with it, although they did have the best cold-weather gear money could buy, and the food was superb. But as sisters, none wanted to be the first to break and disgrace their House.

They had made good time and arrived at the temple a day early. It was a completely restrained reception, for no other reason than the elder sisters last saw the new arrivals as babies when they left Messapth. However, Geflin could immediately tell which one was which. The graduates had not really seen their own reflections for seven years, as there were no mirrors in the temple. The Ceremony of Transition would take place within the hour, where all had been prepared in the great hall. The thirty or so fit young men had little time to impress the sect, as they were taken through to the Arena and were put to the test and little did they know that it was genuinely life and death as the weakest would be eliminated. The tests measured their intelligence, reaction, and strength. The first round all should pass, but the following three rounds got harder in order to sort the wheat from the chaff until there were six left who would begin training and their families would be paid, nine who were offered jobs within the temple; seventeen had failed and believed they would be sent home with the rest of the porters and graduates, and no one told them any different.

The Ceremony of Transition took place. Geflin was Mistress of Ceremonies. Rising from her seat, she walked to the centre of the great hall, to her own House's graduate, whom she took to the initiate Geflin. They bowed solemnly. Graduate Geflin presented a key to the right hand of the initiate Geflin and said, "Sister, this is the key to all I have here, and it is yours." She asked her sister to follow her to present to her master, who took her hand and vowed that he would do his duty and that she would be ready for graduation in the allocated seven years' time. This was replicated six more times, and then the ceremony finished.

The graduates would leave at first light the following day, but a banquet was always held to honour the graduates and to demonstrate the skills they now possessed. Everyone was assembled and enjoyed the feast, including the seventeen unlucky young men who were having a great time as the food was exceptional and never had they tasted anything like it. They were unsuspecting and relaxed. After the food had finished, the graduates took to the floor and started their warm-up routine. They were now beautiful young ladies and the engines in the young men started to get into overdrive. They all came on to the floor to show off but lay slain on the floor in less than a minute. The masters of the graduates applauded, knowing that they had taught them all they could, although time and practice would make them even more dangerous.

Morning came, and the graduates said their goodbyes and started the long trek home to Messapth, and so the cycle began again.

CHAPTER SIX

I ARRIVED BACK at Media Corps. I had decided that the conference facilities were better than Assington's, and there was a tremendous amount of important news to be passed to all concerned. Conrad met me in the conference centre and told me Scotland Yard had sent him the photo-fit of the built-up head of my would-be assassin. He had a hard copy of the photo and showed it to me. The shock on my face was plain to see! I was looking at my own face! Not my face now after being rejuvenated with Utopian technology, but as I looked a few months ago. Everyone that knew me would not have recognised me.

Seeing my expression, Conrad asked, "Do you know

this man?"

I nodded and replied, "It's me as I used to look!" and showed him my passport, which had my old photograph in it.

"Good God!" he exclaimed. "This puts a whole new perspective on the assassination attempt. It appears you have been cloned! Stephen has to be told immediately!" and he rushed out of the room. Stephen had been up most of the night with Robert, sorting out the attack on Messapth, and they had just got to sleep when Conrad rushed in and showed him the photo-fit and my passport. He, too, was shocked and leapt out of the armchair to get to his jacket and his phone, then he dialled a number and barked, "I need all my principals internally tagged today. I will send special transport to you in order to facilitate this. I want you at Media Headquarters within the hour!" A bemused doctor at the receiving end of the phone was about to go to bed but would now wait for the special transport to take him to Sydney, the Australian headquarters of Media Corp and little did he know he would be in London in just over the hour.

Stephen told me of his intentions. "It appears that someone has the ability to clone you, and for that matter, any of us close to you. I am already internally tagged, and my staff know how to check; everybody that can get close to you and your family will similarly be tagged. It is quite painless, and it's no different from chipping your pet; however, you can be traced by it from satellite, so it's a tad more sophisticated. With this in place, any further attempt to clone any of us will be doomed to failure. I have initiated the highest level of security for everyone until I can neutralise this new threat." He did not need to attend the conference as we had decided that the attack on Messapth and the capture of the daughters was on a need-to-know basis. I did not need to read his mind because the concern was written all over his face.

As I made my way to the conference centre, I spoke to David and told him about the assassin having my old face, so the enemy must have somehow got access to my medical records. I asked him to see what he could find out about cloning as a matter of urgency. Over the conference facility, I told the Star Chamber about the attempt on my life and the need for them to get tagged, and that if they had problems in doing this Stephen could help. The President, Felbrig and Charles would have no problem, nor would the Prime Minister and Chancellor.

CHAPTER SEVEN

IT WAS THE FIRST BOARD MEETING of the amalgamated Earth Corp. The members explained the change of policy they had each undertaken and estimated the cost to Earth Corp was close to two trillion dollars. It was an estimate of monetary expenditure which I told them I could cover, should it be necessary, but our major problem was saving the planet and rapidly reducing carbon emissions. I brought Court Leiston into the conversation at this point. He reported that he and his team had replicated white energy in his laboratory in California but were still a long way off being able to use it to power anything, and progress through the Utopian archives was painfully slow. "Four billion years of history to sift through will take time,"

I said. "Perhaps we are looking at this from the wrong angle. The verticular did not destroy the stealth aircraft but miniaturised them somehow and while it had them, it modified them so much that the pilots thought they would not be able to fly them, whereas it actually made them easier to fly, so why don't you ask your verticular about your problem?"

"It might just work," Court said. "The Utopians are all trying to help in finding the key to their technology, and it's like having all the answers to every problem, but to utilise this knowledge we need the questions, and how and why they arrived at the solution. Don't forget that the droids were given the ability to self-improve aeons ago and have become sentient in their own right, so if even if we eventually decipher the archives, the droids may be so far removed from the Utopian original concept of them that we will be no further forward."

I asked, "How are they getting on with the blueprints for the equipment that we need down there?"

"No problem at all," he responded. "They seem to be enjoying the work and you would not believe the improvements they have made to the equipment! Our team of scientists down here are coping well, assessing the damage done to the Diaorderian plain, and the modified equipment they are using should give an accurate idea of how weak the Earth's crust is. From these figures, they should be able to extrapolate a close estimate for how long we have before the eruption we are all dreading."

A surface team member interrupted and introduced

himself as Professor Dave Mac, head of the seismology team working on the surface and all the probes and sensors which were now routed through Flint, Texas, and the world's leading authority on volcanic eruptions. He said, "A civilisation that has existed underground for four billion years must have technology or systems to prevent them from being wiped out. The planet must have been as hostile underground as it was on the surface. The detritus from the Big Bang hitting the earth was considerable and the reason for them going underground; the tectonic plates of the earth were constantly moving due to the activity at the earth's core and must have caused the Utopians a great deal of grief in their early existence. For them to have survived this, they must have found a way to relieve the volcanic pressure. Even if Utopia is an underground continent, the rigours of the earth's core must affect it in the same way it affects the surface." I interrupted to ask him what his point was, then he continued, "You are all focussing on technology reducing carbon emissions to stop the crust from weakening further. The preliminary reports I have read seem to say the crust is weak, and the volcanic activity around the globe is increasing, Yellowstone printouts are giving me grave concerns and I do not want to be alarmist, but I say we have weeks not months, so finding out how the Utopians have survived must be your priority, everything else is secondary."

He was right, of course, and looking at all the conference monitors, I could see the concern on all their faces at this revelation. I asked him, "What do you suggest, as I know the Utopians have no knowledge of this technology? If it exists, it must be with the droids as they do everything for them, but we are still unable to communicate with them."

He replied, "You need a team of potholders to find the underground tunnels which must be there. They would be the only way to remove the pressures that affect our earth."

I asked him, "Professor, if you were to design a system without limitations to cost and feasibility, how long would it take you to produce a blueprint?"

He laughed. "I have been working on it for most of my life! Washington did not have the funds or the inclination and shelved it. The cost would have been greater than the entire space programme and would have reduced the military budget by a third, and since they have powerful lobbyists close to the late President, it got no further."

"I need it in blueprint format so I can show it to the droids. It might just unlock the information we need," I said.

"The latest version was produced by my daughter; it's in virtual reality format, similar to your film on the Armageddon scenario, which will happen to earth unless we eliminate carbon burning," he replied.

Court spoke up, "If you send it to Nigel Wolstenholme, the head of my research centre in Los Angeles, he will adapt it into a readable format for the droids."

"How long will that take?" I asked.

"A day, maybe two," he replied. "I will get his team to work round the clock."

"That's fine," I said. "When it's complete, the professor,

Court and I will go to Utopia and present the blueprints together, as I don't know what will happen and the professor's skills will be needed."

CHAPTER EIGHT

COURT AND I COLLECTED the blueprints from his R&D department in Los Angeles. Nigel and his crew had worked round the clock and, after 24 hours, the film had been translated into what we believed the droids could recognise and potentially help us should the inevitable happen. Professor Dave Mac had said that the Utopians must have been confronted with quakes and eruptions, so they must have counter measures that protect them in order for them to have survived. That was rational, and we had to hope he was right.

We collected the professor from his laboratory. He wanted to take everything but the kitchen sink, but I pointed out to him that our transport would not allow for that, so whatever he needed would have to be fabricated there. "It will take months to fabricate all that I need, and we don't have the time," he said. I said nothing as we entered the verticular, but I watched his face as we descended. He appeared as shocked as were all first-time travellers on the verticular. We had to do two stops on the horizicular for Utopia City, but still, it had taken less than five minutes.

We made our way to the technical area; the small droid was there and even looked pleased to see us. We took the blueprints and laid them out in order. The droid was assimilating the data quicker than we could lay the pages out, and it stopped a third of the way through when three much larger droids appeared at our feet for us to stand on, which we did and were quickly taken to an area where we stepped off. The small droid led us to a large crystal globe, where a door opened, and the droid went in. We followed; the door closed and immediately we were moving quite fast.

We were soon out of the city. The globe illuminating our path, then in front of us, was a vast door, 50 feet in diameter, which looked like metal and must have weighed hundreds of tonnes; it opened for us, and we passed through before it closed behind us. We were now descending rapidly, probably ten to 12 miles, when the globe started to slow. An orange glow appeared below us. The globe settled above it and started to follow the flow of the magma—molten rock—and just 20 metres above it, we should have turned into dust, yet we hadn't even broken into a sweat! Court and I did not understand the significance of what we were seeing, but the professor's mouth was wide open. He did not anything out loud, but his mind did: "The Utopians are protected and have control of their environment. They will never be troubled by any normal tremor or eruption and unlike the surface, their defences are more than adequate!" Our journey continued. It was as if we were on a magma highway, first single, then dual, even three lanes of magma and finally back to one. The magma in the three lanes moved a lot more slowly than the single lane we were following.

Court and I were just taking in the sights, whose importance was lost on us, but Dave Mac understood it all, totally absorbed by the implications of what was in front of him. We arrived back at the large door; evidently, we had gone round in a circle which had taken over four hours but had seemed like minutes, such was the spectacle we had all just witnessed. The droids brought us back to the technical area. The professor's adrenalin level and the use of his speech returned, not that he had ever truly lost it, but for a man who had studied volcanoes and eruptions for all of his working life, he had been stunned into silence to be where no human had ever gone, amongst the magma and its trails, in a civilisation that had control over it and therefore would never be threatened, unlike the surface world.

I demanded of Dave "What you have seen? Can it help us? Yes or no?"

"Yes!" he replied and started to explain how. I interrupted him to say that neither Court nor I would understand the science he was about to impart, it was enough that what we had seen would help.

"What do you need?" I asked, and I thought he was about to hyperventilate, "as it will all have to be fabricated here by blueprints until we are able to communicate with the droids? I know it could be time-consuming, time which we don't really have, but I will leave you here to think about your requirements and will be back in a couple of hours, as I have to see the rest of the underground team."

The news was mixed. The Diaorderian plain was now back under control; in that the crop was no longer at risk, thanks to a vast canopy now under the roof which was channelling the acid rain into gulleys and from there to the recycling system. That seemed an easy solution, which it was, but still impressive as it had covered two thousand square miles inside two weeks. The bad news was the weakness in the earth's crust at this point was greater, but only at the 500-square-miles section where the crop had been affected. It had been mathematically worked out that degradation had penetrated five miles but was still weakening the crust at this point and would continue to do so until it met the magma fields. There was some good news though: because we had stopped the flow, the existing degradation would slow, the worst-case scenario was a year providing there were no violent eruptions close to the weakness in the earth's crust.

We went back to the technical area, but the small droid and the professor were not there. Two droids turned up, so we stepped on them, and they whisked us off to meet the professor. It seemed we were in the middle of the technical area, and there were many small droids in the building we entered where we saw the professor in the middle of a holographic projection of the whole Utopian world above and below ground. I entered his mind and told him we were back, so he looked up and came to join us, with the droid close behind. He informed us, "All of Utopia is controlled from here. These droids work endlessly on the air, it's their climate control. It also has the task of defending Utopia from natural phenomena and controls everything we saw this morning. As far as I can make out, there are sensors that pick up an increase in pressure and it opens and shuts doors to release this pressure and dissipates it through the magma streams underneath Utopia."

I asked if it could get overwhelmed by the sheer scale of an eruption, and he said he didn't know. "But if I had built this, I would know what size of eruption it would take before the system breaks down and cannot control the eruption."

"So, the droids should know at what point the system will fail?" I wondered.

"Well, I don't know how, but you are going to have to find out!" I then told him about the degrading of 500 square miles of the Diaorderian plain, and the calculations of at least a year before it would reach the magma level. I asked if he needed any help, or if there was anyone from the surface who could assist him and he rattled off several names, adding that they were not scientists per se but possibly the best volcano and gadget hobbyists he knew. I was pleased about that, as they should have already been on board after my search for the most qualified scientists.

It took four hours to get his team back to Utopia. The biggest problem was getting immediate leave from their employment, but with some mental persuasion, it was resolved and the five would all keep in contact should their companies need them. Court decided to stay with them, and I would meet him much later at Assington. The professor knew what we needed and would bring them up to speed.

I left for the surface and arrived at Cheltenham Manor. The chaos was more organised than during my last visit. It was a hive of activity, but everybody seemed to know what they were doing and where they were going. I managed to discreetly get as far as the office, where security recognised me and opened the door. My sister raised her head from the desk to say "Hello", so engrossed in her work that at first, she hadn't realised it was me. She ushered me to a seat while she finished what she was doing. I might have been the richest man in the world, but you do not clash with the matriarch of the family!

I had read the daily reports, but they were just numbers, and I wanted her feelings about how it was going, and the interaction with the Utopians who were vetting every candidate using a list of questions drawn up by my niece and nephew who had been in the head- hunting business for years. She told me that everything was going extremely well. Barely any candidates had failed, and we had no subversive elements trying to get in to undermine our mission. By the end of the next month, we would have Earth Corp representatives of the highest calibre in every country in the world. All who left Cheltenham would know what the duties were, and the timescale required to ensure success.

I told my sister I was hungry and went to the restaurant, where the maître-d' was delighted to see me. He showed me to a table where I had a great view of the entire place. Looking around, it was like the United Nations. I could sense the excitement, and it seemed that eating was holding them up, so they rushed through their meals to get back to work, which was a pity as the food was great, and I was certainly not going to rush mine!

CHAPTER NINE

COLONELS GILL AND BERRY RECEIVED their written orders directly from the President. They had flown into Anders, were taken by helicopter to the White House and shown directly to the Oval Office, and informed that they were attached to Earth Corp until further notice. The modified stealth aircraft would remain at Anders otherwise everyone in the USAF would see the changes and start asking questions, so they would requisition a C-130 aircraft to pick it up and bring it to Anders, where any further modifications would be made.

Colonel Gill went to Fort Trent to pick up the slumberland. He knew there would be problems, his orders checked and re-checked, but a presidential order had to be obeyed, and he eventually came away with enough slumberland to do the job, with some small vials for testing on Sheflin to ensure it would affect her like everybody else who had been exposed to it.

Colonel Gill arrived back at Anders Airfield and saw the C-130 being unloaded as he taxied in. The solar stealth aircraft was being pulled by a tug towards their aircraft, but he could see that the modifications made to their aircraft by Utopian technology would not fit the existing anchorages, so he touched his bracelet and contacted me directly. I responded and told him I would be there in 20 minutes.

I exited the verticular. We were on the main taxi runway leading to the pavilions; I could see the solar stealth craft and the Colonels and beckoned them towards the verticular. Some minutes later, we were all inside the verticular, where I said to it, "The modifications made to the two aircraft will not allow the solar craft to fit and it's a vital component in saving not just Utopia but also the surface world in its attempt to eradicate evil." There was a momentary pause, and then the solar craft disappeared within seconds. Inside the verticular, we could see a picture of the craft undergoing phenomenal changes. In a little over an hour, the solar craft was back on the taxi runway, totally altered but now would fit the stealth aircraft perfectly. There had always been a disadvantage that the solar craft could not re-attach itself back to the aircraft once deployed from the stealth fighter. Several prototypes were lost, and the Air Force decided that it would be safer to land it on an aircraft carrier or at a friendly base, but that restricted what the aircraft could or could not do.

We made our way to the modified craft while the Colonels Berry and Gill admired it. The shape had changed; the top of the craft was identical to part of the underneath of their stealth fighters so it would fit like a jigsaw piece. There would be no need for anchorage as the air movement would keep them together during the flight, and it would detach as the aircraft slowed to allow it to deploy. It was a simple solution that had vexed the military for some time, but there was only one way to find out if it was safe, and they both took to the air. The solar craft always could take off but used so much of its power in doing so, leaving it depleted and hampering night-time silent penetration in hostile territory.

Colonel Gill took the solar aircraft, as always, and got take-ff clearance from the Anders tower. As he taxied to the runway, he noticed very few changes in the aircraft apart from its shape, so it wasn't until he moved the electric throttle for take-off did he experience the difference, as he was airborne within three hundred metres and silently ascending and still accelerating. He eased off at twenty thousand feet and went out to sea with Colonel Berry not so far behind. The rendezvous was about two hundred miles off Coney Island. He and Colonel Gill communicated with each other; Colonel Gill slowed his solar aircraft and Berry positioned his aircraft above it. The two aircraft slowly came together with a slight clunk, leaving them as one, which was how they returned to Anders Airfield.

The pilots exited their aircraft and walked back to me. I did not have to read their minds because it was written on their faces, so I asked when they could leave for Mildenhall. "This afternoon," Colonel Berry replied. "It's been a few days since we have seen our families and we would like to have a bit of time with them, as we don't know when we will be back stateside."

"I have a better idea: phone them and tell them to get packed for a month and I will send my plane to pick them up and bring them to England. They can stay at Assington or Mildenhall as my guests, whichever you want, but I want you in Mildenhall sooner rather than later."

I organised the plane to pick up their families in San Diego. They, as well as the pilots themselves, would be safer under my roof until the trials were over. I contacted Stephen Shefford and told him that the slumberland would be at Mildenhall air base within the next five hours. "It is extremely important that the aircraft are not seen by the USAF. You will have to use your best diplomatic skills on the Base Commander to ensure the brief stay at Mildenhall is incident-free, but your orders directly from the President will allow you to use ultimate force, if necessary, which I hope it will not be. I will see you in England. Meet me at Assington and we will go to Mildenhall together by car as it's only 40 minutes away. I will ask the President to call the Base Commander so he will be expecting us."

I arrived back at Assington. I had a few hours to spare while the planes were crossing the Atlantic, although I wanted to be at the base an hour before they arrived. I had remembered my blue chip, so the alarms didn't go off. Moreover, security was becoming used to my instant appearances. I walked to the house, but no one was around, so I contacted security, asked where everyone was, and "shopping" was the reply, so I went to my office. I checked the mail and turned the box on, but there was nothing spectacular, in fact, almost boring. There were no terrorist atrocities, so the brokered thirty-day truce was holding—a good sign that the First Principal, now the Secretary of State, did have the clout to broker a worldwide peace deal—I certainly hoped so.

CHAPTER TEN

THROUGH HIS CONTACTS in the US judiciary, Felbrig had heard before Conrad that a team of lawyers had been put together funded by the Perkins/Arnott legal conglomerate on both sides of the pond and that they had presented a case in front of a judge, claiming the written statements were obtained under duress as there could be no other reason these extremely intelligent people could not keep silent and admit to such crimes as they had been indicted for. The judge, who was in the pocket of Arnott and co., had ruled that those statements were inadmissible—and similarly in the UK, where they had all been released on bail. The bail was set at ten dollars since I had taken all their money. He also ruled that the Supreme Court would be the only place the defendants could be tried since they were in government, citing some little-known reference to the US constitution—again, it was the same for those in the UK. The Supreme Court's workload meant that it would not hear the case for 11 years, and four years in the UK.

There was no easy way to break this news to me; Conrad wanted to do it in person. I was speechless. My anger had to be suppressed; it was yet another problem to resolve. Felbrig and Rodbridge were in the Oval Office when I contacted them.

Felbrig was already on the case and advised me that the President had executive power to order the Supreme Court to hear the case immediately if national security was at stake, so this had been done with a date for the first hearing set for three weeks ahead. Because the legal team had gone with the Supreme Court route, they would not get long extensions to prepare their defence and the case would be heard on the due day, ready or not. The prosecution was ready to go. "The truth triggers are still in place which Monk and I placed in their minds, so if the same questions are asked, the answers will be the same," I said.

"We will give our evidence first and full disclosure will be given to the defence team, but they don't have to disclose how they are going to defend their clients, such is the law," Felbrig added.

I felt a little better that stateside it was all in hand. I contacted our Prime Minister, who was already in conference with the Attorney General.

Our Supreme Court was relatively new, and I told him I had spoken to the President and that their case would be heard in three weeks. "Can we not do the same?" I asked, "It would be unfair that the Americans would have been on trial and the outcome already known, so I believe the trial here should be held at the same time." The Attorney General agreed and said he would talk to the Supreme Court judges to find out their views, but it would not prevent the old Cabinet from taking their seats in Parliament, because only the electorate could remove them from Parliament and most of them were really popular with their constituents. "The old Cabinet must be suspended from Parliament to prevent them from taking an active role; if they are so popular with their electorate, then we must have by-elections in their constituencies and put our own candidates up against them. If somehow, they are acquitted, the Prime Minister has several candidates to replace them all. If their constituency party decides to stick with the incumbent MP, then we would have to ask him to resign from the party and stand as an independent."

I could feel my blood pressure rising again over the legal and political complications of the situation. Was I warming up to become a democratic dictator, the first of its kind, following the public's concern and acting in the interest of the public to do the right thing, suspending Parliament and the judiciary until they could be trusted to act correctly and do what the electorates want? I was sure I had the power to do this, but it was just a thought which momentarily passed. I had to live and work within the law and use diplomacy and politics to convince everybody that my way was the right way and the only way to save our planet.

and use diplomacy and politics to convince everybody that my way was the right way and the only way to save our planet.

CHAPTER ELEVEN

WHEN STEPHEN SHEFFORD ARRIVED, we still had three hours before the aircraft was due to arrive at Mildenhall—or so we thought—then Colonel Berry informed us that they were 90 minutes away. The modified aircraft were twice as fast and had not needed to refuel in flight because the gauges still showed three-quarters full, and they seemed to run on air. "Well, you might as well slow down as it will not be dark for another two hours. You're landing at Mildenhall, instead of Lakenheath, where most of the plane spotters gather, so with a bit of luck, you will go unnoticed at Mildenhall. We will be at the base in an hour. You will have no radio contact with any traffic control and will land without their assistance. I will ensure it's safe to do so, but if you need to contact me, use your bracelets and maintain radio silence from now until you're in the hangar," I instructed him.

We left Assington for the base. It was the first time I had been in the new car, and my chauffeur, Trevor, was keen to point out that it was impregnable from any hand-held weapon. It also had countermeasures for rocket attacks like the ones the aircraft are equipped with, and he spent the entire journey telling me every single thing that made this vehicle special. We arrived at the base and still had to go through the security protocol. What Trevor had forgotten to tell me was that the car was also an armoury, with guns of all types secreted about the vehicle, and some very alarmed base security personnel easily found them. I reassured them that we were entitled to carry them and went over the scanner when everything went into alarm status, and I had to reassure the scanner operator that all was in order. With the security checks out of the way, we were asked to follow a USAF police vehicle that would take us straight to the Base Commander.

The Commander had an honour guard on parade. He had never had a direct order from the President of the United States, and he would not miss any opportunity to impress. Trevor opened the door, and we both got out; the honour guard stood to attention, and the Commander, smiling from ear to ear, held out his hand. We shook hands, and he asked whether we would do the honour of reviewing his guard. I could have implanted in his mind but took to whispering in his ear, "Did the President not tell you that this was a top-secret mission, on a need-to-know basis?"

He nodded.

"Well, this is not a good start," I hissed. I told Stephen to inspect the guard as he had been in the elite armed forces, and these guys had really done well with a maximum of three hours' notice. I left Stephen doing his bit and walked into the Commander's office, where there must have been around thirty military personnel and enough food to feed the whole base.

I beckoned the Commander over and asked if I could have a word in private. We were just about to leave when Stephen returned and joined us; I had never seen him so angry. We walked to the private office, and Stephen exploded once inside. "The mission was so top-secret the President spoke to you personally and told you that, once we arrived, you had to do exactly what was asked! We haven't fucking asked for an honour guard or a fucking banquet, for fuck's sake, we didn't want anyone to know we were here!"

The Commander was not used to being spoken this way and retorted, "You are on the most secure base. No one will know about you outside of this base."

"Commander," Stephen replied, "how many people on this base, including civilians and contractors?"

"Well, it ranges from 16 to 18 thousand in total."

"How many will be leaving the base to go home?"

"About half."

"And what do you think they are going to say about

today?" The implications of his actions suddenly dawned on the Commander. Realising why we were so angry, he became very contrite and asked what we needed, and so we got down to business.

He left to instruct his staff to take the food to the mess hall and that everyone should leave the building, as his office was now under presidential control. Only those with presidential clearance would be allowed in the vicinity, and that would also apply to other parts of the base. Then he returned to his office. Stephen removed a gadget from his pocket, walked carefully around the office, and after a couple of minutes, he went outside to all the other rooms, came back and announced, "It's all clean."

He told the Base Commander that two highly modified stealth fighters would be landing there in the next hour, "Colonels Gill and Berry will be the pilots"—instant recognition from the Base Commander at these names—"and they have presidential orders that until further notice they are assigned to Earth Corp." I told him that the aircraft would be landing after dark, the pilots would not require tower assistance, and for the roughly 20 minutes while they were on the ground, total blackout would be required. Stephen continued, "Now, we need a hangar to fit them both in, which needs to be somewhat isolated, so it does not interfere with your day to day running of the base. Nobody from the base can come within two hundred metres without risking being shot. Your security will be three hundred metres from the hanger. That will give us a hundred-metre cushion for accidents, but I can assure you that if anyone gets to 50 metres from this hangar they will be taken out, are you clear about this, Commander? Taken out means dead."

"But…" the Commander began.

"No buts; if a person has ignored your security and mine, then they will be deemed hostile, and ultimate force will be used."

"One of Stephen's men will guide the planes to the hangar, and it will be secured by his men exclusively. The aircraft have just one mission and it should all be over within the next 14 days. The success of it depends on secrecy and will save the lives of countless thousands of people around the world," I added.

"Now let's get down to business," said Stephen as he got out his laptop. We had the base up in real time and carefully scrutinised every inch, asking the Commander questions. About four hundred metres from the fuel bunkers and a little to the right of the main runway was a very large building. "What's this?" he asked.

The Commander replied, "It was the fuel depot maintenance shop, it used to be a hangar." "Do the hangar doors still open?"

"Of course, they will!" Stephen zoomed in closer, then out again.

"Perfect!" he announced. "You have under an hour to turn the depot into a hangar." "Impossible!" the Commander objected, "It would take days to return it to being a hangar." "Ok, a storage area for two special aircraft," Stephen said. "Get the guy in charge and order him to take whatever steps are necessary to make available a hundred square metres and he has an hour to do so. If it's manpower, you already said you have over 14 thousand personnel. Make that call." So, he did. There were some excuses, but the Commander ordered them to make it happen. Every base resource they needed would be available. Stephen would ensure that the time deadline was kept. The Commander gave him the passes and went to the hangar to ensure compliance.

It had been dark for about 15 minutes, and the hangar was ready when Stephen came back and asked the Commander to contact the control tower and ask whether they were expecting any more incoming flights. One was due in ten minutes, then no more until the morning. "That aircraft must be parked as far away from our hangar as possible. The flight crew will be the only off-load. Whatever else is on, it will wait until our consignment is in the hangar and under our guard. The control tower can take a break until everything is in place. As soon as that incoming aircraft is on the ground, our security team will helicopter in and secure the hangar. We need a complete blackout on the runway, so when the tower takes its break, ensure that all lights are out. Our aircraft will use their own technology to get on the ground," he stated. The Commander issued orders for all this.

We heard the last plane—an old Starlifter that was far too noisy by today's standards but presumably still serving its purpose, although its carbon footprint was immense. It taxied to the far end of the runway and was told to exit the runway and go to holding bay A6. Transport would collect the crew from there and unloading would take place in the morning. The crew had barely time to finish their de-brief before the transport arrived and steps were attached to the aircraft. The speed everything was happening amazed them, even more so when the transport hurtled along far over the base speed limit. They were halfway along the road adjacent to the runway when the control tower lights and runway lights went out, and for a few minutes, everything was blacked out so only the lights of their vehicle led the way until they got into the base, where it seemed only the runway and control tower had been affected as the lights were on there.

CHAPTER TWELVE

JOHN TURNER HAD GOTTEN ALL THE SHOTS of the C-141 Starlifter he wanted. His plane-spotting interest was cargo, which was of no interest to all the other anoraks who spent their whole time at Lakenheath watching fighters. He had been following this one's journey from Seattle and was disappointed that it had landed in the dark, but his state-of-the-art camera and radio equipment had followed its journey, and he was well pleased with what he had got. The runway lights went out as he walked back to his car.

He looked back and noticed the control tower lights were out as well. Strange! he thought. In the thirty-odd years he had been watching, this had never happened. He saw that the base still had light, it was only the runway that was dark, so he put it down to a power failure but as he got to his car, there was an almighty whoosh, the air became unsettled and two black objects descended onto the runway.

He had packed up all his gear. The only thing he had handy was his phone, so he just hit the capture key. Whatever had landed was fast and disappeared at the end of the runway. He saw vehicle lights turning round, and then darkness returned. He had to hurry home and download the pictures from his phone to see what had landed at the base and share it with all his plane-spotter friends! But no matter what he tried, all he had was a pair of black shapes.

He knew that something special had arrived at Mildenhall, and he was going to find out what but what he didn't know was that if he became a nuisance, we would be entering his mind and altering it!

CHAPTER THIRTEEN

WHEN COLONEL BERRY ADVISED me that they were 20 minutes away and descending rapidly, I informed him that the last inbound aircraft had just landed, and the runway lights were off. Once on the ground, he should follow the vehicle off the runway to our secured hangar and meet me at the Base Commander's office. The aircraft taxied to the secure hangar, where both were put under canvas, so nothing was visible. Even in the unlikely event that someone should get through both security fences, there would be nothing to photograph. I was pleased with this outcome as Stephen had said that every plane-spotter in the country would be descending on Mildenhall. "Now that everyone at the base knows of a highly secret arrival of aircraft with their own security, we might as well have put the arrival on Facebook. It's human nature when something unusual happens at the base that the civilian workforce would tell their families and friends, who in turn will tell their friends that there's something top-secret happening at the base, it will be common knowledge by morning, thanks to the Base Commander."

Colonels Gill and Berry were shown into the Commander's office. They both knew him, but I asked him to leave after the pleasantries. He thought he might be privy to what the secret meeting was about, but he was wrong. Stephen opened the door for him to leave and beckoned one of his guards to stay outside the door so no eavesdropping could take place. Colonel Berry had a small stainless-steel cylinder in his hand. "In this cylinder, there is enough slumberland to put the whole base to sleep, and the remainder will stay on the aircraft until needed," he told us.

Colonel Gill gave us what looked like gas masks and said, "You will need to use these if you don't want to be overcome by slumberland, these are no ordinary masks as the membrane has been specifically designed to stop the spores entering the mask, so providing you wear gloves you will be safe from exposure to slumberland." Stephen took the canister and masks and used his bracelet to contact Pat Smith, telling him to be in the Prague office in 20 minutes. Stephen and I walked out of the office with the Colonels, I told my chauffeur to take them to Assington, and we would make our own way back.

I summoned a verticular which arrived instantly. We both got in and arrived outside Stephen's Prague office in ten minutes. It would have been quicker, but I had to convince our transport that the items we carried were necessary and critical. We were travelling directly to Prague and would not need to stop in Utopia, so if even if they posed any threat, it would not be to Utopia.

CHAPTER FOURTEEN

PAT SMITH HAD JUST FINISHED DINNER with Sheflin at her apartment when he got Stephen's mind message. He went to her fridge, where there was only local lager, and he said to Sheflin, "I am going to get some Australian lager. The local stuff is too gassy." There was a slight frown and then a big smile. "I will have a shower and then you can convince me that bloody Aussie lager is best," she said.

The journey to the office took about 15 minutes, and he arrived on time. He went to the kitchen and got a case of lager, then went to find his boss. When he entered the office, he found a large bunch of flowers completely sealed in cellophane on the table. Stephen said, "When it comes to romance, Australians are pretty piss poor. Sheflin is the key to a successful mission. Romance is what women like, so take these flowers and start getting romantic! A case of lager will never hit the spot! We have to get all her sisters neutralised." He handed Pat six top-secret user documents. "These must be sent first and then two days later the communication devices will be sent separately, which her sisters will be expecting." Pat put the documents into his jacket, picked up the lager and flowers and got to his car, where he gently placed the case of lager on the rear seat and threw the flowers on top. "Romance be buggered. All these sheilas really want is a good seeing-to, and I am the man to do that!" but his opinion on women was about to change for life.

He arrived back at Sheflin's apartment and rang the bell. In front of him was the case of lager, behind his back were the flowers. Sheflin checked the CCTV and pinhole in the door before opening it, saying "I do hope this lager is as good as you say or I might have to kill you!"

"Perhaps these might change your mind?" he asked and gave her the flowers. Pat could not believe her reaction—the smile went from ear to ear. She ran through to the kitchen for scissors and in seconds were out of the wrapping and she inhaled the beautiful scent of the flowers. "Oh, Pat! This is the best thing that has ever happened to me. You are the most wonderful man I have ever known!" She had no vases in the apartment and had to leave the flowers in water in the sink. She came towards him and kissed him like she really meant it; he picked her up and carried her into her bedroom where they made love. This time it was not just sex but two people in love, a totally different experience for both of them. After two hours, they were exhausted, lay side by side and fell into a deep sleep.

Pat's phone alarm went off at its normal time, 06.00. He quickly turned it off so as not to wake his lovely Sheflin. Full of love, he decided he would make breakfast and let her enjoy it in bed.

Half an hour later, he put her breakfast on a tray with one flower from the sink in a champagne flute and took it to the bedroom, placed the tray on the bedside table, and gave her a gentle kiss to wake her. Nothing. He gave her a gentle shake, nothing. He checked for life signs; they were all there. He started to shout, nothing. She was out for the count. He went into the lounge and phoned Stephen. Stephen was surprised to hear from him so soon. "It's Sheflin! I can't wake her. All her vital signs are there but she will not wake up!"

"There is nothing to worry about, she may be asleep for a couple of days, but what I can't understand is why you're not affected," Stephen told him.

"We are trying a drug that has no side effects. It's been tested on three army bases. Everyone exposed to the drug sleeps between 24 and 48 hours, then they wake up and all that has happened is they have lost at the most two days of their life. They wake up as if they have only had a normal night's sleep. You should have been affected the same way, so it must be the bracelet that has neutralised the drug. If that's the case, it's even better news as our forces will be immune to the drug when we enter Messapth."

"We didn't get the chance of sending the documents to the other sisters, the flowers saw to that, so if she's out for two days, it could be a problem and put our schedule back a couple of days," Pat said.

Stephen replied, "I am coming over with Robin and see if he's able to do the Sleeping Beauty on her."

"He's not going to bloody kiss her!" exclaimed Pat to which Stephen replied, "You've become a jealous bugger!"

I had gone back to Assington. Stephen had told me the drug had worked and now the problem was to wake Sheflin or put the schedule back two days. I assured him he need have no fear; Prince Charming was on the way. We met at Sheflin's apartment. I went into the bedroom and entered her mind. I could see that the drug had blocked her slumber region and that the drug was slowly degrading as her immune system had kicked in, but it would take at least 36 hours before her normal sleep pattern would return, so I activated her immune system to make it work much faster. In seconds, I could see the degradation was now much faster, and at this rate, she should be fully awake in an hour. Mission accomplished. I told Pat she would be awake in an hour, so best if he cooked another breakfast so it would be ready when she woke up.

CHAPTER FIFTEEN

STEPHEN AND I WENT BACK to his Prague office and discussed the neutralising of the remaining sisters. We knew now that slumberland would work on them and Messapth. "These are very clever women, and I am sure they would notice the change in their daughters. When Sheflin went back, she felt uneasy, and it's quite possible that her mother noticed it, but as there were more important things on the agenda it was not considered, but if all six are different when they go home, it will be noticed, so we must allow them to deploy the explosives into all the Star Chamber's aircraft. We know that the explosives will only act at altitude, so if the pilots keep the aircraft under a thousand feet, they should be safe and we can orchestrate a mayday and the media can be relied on to inform the world of the demise of prominent businesspeople across the globe," Stephen said.

"We seem to be dotting Is and crossing the Ts prematurely. Between now and the deployment of slumberland are the sisters really going to do that much harm?" I wondered.

"Our main problem will be if the sisters do notice a difference in Sheflin, so if she notifies them that she has deployed her canisters, they will be under pressure to deploy theirs," he replied.

"They are going to have a problem now that Rodbridge is President, as it will be difficult to get close to Air Force 1; they may have to rethink the strategy," I remarked. "It was always going to be hard to get Rodbridge as he has his own airfield, but to them, no one who was at the Star Chamber meeting can remain alive or the action to recover Media Corp. for Bruce Kennett will undoubtedly fall at the first hurdle, so we underestimate the ingenuity of these ladies at our peril. I will talk to all involved and tell them not to fly for the next 13 days until we have removed the threat of Dark Seven. If they need to travel, I will arrange it," concluded Stephen.

CHAPTER SIXTEEN

SHEFLIN PEACEFULLY WOKE UP. Pat had cooked another breakfast and presented it to her. She was overwhelmed and wolfed it. She realised she was well out of time for her routine—her workout took nearly two hours, and she was now four hours behind her normal day, but she did not care. Pat took the tray away and then came back into the bedroom. "You have put me hours behind, and I have missed my workout, and it's all your fault!" She grabbed him, tore his clothes off, and made love again. It was fast and furious, then over. She told him, "That will make up for my missed workout!"

"If that's my punishment, then rest assured it could

become a regular event when I am here. It might give us an edge when we exercise together!" he replied, and they both laughed.

As he gathered his clothes, he handed her the instruction manuals for the top-secret devices, saying, "I will have the devices in a few days, how are you going to send them?" to which she replied "UPS—we use them all the time. Only sensitive information goes through trusted couriers, where no traceability is the prime requirement. Even the devices will go UPS as we can track them all the way and it's safer, other than delivering by hand."

Pat went back to the Prague office, and they arranged to meet later. Sheflin phoned her sisters and told them the instruction manuals were on the way to them and the communication devices would follow within a few days. "I have deployed all my canisters and the Swiss, Italian, and German part of the Star Chamber should be neutralised as soon as they take to the air." The sisters said that all their canisters would be deployed within the next 72 hours.

She questioned Geflin's response, as her American targets were now ultra-protected, as circumstances had changed, and they were the government now. Geflin laughed. "I have had more shags on Air Force One than any President. I have been through all the pilots and co-pilots. I even have security clearance in my own right. It is easier now than if I had to get into Anders Airfield, which has always been a problem. All the security there must be eunuchs, but the US military are driven by their dicks, so it's easy to get what you want. Charles Dunedin could be difficult as he will not fly, so I may have to turn his lights out personally, but rest assured I have no problem with the timetable."

CHAPTER SEVENTEEN

THE HOUSE OF DEFLIN WAS UNIQUE within Dark Seven. Deflin had met a man during the seven years after leaving the school in Zurich. He was a couple of years older, but Professor Roger Bane was the most intelligent and gifted person in cloning; he was at the very top, and where he led others could only follow. Dark Seven had funded all his research and allowed Deflin to marry him and set up home in a village just outside Cambridge, where he would be close to his faculty and research centre with the pick of the best students, and what seemed to be unlimited funds for his research.

At home, he had duplicated his laboratory, at his wife's suggestion, and she assisted him there with his research, where between them they had developed a human clone from DNA of a blood sample. It took just over three months for the clone to become an adult. The professor's aim was to create a clone for organ donation to the rich and powerful, however, Deflin had more sinister motivation and while her husband was away at university each day, she was trying to go one step further, to bring them to life and replace those rich and powerful people.

Deflin had been at the council meeting when Bruce Kennett had arrived and knew the problem he had losing his empire to me. She had been working on a technique using a DNA profile to programme an existing clone. She accessed Addenbrooke's files on the off chance that I might have been a patient or screened at some point, and bingo! I had been, so she took my profile, used one of the clones and programmed my DNA into it. The next step was to give it life, which had been successful on cloned animals. This step was a giant leap, and one her husband would not have allowed, had he been there.

Deflin punched the buttons and began to programme my DNA into the clone, which started to take my shape. She programmed it to ride a motorcycle and to shoot, and she energised the clone to life, and to her amazement, the programming was successful. The motorcycle had been purchased, all identification and false number plates fitted, the clone had been programmed to ride it and off he went to assassinate me.

Deflin knew that one day she would have to kill her husband, but the time was not right yet. In her house at

Messapth, an identical lab had been constructed, but she did not have the same vision and expertise in this science as her husband so he would be safe for the time being, although she would have to prevent him from going to the lab that evening so he would not see that one of his clones was missing. It would not be hard. A threesome with their daughter would exhaust him, so everything was prepared for a night of debauchery.

CHAPTER EIGHTEEN

I LEFT PRAGUE and returned home to Assington. David had researched cloning as I had asked him to do and bought his preliminary results, which he handed to me, and we went through them together. There were hundreds of labs working on this branch of science, but very few at the top, and the one name which kept cropping up was Professor Roger Bane, who had published the most papers on the subject. The others always referred to his research, so he clearly was the man most likely to know who could create a clone of me and make the attempt on my life.

David gave me the scientific data on the guy, so I spoke to Conrad and asked if he had anything on him in Media

Corp. Within seconds, pages of information were being downloaded on my computer, most of it on his family life and his notoriety, just a bit of academia. A clever guy like him would earn quite a lot of money, but looking at photos of his house, it was larger than Assington Priory, and it would take a considerable sum of money to keep it in good shape. Things were not adding up.

Stephen Shefford was still in Prague, and I asked him to check Bane out thoroughly. I sent him all the stuff that David and Conrad had given me, and I continued wading through Conrad's file on the professor. There was a whole gallery of his photos, but barely any photos of his family; in fact, his wife and daughter were clearly deliberately omitted; I could not find any photos of them. Why was he so careful to ensure their anonymity? I spoke to Stephen again and asked that Bane's wife and daughter be included in his checks. "It's a gut feeling. I believe this is the guy who created the clone that tried to kill me."

He said, "I will be in Assington just after midnight. Relax, have a drink, don't even think of doing anything other than going to bed. I will see you in the morning and talk to you then." He knew I was thinking of taking a little trip to Cambridge, and now that was off the agenda until tomorrow. I had the whole evening off, but I just had to talk to Herr Hoffman to find out how much the professor was worth and where the money was coming from to support his lifestyle. I would have all the information available on him by the morning and then we could agree on a course of action and implement it.

CHAPTER NINETEEN

I **REALLY HADN'T HAD THE TIME** to look round my home yet. It was a hundred and 60 acres and I had only really seen the parts I lived in. I would find my wife, and we would explore together. I took the easy way to find her, touching my bracelet to enter her mind. She was busy, the twelve houses were built, and it was now time to make them homes, so Sue was talking to all the family, making sure that each house was right for its family, paying her usual attention to detail. I caught up with her at Peter's house and asked her how it was all going. "Well, to be truthful, it seems that all the family want to stay at Cheltenham and really they are just going through the motions about Assington," she told me.

"I can understand that. They are being waited on hand and foot, living in luxury, with excellent food, and because they are our family, they are VIPs, and anyway, their work is in Cheltenham," I replied.

Should we fail to stop the eruption, we would still have time to get them there, and perhaps we should be looking at the houses as storerooms, just in case. But then I wondered what right we had to survive when so many would perish? Yet another dilemma.

We left the houses, passed through the woods and walked towards our boundary wall across acres of wildflowers and pasture—a natural habitat for all the animal residents. I told her what was happening and the progress we were making; there were so many problems to be resolved, but I assured her I was on top of them all. I realised it would take days to look round the estate, so we started to walk back to the Priory, bumped into security, and they gave us a lift back.

There seemed to be a permanent barbecue on the go. I really had no idea how many people were employed to look after the three of us, apart from Sue's chauffeur, Trevor, and his wife, both employed by me. All the other people were with Stephen Shefford Security, and it suddenly occurred to me that we had never talked about costs. He was wealthy, but this was business and all the arrangements needed to be put on a business basis.

It must be an Australian thing—the prawns were huge, the steaks massive, and the barrel of beer seemed to last well, but Trevor was taking care of that as he was in the trade before working for me.

It was the first time in weeks that I felt relaxed; I am sure that was due to the feeling that we were in total control of our agenda. In as much that the people who wished us harm would be neutralised, there remained the unanswerable question of how safe the planet was, and only time would tell.

It was just past midnight when Stephen Shefford arrived. We were woken up by the noise of the helicopter's rotors. I felt as though I should get up and discuss things with him but decided to stay where I was until the morning.

CHAPTER TWENTY

I WAS SURE SOMEONE WAS COOKING bacon under my nose—the delicious smell woke me just after 8 am. I showered, dressed and went in search of that aroma, knowing that our kitchen was fully ventilated, so smells disappeared into the atmosphere; why was I not surprised that breakfast was on the barbie? It was wonderful, the taste and smell abundant in every mouthful.

Stephen appeared just as I was finishing my breakfast, and over coffee, he told me that my instincts were right, "It seems that Sheflin's sister Deflin is also the daughter of Professor Roger Bane. I have checked with Sheflin and Bane's wife is the only mother of Dark Seven to have a life outside Messapth, she does not know why but it is

extremely important to Dark Seven for this to continue."
We looked at photographs of his daughter and wife, and
like Sheflin, they were beautiful. Roger Bane was a geek; he
really had nothing going for him but his intelligence.

Herr Hoffman's financial report showed that there were
several corporations and benefactors who supported his
research with large sums of money such that he would
never run out, but all these came from one source, a small
private bank in Paris, which had enormous funds at its
disposal, complied with French banking law, and had been
given the all-clear on money laundering from the French
security commission, the EU commission and the
European Bank.

"Yet Herr Hoffman, with all his clout, has not been able
to talk to anyone at the bank as the directors are on holiday
for August and cannot be contacted. Herr Hoffman's take
on this is that the bank is laundering money, how it got its
accreditation he will investigate further, but it will take time;
suffice it to say that Professor Roger Bane's research is
funded by illegal money, but it's clean when it arrives at his
bank," I summarised.

Stephen said, "It was just as well you didn't go to
Cambridge; you would have been no match for those two
women; I suggest that we wait until the daughter is taken
out of the loop, which will be in the next three days, and use
her to neutralise her mother. The mother takes frequent
trips to Ankara. It seems that she is the principal benefactor
to an orphanage just outside Ankara, but checking by
satellite, it has a runway and a Learjet parked on it. I

checked out the ownership, it's the same company that leases out Sheflin's plane. It's a good cover. She actually puts in a lot of money and everyone at the orphanage thinks she is an angel, according to my people in Turkey. We have forestalled any more cloning by using the chips, so that's not a major issue. I will have satellite surveillance on the premises and track her movements, and with Court Leiston's help we can get into their computers and find out what's really happening, so my advice is to concentrate on Sheflin's sisters as agreed, take control of Messapth, which will leave Deflin—the mother—isolated and although extremely dangerous, she can be taken out at our leisure one way or another."

I reminded Stephen that "another" was not sanctioned, and the intention was that these dangerous people would live to regret the evil they had perpetrated.

I checked my emails. The Star Chamber members had immediately started to implement green policies. Chow En Lie was having great difficulty because even though these changes would be funded by Earth Corp, politics was still be involved as all changes had to go through a bureaucratic process. It could be years before our merger was ratified, so I hoped we had that time.

Better news from America, the election date was now confirmed as 23rd September. The unelected President, Rodbridge Anders, would stand as an independent, in view of which both Republican and Democratic parties would put up candidates as required by the constitution but would not contest any state purely because of the impending disaster that would turn America into a crater.

Rodbridge had officially told both the Senate and Congress, the House of Representatives, that he would only be at the helm for this period, but he wanted the American electorate to confirm that they understood what might happen to them and to show support for his efforts. It was a similar situation in the UK and the rest of Europe; it was universally accepted that the world was facing an impending disaster of a magnitude that was beyond politics, but we needed to have the people's visible support; unopposed elections were taking place everywhere, with Earth Corp being the only party on the ticket.

Herr Hoffman's email made some interesting reading. A serious amount of money was channelling from the northern hemisphere into Swiss banks and being drawn into banks in South America, Australia, New Zealand and the South Pacific Islands. Most of these funds were for property acquisitions, so it seemed the wealthy were finding boltholes where they planned to survive the imminent eruption. "Unfortunately for them, the volcanic cloud will be so immense it will cover both hemispheres and in time both ice caps will merge, there is a possibility that small parts of the Pacific Ocean may be unaffected, and that's about the only place where survival just might be feasible, but with the prospects of a slow, lingering death, as the ice age will last over a hundred years. On the positive side, gold and precious stones are having a revival, and have reached an all-time high with no signs of a weakening market," he reported and added that he felt it was due to their state as hard currency and to a lack of faith in electronic money.

I picked up the phone and told him to sell my gold and precious stones to increase our cash reserves to five hundred billion pounds. I did not know why I wanted this arbitrary sum of cash, but it just seemed the right thing to do. I went to tell Sue I was off but would be back for dinner.

CHAPTER TWENTY-ONE

I ARRIVED IN UTOPIA and made my way to the technical area, which was humming with droid activity; I discerned a sense of purpose in them and that something had changed. I found Professor Dave Mac, and from the smile on his face when he saw me, I did not need to read his mind. I knew I was going to get good news.

He told me that the communication with the droids had been solved, sign language! "One of my team's son is deaf and dumb and is able to sign. He taught the droids to sign and now they are fully up to speed on the problem that faces us all. The machines that make the tunnels you saw yesterday are now back online and have started new tunnels, where the earth's crust is weakest; it appears that the existing tunnels terminate at the Mariana Trench in the Pacific."

He took me to a display showing twenty-five red dots in line—which were the tunnelling machines, all moving but some faster than others. I asked how long it would take. "Amazingly, they are covering about a hundred miles a day, I estimate the trench to be about three thousand five hundred miles, so in roughly 35 days the first pressure tunnels will be complete, then they will come back and start again a mile lower each time until we have a hundred tunnels. They are contained within a circle one hundred miles in circumference, and if necessary, we will blow them to make one huge tunnel."

"Isn't that a bit over the top?" I queried. "When Krakatoa exploded, it left a ten-mile crater on the seabed. I am factoring in a safety margin of ten, and hoping that will be enough," he replied.

"I am sure your calculations will be fine. Can I meet your guy who taught the droids sign language, as I would like to thank him?" I added. We walked over to him as he was giving instructions to a droid, who relayed them to whichever droid would accomplish the task. I thanked him. I read his mind and there was a deep sadness about his son, mute from birth. I told him we could be able to help and asked if it would be alright if I tried. It would only take us about 30 minutes to get to Tucson, Arizona, and I summoned Monk to travel with us, as we would need his skills, which he had been using longer, although, in theory,

I should have the same level of skill.

In a short while, we were walking up his front path. His son was playing on a swing and hadn't noticed us, so he walked around to face him. A huge beaming smile consumed his face when he saw us and he jumped off the swing for an almighty hug from his dad, who carried the boy indoors.

He introduced us to his wife and told her what we were going to do, but Monk had already started: the neural pathways that coordinate speech and hearing were being fixed, and within two minutes of us arriving the boy was making and hearing noises.

His first word was "Mummy". Monk was also uploading into his mind the vocabulary he would need for his age. Tears streamed from the eyes of both parents, and their son could not stop talking. I told the father to take the rest of the day off; he would not be needed until the following day when Professor Dave Mac would pick him up.

CHAPTER TWENTY-TWO

MONK AND I TRAVELLED back to Assington, where we would meet the team that would be capturing the six sisters and a Dark Seven mother. I felt that there was an over-reliance on the slumberland drug, although the text on Sheflin was successful, but only time would tell.

The parcels containing the drug would be delivered over the next few days, monitored by the security team. "The first parcel was delivered today to Sheflin's sister in Sydney. Stephen Shefford has a surveillance team monitoring her, and also the satellites with heat-seeking and infra-red capabilities will be assessing whether the drug has worked and whether she is unable to put up any resistance," we were told.

I insisted that Monk and I would be there because it had taken both of us to achieve mind control over Sheflin. She was aware of our abilities and would have taken us out first had she the opportunity, but she had been restrained physically so it was purely a mental fight, but it was still difficult and Sheflin herself said she was the worst practitioner of her martial art amongst her sisters.

Stephen was making use of my office. We all sat, looking at computer screens, and watched as the first parcel was delivered; Sheflin had told her sisters that they had to sign on receipt, such was the importance of the communication device. It would take the best part of a week to capture those that were outside Messapth and neutralise them, providing everything worked to plan. The plan was very good, providing slumberland worked, as the biggest task was to nullify Messapth and its inhabitants, and for that, we would have to wait and see.

I was looking at a freeze-frame picture of the recipient of the parcel. Sheflin was beautiful, but her sister Caflin appeared even lovelier, or maybe it was just beauty being in the eye of the beholder. For all her looks, she was undeniably evil, and we all had to remember that. Each communication device carried a separate electronic signal that Stephen now turned on so that we could trace them anywhere in the world. Sheflin had warned all her sisters that trying to use their device without following procedures in the handbooks that would be sent separately would cause it to self-destruct. She had advised them to take their device to their own safe houses, which were not known to any other sister. We needed that information so we could completely close down their operations on each continent.

The communicator was on the move, and we were following live on the screen, but I felt sure this would take some time, so I asked Stephen to let me know when we had the address, and I went to read the latest reports on acquisitions.

The preliminary reports from Africa and the Indian sub-continent were unanimous in stating that there was an abundance of silicone; all had coastal areas, so sodium chloride was plentiful, hydrogen was everywhere, so we had the basic requirements to produce white energy, but we had to find water to sustain people in these areas. Desalination plants were expensive and would have to be run on fossil fuels, which would be self-defeating since we were trying to eliminate their use. Sunshine and heat we had, so solar power was a possibility, but the carbon footprint from making the panels was greater than from the short-term use of fossil fuels until we could adapt them to run on white energy. The costs were staggering: the oil/electrical desalination plants were $1.5 billion each, and we needed ten. The solar panels were slightly dearer but required an area the size of Suffolk for deployment.

We had to find a natural source. I knew that Utopians took holidays as we did and there were huge underground freshwater lakes; indeed, Monk was an avid sailor who spent all his free time on his boat, as did most Utopians. Sailing was the Utopians' favourite pastime, and the lakes were all well documented and mapped, but I wondered how we could locate these lakes from the surface, with the possibility of tapping into them to get the water we needed.

I went back to Stephen, who was still monitoring Sheflin's sister and asked him about the satellites he used, whether they could search beneath the earth's crust, but he didn't know. To find out, he spoke to someone in the American military and posed the question. The reply was that radioactive elements could be traced about a mile deep, but if they wanted to go further, they could use the geo satellites the oil companies used for finding oil reserves and precious metals.

I spoke to David to find out who owned these geo satellites and was advised that they were built by Geothermal Technologies and used NASA for launching, and there were over two hundred in orbit delivering data for a price. Based on previous finds, the programmes running the satellites yielded 87% accuracy in identifying the presence of oil, but drilling was necessary to confirm that.

I asked David to find out if we could change the parameters of the programme to locate water instead of oil. Earth Corp had now hundreds of scientists, specialists in some form of geology, so I posed a question for them all and flagged it as a priority, "How can we locate water that is deep underground? I know that there are at least four freshwater lakes of monumental size and I need to know how to find them." I pressed the send button and went back to see how the pursuit of Sheflin's sister had progressed.

CHAPTER TWENTY-THREE

THE FLASHING DOT ON THE MONITOR came to a standstill, so I assumed that the location of Caflin's safe house was now included in our dossier. Stephen had all satellites now focused on that house, and we could see that the only way in was a single-track road or by foot. The telltale infra-red signals were scattered all over the property. Anyone trying would have great difficulty getting to the house unnoticed.

She was at least 90 minutes away from her home, and we were 45 minutes away with the team in position to capture the second sister, the same team we had for Sheflin, in case slumberland did not work and she had to be taken by force. There was enough time for me to spend some of it reading the mountain of important reports, so I clicked through them rapidly.

Once I was up to date, I shut down and went in search of a coffee. I found Sue in the kitchen, helping out. "Any chance of a coffee?" I enquired, and without looking round, she pointed to the percolator and said, "Help yourself!" which I did, and took my coffee into the garden. I marvelled at the number of people in evidence, all looking after our welfare; I had barely any involvement in our security, as Stephen had told me many times.

I was going over in my head all the reports I had just read. There were about four hundred and fifty companies around the world with the potential to clean up carbon emissions but were just idling along with no clear direction because the power generating and oil companies were only just scratching at the surface of the consequences of burning carbon. I had warned them as a major shareholder that they must clean up or be closed down, but that would be the last resort since the ensuing gap in energy supply could not be bridged from renewable sources, potentially leading to power cuts, which would not be tolerated by the public at large. I had to develop another strategy.

I spoke to Herr Hoffman and told him to buy stakes in those companies and inform them that funding would no longer be an issue and they should prepare to clean up the world, starting with the worst polluters. I told him they should offer the oil companies and generators of power a no-deposit ten-year lease-purchase deal for the equipment at 5% interest. All governments would allow 100% of these costs to be offset against their tax liabilities, and any companies failing to comply would have an additional carbon tax of 15% of monthly turnover placed upon them, with immediate effect.

Herr Hoffman pointed out that those allowances did not exist under present law, to which I replied, "Not yet, but I assure you that there will be announcements within the next 48 hours by all governments that legislation will be put in place in order for the lease-purchase scheme to operate."

"How can you be so sure?" he asked. "Easy, the President is a businessman first, and it's a no-cost option for his company. He will do the right thing. I am just about to talk to him," I stated.

"OK," he agreed, "I will get my team on it, but you realise every time you enter the markets you set a false demand and send the wrong signals to the experts and they tend to follow and push the market higher than it really ought to be, pension funds take advice from the experts and vast sums are invested which affect ordinary people."

"I do realise, but most of us will be dead if we don't stop burning fossil fuels, so saving the planet first is my priority," I said.

"Point taken!" he replied.

After three unsuccessful attempts to contact the President normally, I touched my bracelet, and we were communicating immediately. I told him the proposition and straight away. He thought as the Chairman of Anders Corporation looking at a good deal and assured me "Anders will be the first to sign the lease agreement."

"Mr President," I said, "I want you to address the nation. Your ambassador to the United Nations must extol the virtues of the leasing scheme. You must also get all the Star Chamber members to embrace it and use their influence to ensure full subscription to the deal. Make that speech 48 hours from now; the British Prime Minister will do the same."

I spoke to him next. He told me he would be in contact with the EU and hoped they would also relay the message, but his main concern was whether we could deal with the volume of demand if every carbon polluter placed an order in five days. I agreed that we couldn't, so we would just start with the worst polluters.

CHAPTER TWENTY-FOUR

I TOOK MY CUP BACK to the kitchen. I wondered why Sue was still busy in there and asked. She said she was worried and keeping busy was her answer; of course, her bracelet worked, so she could see all the concerns in my head.

I went back to see how things were regarding Caflin. She appeared to be heading home. It was nearly midnight in Sydney. We were now following by satellite only, as the communicator was at the safe house. It was like watching a reality programme on TV. Stephen noticed that she did not seem to be going straight home after all. We soon understood why—her car stopped at an apartment complex. She went to the door, buzzed and spoke into the intercom, and then went back to her car and waited.

Two minutes later, a guy stepped out and walked to the car. Stephen zoomed in on his face, but it took the computer a few minutes to get a name. "Shit!" Stephen exclaimed. He had already clocked who the guy was. "It's Huey Harris, the lead singer of the Twingos. My company's assigned to protect him and the rest of the group!"

I wanted to know what the problem was, as we would not kill him. "If she takes him back to her apartment, he will not be affected by slumberland, if what Robert Saxham thinks is correct. So, she will stay asleep, and he will be unable to wake her, assume it's a medical condition and call the emergency services!" he explained.

I touched my bracelet and was in contact with Robert Saxham. I asked, "Can slumberland be targeted to an individual who is not in the same time frame as someone already exposed to it?" He didn't know but told me, "No one has died from it, several thousand people have been affected by it and there have been no side effects, so far only directly administered. I don't know, and I don't know who to ask, sorry!" I sought Monk; he reassured me that our power over Huey's mind would keep him safe and out of harm.

I turned back to Stephen and told him we would be leaving for Australia immediately to dart Huey Lewis with slumberland so he would catch up with his girlfriend when he slept, and to reassure ourselves we could satisfactorily sort out any complications with his client.

"Robin, you don't understand. He has 24/7 security, and my guys are the best. They are part of his life, his shadows," he protested.

"That's all very well and I accept what you say, so they will have to give him the slumberland, then. You need to contact his minders, and we must meet with them so they can ensure that he is subjected to the drug before he goes to sleep," I concluded.

We had assembled the team within 45 minutes and were gathered close to an exclusive Thai restaurant in Sydney. It was just past 1 o'clock and Stephen walked off to find Huey's minders. They were on duty, very alert and professional. He instructed the senior minder to take a bunch of flowers into the restaurant and make sure that Huey smelled them as well as his companion and to stay with him until he did, even if it meant he had to smell them himself.

The minder took the flowers into the restaurant, summoned the maître-d' and gave him a password to repeat to Huey which he would recognise as from his minders and know that ignoring it could be dangerous and indeed might well be.

Huey responded correctly, excused himself and then came back with a huge bunch of flowers, allaying any fears on the part of his partner. They both ingested the full fragrance of the flowers and would now succumb to slumberland the next time they slept, whenever that would be!

All plans can go wrong. It was my fault. Young people do stay up at night-time and sleep daytime, but I had incorrectly assumed that they would sleep at some point when it was dark, only now I could see it would not happen anytime soon. My idea of capturing the six daughters of Dark Seven using the time zones to our advantage would not work.

They should all have been exposed to slumberland and when they slept, it would be for a minimum of 24 hours and a maximum of 48 hours. The plan was not dead in the water, we just had to think it through.

I suggested to Stephen that we would take the team to his offices and have a rethink, as nothing was going to happen there for at least an hour. He made a call and four vehicles arrived to take us all.

Stephen, Monk, and I were now in his office. "Let's get all six daughters on a screen with the time they each received the communicator," I said, "and on each screen put a twenty-four-hour countdown clock from that time. We are within 45 minutes of each daughter, so we can capture them by monitoring when they sleep, targeting them in order of when they sleep. We do have a window of 24 hours, so we just have to monitor them all and we can leave the team to do that while you show me Sydney."

Monk and I followed Stephen to a vehicle. I asked him to pretend we were tourists and do the normal thing. I could tell his mind was still on the job in hand and he was a reluctant tour guide. "Chill out! We can do nothing until they sleep, and in the worst-case scenario that slumberland does not work, we still have an effective team to take them aggressively if we have to," I reassured him, "so relax and show us your city."

It worked—well, sort of. He drove us to the highest point that overlooked Sydney and its harbour and pointed out all the significant sites; the views were spectacular, but we seemed to be looking at a postcard rather than the real thing.

Next, he took us to a restaurant where all the tables had a panoramic view overlooking the city. The owner recognised Stephen and took us to a table himself, summoning a waiter for drinks. Stephen ordered bottled water, and Monk and I would share a bottle of Chablis.

The waiter scurried off, and the owner handed us all menus. I was not feeling that hungry, so I just ordered some prawns in a green Thai sauce, and Monk chose the same. Stephen opted for a house speciality, a Roo burger.

The service was excellent, and our meals soon arrived. I had never seen prawns this size—they were huge and cooked to perfection, and the burger was in itself a meal for two, including the trimmings.

We did the meals justice. Stephen had not eaten properly for two days, just grabbing bites whenever he could, and I could sense he was more relaxed now that his hunger had been satisfied.

As the second bottle of Chablis arrived, Stephen's phone rang, so he waved the bottle away and took the call, anticipating that we would have to leave at once as it was a forty-minute drive back to his office. Monk and I were disappointed, as the Chablis was excellent, but business had to come first.

CHAPTER TWENTY-FIVE

BACK AT THE OFFICE, we were updated on the daughters. We should have foreseen that they were young people and being up at night and sleeping during the day was their thing. The daughter based in Hong Kong had received her parcel, and we had to assume she had opened it and gone back to bed instead of taking it straight to her safe house as she was told because the satellite infra-red and heat sensor showed just one red spot which was not moving about.

I contacted Robert Saxham and asked him how long it would take the drug to work; he said he would make some calls and get back to me. Stephen phoned Pat Smith, asking him to get Sheflin to contact her sister in Hong Kong. We all watched the screen for the slightest movement, but there was nothing, so it was decision time. "Let's go and get her!" I announced.

We arrived at Hong Kong International Airport. Stephen's company looked after most of the world's international airports, so the verticular could materialise in the private staff car park. The air ambulance was ready for immediate take-off, the ambulance was ready to collect its patient, and the rest of the team bundled into cars.

Stephen, Monk, and I put on the paramedics' kits. Stephen drove, and the cavalcade left rapidly, lights and klaxon sounding. Hong Kong traffic was dreadful any time of the day, but the universal emergency vehicle protocol worked, and we arrived in 15 minutes.

The security barrier raised to admit us to the complex, and we pulled up outside her apartment block. We got the stretcher out of the ambulance while the rest of the team secured the area, cancelled out all the CCTV and neutralised the security of the complex, so when we left there would be no evidence that we had ever been there. Stephen put his universal card into the security panel and the door opened.

There were four lifts, and we used them all, holding them on the top floor. We approached Feflin's door, Stephen opened it, and the team rushed in with tasers and white light guns at the ready, but it was all clear so that only left the bedroom. Had she been awake, she would be aware of us and prepared. The team burst into the bedroom and surrounded the bed where this beautiful woman lay. Monk and I approached the bed and confirmed that she was out for the count.

On her bedside table were several bottles of sleeping tablets and flu pills. She had flu, that's why she didn't go to the safe house.

Stephen looked for the communicator. He soon found the safe, opened it and retrieved the communicator, but left a considerable amount of money and jewellery which he later estimated to be worth well over a million pounds, the float for evil.

Monk and I entered her mind. We had to unlock her history to change her mindset. Once again, I was appalled at what a member of Dark Seven had done. We started to eradicate the history first so that overwhelming remorse would not make her suicidal when she woke up. Next, we nullified and replaced all evil tendencies with level and balanced principles based on good.

When we had finished, Stephen instructed his men to cuff her, shackle her ankles, and strap her to the stretcher before taking her to the ambulance. I said that would not be necessary, but he retorted, "I still have people in hospital from capturing Sheflin, and I will not be taking any chances!"

The convoy returned to the airport, and we sent her on her way to Prague. *Two down, five to go,* I thought. Will they all be this easy? Slumberland certainly works.

We had now neutralised two daughters, but what Monk and I had not realised was that they had a system of contact between them, which ensured the security of all the seven.

Sheflin remained in contact with her sisters, but Feflin would be out of touch for at least nine hours on her way to Prague. It was lucky that this was in her mind, so we found out when we entered it, as her flu had stopped her from her usual routine, and she hadn't wanted to do anything but sleep.

We were in a dilemma. Slumberland could last up to 48 hours. The security protocol might be triggered and alert Messapth, which we needed to avoid at any cost. We needed Dark Seven to be completely unaware of anything other than business as usual.

Sheflin gave us all the contact numbers and Stephen already had Wisconsin monitoring and recording at all those numbers, so I asked him to send all that information to David to work out how much time we had before their alarm system was triggered. If there was a pattern, David would surely find it.

CHAPTER TWENTY-SIX

BACK IN THE HONG KONG OFFICE, we now had just the five screens. In Australia, Caflin and Huey had left the restaurant for an exclusive club, which closed at 7 a.m., so I imagined that they would be there until the end unless their desire got the better of them, and they left earlier to indulge their lust.

I didn't realise that the club had private rooms where horny couples could satisfy themselves without leaving the club, and of course, that was what they had in mind and why they had gone there. We now had the major problem of how to extricate them from this club. Certain staff had to be retained to look after their guests, but if they could not wake them, they would panic and call the emergency services.

I turned to Stephen, who said, "We will be the emergency services, no problem, but what to do with Huey Harris is our biggest difficulty. We can't leave him there, so he will have to come too unless we make him disappear permanently."

"Not an option," I said. "We will take him to Prague."

"You can't. He is on tour with the band and has a gig tomorrow at the Sydney Opera house. I think people will notice if there is no lead singer!" objected Stephen.

"He won't be awake for it, anyway. He could be out for two days," I said, "unless I wake him up. I will enter his mind on the way to the airport and see what sort of relationship they have and go from there. We can either kidnap him or wipe his memory clean and return him to his apartment."

Caflin and Huey had started on the second bottle of champagne, and Huey was just about to top up their glasses when Caflin put a hand over his, her other hand on his crotch, and started gently massaging. On cue, he rose to attention! He summoned a waiter and asked for a key to their usual room, picked up the bottle of champagne, and led her calmly to their room.

Once inside, they resorted to more urgency. Their clothes were scattered around the room, and the next hour was filled with hectic lovemaking until Huey was exhausted. Caflin had an abundance of energy and never tired but had got used to burning her men out. In Messapth, the luxury of having all the men she needed to sate her sexual appetite was the main reason for going home.

She had tried sex with three men she had picked up in a nightclub in Fiji, local men who couldn't believe their luck, the sex had been sustainable for a few hours and she had really enjoyed it, but they were so full of themselves, bragging with each other about who had been the best lover, and it left her no option but to kill them and feed them to a couple of great white sharks from her boat on the way back to Sydney.

When the last piece of them had disappeared, she made a radio call to the Australian coastguard and told them of the shark attack while they were swimming; they had sacrificed their lives in order to save hers, she claimed tearfully.

She had to make a statement when she returned to Sidney and handed over their possessions so the next of kin could be notified, but she heard no more about it after that.

Huey had been on the road for six months and five concerts a week were taking their toll on him. Caflin smiled as he fell into a deep sleep, and she followed shortly after.

It was now 7 a.m. and the owner of the club wanted to lock up. He checked each room—normally, people had their fun and returned to the dance floor, but there was no answer when he knocked on their door, so he let himself in and found the two guests still in bed.

He recognised Huey straight away, tried to wake him, but got no response. He tried the woman...no response, panic taking hold of him. He thought they must have taken some illegal substance they had got at the club.

He rushed out and called the emergency services, but

the call was intercepted by us, and within ten minutes Huey and Caflin, were under our control.

Monk had explained to me that removing a memory from a mind was time-consuming as the brain often stored them in different parts with a traceable pathway leading to the memory, much the same as a computer does—if you put in a full search containing the key word, a list of files are shown, the brain is far cleverer as it puts the memory in order of events.

We had decided that for Huey it would be quicker to add a memory about that night, leaving the club, being dropped off at his apartment and going to bed, and we programmed his mind to wake up eight hours later after removing the effects of slumberland. Two security guards took him back by taxi to his apartment, with the cover story, if needed, that he was drunk and needed to sleep it off, and the paparazzi didn't need to find out.

Huey was now back in his apartment fast asleep, having had a wonderful time, and Caflin was on her way to Prague. We had rid her of evil while in the ambulance, and when she woke up in Prague, she would be full of remorse for the things she had done herself or condoned being done by others.

As we arrived at the airport, her phone rang. The caller identity was "mother", but we couldn't answer it. My whole body went cold; Messapth was calling a daughter. Surely no answer would start alarm bells ringing. At the very least, it would raise concern.

I told Stephen we would use my transport instead of the

plane, and we were in Prague 30 minutes later, where we now had two sleeping daughters.

Sheflin had arrived, and I said "Caflin's mother phoned her about 40 minutes ago, she was unconscious so could not answer. Do we have a problem?"

"Yes, you do!" she replied. "Not answering a call from your mother definitely starts alarm bells ringing, we only have a five-minute window to reply."

I asked what would happen then, but she said she didn't know as it had never happened before. Stephen speculated, "They would probably go on alert, another mother would try to contact her daughter and if also unable to get a reply, the level of alert status would raise."

"We have three daughters, including two unconscious, so it depends on which mother tries to contact her daughter next. If they all do, then we do have a problem, as Caflin and Feflin have changed their mindset and even if they were conscious, they would not be able to focus properly and their mothers will know that something is wrong," I said. "We are going to have to take out Messapth now!"

Stephen said, "Our plans are turning to shit. Slumberland works, so we take out Messapth. These are clever females, and you don't know what contingency plans they might have for our attack on their daughters, so best we just put them to sleep. At least that will give us time to capture the remaining daughters and hopefully a twenty-four-hour window to neutralise Messapth."

CHAPTER TWENTY-SEVEN

COLONELS BERRY AND GILL were still at the base on standby mode. I told them that everything seemed to be going tits up, so I wanted Messapth taken out that night, and I asked them if that would be a problem.

There was a slight hesitation before they replied "no". "Then let's do it," I said. "And good luck!"

"Stephen, how dangerous would it be for us to be there while the dosing is taking place, can we protect ourselves with the masks, so we are not affected?" I asked. "Don't even think about it!" he replied. "We will watch via satellite until all the heat signals are dormant and there is no activity. We can use Utopian transport then to get us inside Messapth while we wait for our helicopters to arrive bringing our troops and take out Dark Seven and all its evil for good."

Confirming what Stephen had said, Monk told me, "We can only neutralise the effect of the drug while we are awake. This drug just makes you sleep longer, so if for any reason we are exposed to it, we will all be affected in the same way. Our immune system will not find the drug harmful, so will not kick in. We are vulnerable."

I had to accept their judgement, and that I had to change my mind, but I did find the waiting hard.

David had analysed all the communication data from the last seven days using the sisters' phones, but he could find no link that would signal to the rest of them that one was in trouble. We did not hold sufficient information yet although we could get it, now we had their numbers. But that would take time, so I put it on hold until we had taken Messapth.

CHAPTER TWENTY-EIGHT

OBLIVION KNEW HE WAS GETTING WEAKER, and the Convergence was getting stronger; if he did not do something relatively quickly to upset the balance between good and evil, he would never be strong enough to overpower Infinity to conjoin with Eternity and put the Universe on a path of evil which would make him omnipotent.

Earth had always been his nemesis. No matter what he had tried in the past, he could not eliminate the Utopians, and it was the Utopians who were increasing the power of the Convergence as they were now entering the final part of human evolution to become part of the Convergence at the point of natural death.

He created a super-enriched hydrogen bubble of molten lava at the Earth's core, the size of Utah. This would slowly rise to the Earth's crust, pushing vast amounts of lava before it, taking out the whole of Utopia and pushing upwards through the crust to erupt on the surface.

CHAPTER TWENTY-NINE

GEFLIN AND HER ENTOURAGE ARRIVED in Lhasa and went straight to the four-star Sheraton Hotel. The daughters had forgotten what luxury was like after seven years in primitive conditions at the monastery, but they soon adapted to it!

Jojhinda Ravagit was already at the hotel. His family had been on the payroll of Dark Seven for centuries. His task was to create identities for the fourteen-year-olds. With all the social media available to kids, any teenager without a Facebook profile, Twitter account, and school friends would stick out a mile, so whole new identities had been fabricated from the age of three, which would have to be learned by the girls. This would take two weeks and then they would travel to Messapth, then on to Paris and Rome to shop before attending the Swiss finishing school for the next seven years.

The girls were excited about this part of their training after the austere living at the monastery—the fine clothes, the food, and most of all the fun, their sisters had all told them stories about their time at the school and they couldn't wait to get there.

The first time Geflin realised something had gone wrong was when her corporate card was rejected, checking out of the hotel—embarrassing, but her personal cards still worked.

She hadn't spoken to her house since arriving at Lhasa some three weeks ago, so she phoned her daughter in New York. No answer. She rang her household in Messapth but could not get through.

She was becoming really anxious that something was very wrong. She went in search of the daughters, who were finishing breakfast, and she told them to contact their mothers, but all tried and all failed.

"Something very bad has happened, and it seems we are on our own," she told the daughters. "We must find out what has happened so we will go to America as all my contacts are there, and we can do all the shopping in New York once I have found out what has gone wrong." The daughters were disappointed at first, but then again, New York sounded marvellous as they would probably never go there once, they started at the finishing school.

Geflin had several aliases, but she had not bought proof

of those identities with her. She phoned Jojhinda and told him she needed another identity, giving him a name she had used when she was looking after the Americas, and for which the paper trail was verifiable, as it was one of the first people she had killed when taking up her seven years in America.

There were never too many identities, and she had all the proper documents for this one in a safe deposit box along with over a million dollars in cash, but she needed to get back into the States.

Jojhinda flew back to Delhi, saying it would take two days to get her American passport, so she went with him and told the daughters to get ready, she asked reception to book the flights but found that there was no availability in any class on all aircraft for the next few days, so she chartered a Learjet, but it would not arrive at Lhasa for five hours. She could have chartered a plane at Lhasa to fly herself, but her pilot's licence had insufficient hours as she had not flown a plane for over two years.

She asked reception to book taxis to take them to the airport and where they would wait in the VIP lounge for the jet.

The flight to Delhi took about two hours. They took taxis to the Crowne Plaza and prepared to wait for her American passport.

Meanwhile, she had only ever passed through Delhi and decided to do the tourist trail, so she asked reception to organise transport for them all.

While she waited, she started to look through the daily

papers. Inside the Delhi Times, she saw a picture of a recovered old master painting by Goya which would be auctioned, with the proceeds going to a charity. Rage bubbled up inside her because that painting took pride of place in her house in Messapth. What on earth had happened?

She went into the hotel's coffee shop/internet café, where she started to scan back issues of American newspapers, and there it was: a large collection of stolen paintings had been found three weeks ago, all but a few were going back to the legal owners or to the insurance company which had paid out, and with the consent of the legal owners, some would be auctioned. The article showed all the paintings, with which Geflin was familiar as they had come from Messapth.

Her mind raced; very few people outside Messapth knew of its existence, yet somehow Messapth must have been compromised. She must find her daughter, who could tell her everything that had happened, but why hadn't she answered her phone? She tried to console herself with knowing that she would be in the States in another two days, but not knowing the answer to her questions was infuriating, and a deadly rage was simmering.

She would not be taking any prisoners in her quest for the answers, and the anticipation of killing made her feel a little better.

Geflin booked direct flights to New York for them all. The daughters had to get visas, and it would be a good test for their new identities.

Jojhinda was as good as his word, and the passport arrived on time. They got taxis to the American consulate where they were fast-tracked, and within an hour, they were back in the taxis, picked up their luggage from the hotel and were on their way to the airport.

The Air India flight was direct to JFK but would take over 15 hours. She couldn't get eight first-class seats and had to settle for business class. They arrived at the VIP check-in and effortlessly went through the formalities.

They boarded the Dreamliner, which took off on time. They would be served lunch, dinner and breakfast during the flight, which would break up the boredom of a long-haul flight, and the daughters were happy watching all the films.

It was Geflin's first trip on the new Boeing flagship, and being a pilot herself, asked if she could go into the cockpit. The stewardess said she would ask the pilot, but it was doubtful, as to prevent hijack; the cockpit was sealed, and it could only be opened from the inside. She duly asked the captain, who turned on the CCTV and looked at the passenger who had made the request. He had never seen anyone so beautiful! He told his first officer to take over so that he could go into business class and explain personally why he could not allow a passenger into the cockpit.

He handed over the controls, punched in the security numbers and opened the door, then went through first-class to business to speak to Geflin. He explained the new rules on all aircraft because of the threat of hijack and apologised, explaining that it was out of his hands.

Geflin studied the captain. He was a very handsome thirty-something, and she knew that she could do anything she wanted with him. She gently touched the inside of his leg; he didn't flinch, and she knew she had him. Her hand continued up his leg. He had started to sweat; she got up and led him to the toilet, but he took her to the first-class cabin, which had two unused bedrooms. In one bedroom, he locked the door behind them and tore off his uniform. Geflin slowly took her clothes off, and within minutes, they made love. It had been some time since she had sex and wanted it as badly as the very obliging captain, and they were occupied for over an hour.

CHAPTER THIRTY

THEY ARRIVED AT JFK AIRPORT on time. She could not understand why she could not contact the daughter who controlled the Americas, but it was a hindrance rather than a concern as she was sure there would be a good reason.

The passports were closely scrutinised as always, but they passed through arrivals to collect their luggage without a hitch.

They took taxis to the Waldorf Astoria. It had been many years since Geflin last stayed there, but it was her favourite hotel. She just enjoyed the opulence and courtesy that had been shown to her during previous stays. The taxis arrived, the doors were opened, and they all got out and went through to reception.

She realised that the doorman had recognised her, so had many other staff members, so she would book in with the name they knew and not the name she had used to enter New York just hours ago.

She would have to book into the Mandarin using the other name as that was where she gave customs as her temporary address. Although an American citizen, she had been out of the country for several years and with the new border controls since 9/11, all Is must be dotted and Ts crossed, or anything untoward would be flagged and investigated thanks to the prolific flow of electronic information.

The manager had been buzzed by the doorman and greeted Geflin at reception. Two adjoining suites were found for her and the girls.

The long flight had taken its toll. The girls were excited to be in New York but were also jet-lagged as they had missed a night's sleep. It was 09:30 in New York, and the hotel was still serving breakfast, but they all declined it and went straight to their suites where their luggage had already arrived, and all the daughters took to their beds.

Geflin set the alarm for 13:30; she too would feel better with some sleep.

The alarm sounded. They all got up and made their way to the hotel gym.

The gym bustled with had a mixture of hotel guests and members. As guests, they would be provided with their own personal trainer, but the offer was declined because they had a strict routine they insisted on following, and all they needed was the use of the mat and the pool. The other equipment available was not needed.

Geflin headed to the pool, intending to start with fifty lengths, then do her mat exercise. The daughters started on the mats, and the personal trainers soon realised these young ladies were superbly fit, and the speed of their actions would have been unbelievable if they had not seen it for themselves.

They continued for over an hour. The practiced eye of a trainer could see there were slight differences in how each performed, but it was so marginal he thought they must be a team and training for the Olympics.

They completed their mat exercises and did not even look out of breath. After they finished off in the pool, Geflin started her own routine on the mat. She was as quick but had more flair and grace. She knew she was being watched—most of the gym had stopped to look, but she enjoyed being watched and did not disappoint her viewers.

Geflin and the daughters returned to their rooms to shower and dress, had a light lunch, then took a taxi to the Mandarin Hotel where Geflin booked them all in for three nights, saying their luggage had been put on the wrong flight and would catch up with them later.

She went on in the taxi to retrieve her safe deposit box, leaving the daughters at the hotel.

She went through the security checks and was soon reunited with her money and spare identity. The keys to her house in New York State, the car keys and credit cards would be useless, battery dead and out of date, respectively.

The house was in a secluded area and hopefully intact, so she would use it as her base but go first to find her daughter and start to unravel what had happened. She knew the address of the New York flat and would go there that night. She worked better in the dark, and if there was anything untoward, she would be prepared for it, but first back to the Mandarin and pick up the daughters to go shopping.

The daughters were not yet tested in the field. Their abilities were of nominal value to Geflin; they would not be a full asset for another seven years, and just then potentially more of a hindrance than a help, so she decided that they would stay at the Mandarin and she at the Waldorf, giving her more flexibility.

She would have to get them into a private school; The Chapin would do, and she would phone the principal after discussing it with the girls. The daughters were quite content to start their schooling in New York instead of Zurich, and the principal was happy to take seven new girls. The first semester started the following week, and they could board there as well. So, with that sorted, they went shopping.

They returned to the Mandarin later in four taxis, two of which were filled with the shopping, requiring the hotel porters to take it up to their rooms.

CHAPTER THIRTY-ONE

THE DAUGHTERS WERE SO EXCITED about their new clothes, which they couldn't wait to try on and they put on their own fashion show. Geflin told them that dinner would be at 20:00, and she would be away for most of the evening and would not see them until the morning, as she would stay at the Waldorf that night. Everything they might need was available at the hotel, so there would be no need to leave it. They nodded their agreement.

After an excellent meal, Geflin left them at about 21:30. She took a taxi to two blocks away from her daughter's apartment, went down into a subway to the ladies' restroom and changed into a black jumpsuit that made her nearly invisible. She put her original clothes into a left luggage locker and slipped out into the night. Her field-craft might be a bit rusty but nobody, except a true professional, would know.

She reached the apartment building. Keeping to the shadows, she looked for any signs of danger, anything unusual, anybody watching the building, and took over 15 minutes to make sure it was safe. People were coming in and out of the building. Stealthily, she made her way to the entrance lobby, keeping to the dark side, and when someone opened the door, she slipped into the lobby unnoticed.

She took the lift to the top floor to her daughter's apartment, where within minutes, she was inside and had isolated the alarm, pulled all the blackout curtains and then turned on the lights. Room by room she checked, but there was nothing to be found: no clothes, no food in the fridge, the bathroom was empty, even the floor safe was open with instructions on how to reset it, and all the surfaces had dust which looked like it had accumulated over a fortnight.

She had noticed some realtor's "for sale" signs as she reconnoitred the building. She thought one of the signs must be for that apartment, so she would check it out the following day.

She left the apartment and returned to the subway, changed back into her clothes and rented a car to go to her safe house, where hopefully everything would be working. It would take two hours at that time of night, so she would get there just after 01:00.

CHAPTER THIRTY-TWO

AFTER DINNER, the daughters made use of the beauty salon and were so pleased with their transformation into beautiful young ladies that they decided to go for a walk in Central Park, convincing themselves it couldn't do any harm, and while they did not like disobeying Geflin, she need never know. So, they changed into their designer tracksuits and trainers and left the hotel, crossed the road, and entered Central Park.

It was just getting dark as they started to jog, and they had gone deeper into the park when suddenly a young man leapt out in front of them, stopping the girls in their tracks. "What are you doing in my park?" he demanded.

The young Deflin replied, "This is not your park; it's for everyone!"

Several other young men emerged, and the girls were seriously outnumbered. "I am the leader of the Cruz gang, the most feared gang in New York, and this is my park, and you must pay to enter it. Give us your money!" he ordered.

"We don't have any!" Deflin replied.

"You're lying!" he said and brought out a large knife from behind him.

Deflin casually approached the young man, not intimated at all. What happened next was all over in seconds: she seized his arm and twisted it to stick the knife into his own throat. He was dead before he hit the ground, but it took a few more seconds before the rest of the gang realised the leader had been killed, and they went for their knives.

A minute later, twenty-seven members of the feared Cruz gang were dead, all of them with an expression of agony on their faces, except for the leader, who looked more shocked. Deflin had used his own arm so there would be no other fingerprints on that knife or any of the others.

The whole gang was wiped out in minutes, and the girls had not broken into a sweat or ruined their new clothes with a trace of bodily fluids. They also had only used their hands as they did not want to scuff their trainers.

Deflin had a look round to see if there were any witnesses, but none were evident, so they left the gruesome scene for someone else to find and continued jogging as if nothing had happened.

Deflin was wrong. The doorman of the Mandarin had asked a porter to follow them as guests of the hotel to make sure nothing bad would happen to them.

He had kept well out of sight but had phoned the police as soon as his charges were confronted by the gang leader. The gang had been a nuisance for months, and he hoped they would be caught in the act.

He heard the police sirens, and so did the daughters, so they doubled back to the hotel after all, where the doorman was very relieved by their safe return as he too had heard the sirens.

The girls showered and washed off their three-thousand-dollar makeover, then hid their tracksuits and trainers until they could dispose of them properly if necessary. Then they all got into their beds and waited for the dreaded knock on the door by the police, but it never came.

The porter was the only witness, but he did not stay at the scene to speak to the police; instead, he went back to the hotel where he told the doorman what he had seen. The doorman said that the girls had done the hotel a great service and to stay quiet about it because if the girls were as lethal as it seemed from what the porter saw, he would not want them as enemies.

CHAPTER THIRTY-THREE

ALL THE LOCAL NEWS TEAMS covered the story. The police appealed to the witness who had phoned them, but it was clear from their attitude that whoever had done the killing had rid New York of a feared gang and people should be grateful. It would also mean that the gangs that controlled other parts of the park would stay out for the foreseeable future.

Geflin took the interstate up to Kingston as she listened to the radio and heard the news of the murder of twenty-seven gang members. Police believed that it was a gang-related territory dispute. She did not give any thought to this.

She reached Kingston and made her way to Wood Road. Her safe house was at the very end, where the road turned into dense shrubbery. She got out of her car, reached through the shrubbery to find the keypad, punched in her numbers, and the first 12 feet of shrubbery parted. She drove in and the disguised gate closed behind her.

It was another mile before she reached her house. The gardens were seriously over-grown, and she could hear scratching on the paintwork of her rental car. She could barely make out the road, but it reassured her that no one had been there in her absence.

She fought her way to the garage, where she filled the generator with the fuel from the rental car, using the headlights to see, although it took two attempts before it burst into life and the garage lights came on. She threw a switch to turn on the power in the house.

Geflin had purchased a laptop and all the equipment required to get online. She tried everything to get in contact with Messapth, but messages came back undeliverable.

She used Google Earth and paid for real time to scan Messapth, where she could see activity and tried to zoom in on the communications centre—the building was there but all the satellite dishes had gone, so that explained why she could not reach them. She phoned a contact she had acquired several years ago and asked him to get her satellite information on Messapth over the last five weeks; he told her he would get right on with it, and she should receive something in the next two hours.

Geflin next concentrated on finding her daughter. They

had both used Facebook, so she accessed her daughter's profile to see nothing had been updated for 14 days, whereas she posted four or five times a day before that. Her last post was just after midnight, 14 days ago, and since it ended "night", Geflin assumed her daughter would have gone to bed.

She checked the other daughters, but their activity had stopped more or less at the same time, within 48 hours at the most, and the last posts were in the early hours of the morning, so whatever happened was to all of them.

"They must have been drugged. Why?" she pondered. "Their cover is a closely guarded secret, unable to be blown by anyone else alive, so it could only be one of the daughters, but which one? It has to be Sheflin. She was the first to disappear from Facebook, but why? We have the best lawyers. She must have volunteered the information as it could not be got by force, drugs or torture because they are trained to withstand that. She must have turned against the entire family, the whole of Dark Seven!"

Her laptop bleeped for incoming mail, and there was a link to download five weeks of satellite pictures for the co-ordinates she had given.

She opened up the attachment and started to scrutinise the material. There was nothing abnormal for the first 12 days, but on the thirteenth, an aircraft had landed; she zoomed in and got the aircraft identification number. She gave that information to another associate, who informed her that it was chartered by Shefford Securities. As she scrolled through the next three days, she saw two other planes and three helicopters land. By zooming in, she could see that the people put on the first plane to leave were mostly males, and after that took off, the helicopters started to load the contents of the treasure house of Messapth. She couldn't see each item but assumed that it was everything of value. Where was it being taken? She spoke to her associate again, asking for the flight plan. He was back in minutes to tell her it went to Zurich. "Thanks," she said, "I owe you."

One thing puzzled Geflin. She saw activity all over Messapth; re-running the film time and time again, she could see the people who were ransacking Messapth, but they just appeared; they hadn't been dropped off by any helicopter, she was sure of that.

If all their security had been breached, the secret way into Messapth by foot could have been compromised, worse still Sheflin might have shown them the way, but over the first day's activity no one had appeared from the entrance cave, so how did the bastards get in?

She was spending too much time on this problem. She had to accept that "they" had got in and taken away Dark Seven's wealth. Her priority was to get it back. She had contacts in Zurich; the finishing school was primarily devoted to Dark Seven, although the staff did not know of its evil nature, and they were well rewarded for the work they did in fine-tuning the girls into adulthood. She looked at the time; it would be nearly 6 am when she got back to the Waldorf.

During the journey back, she took stock of the resources

available to her: one million dollars, seven deadly fourteen-year-olds, and seven deadly twenty-one-year-olds just about to complete their schooling in Zurich. Would that be enough? They would be all seriously pissed off to have lost the lifestyle that they had been looking forward to. Surely, that would focus their minds on reclaiming what had been stolen from them. Answers awaited in Switzerland, and that would have to be their starting point.

CHAPTER THIRTY-FOUR

A MILLION DOLLARS could sustain a reasonable lifestyle, but that would not satiate the vengeance which was rooted deep in her soul. The perpetrators would die painfully, and for this, she needed more than a million dollars, so she went through a whole list of criminal ways of increasing her cash supply: kidnapping, extortion, fraud, e-crime...they all took so long to organise; drugs—invest a million dollars but cutting and distribution would still take time. Then it came to her in a moment of inspiration. "Colombia, the drug cartels. We will rob one of the drug barons; they carry tremendous amounts of cash reserves, and the authorities would not care too much, probably we would be doing them a favour."

She needed to travel to Bogota and seek out her old main contact. Although it was over 20 years since she had needed to use this contact, she still knew how to find him, and if he was not available, she had plenty of other options which would suffice. She booked a flight to Bogota.

Geflin contacted her daughter in Zurich; she used her decoder. Although relatively primitive, it would inform her that Messapth had been compromised and was no longer safe. "I need all the girls to be in Bogota within seven days. Please make sure that they all arrive in Bogota on the same day but on different airlines via different countries, because I have not found out who initiated the attack on Messapth, so everything we do might be compromised," she instructed her daughter.

Geflin explained her plan to the girls. She booked flights for them to Florida and told them to charter a boat there for at least one month. "When at sea, use your charms to find out how to operate the motor cruiser, and once you are conversant with its operation, kill the crew and throw them overboard. Make your way to Colombia and then to the River Sinu where we will rendezvous."

The girls were quite excited about going to Florida and they had a whole week to get to Colombia so that they would have time to do the Disney thing before setting off.

Geflin gave her daughters a quarter of a million dollars in cash for the charter and any other incidentals. Taxis were ordered to take them to JFK; she signed them out of their hotel and herself out of the Waldorf, and re-booked reservations for them the following week, just to keep the authorities happy, should they feel inclined to investigate their whereabouts.

Using fake names and addresses, Geflin bought mobile phones with worldwide coverage for use only while on this operation.

At JFK airport security, the daughters went through swiftly; their flight left first. Geflin took her flight to Bogota and during her twelve-and-a-half-hour flight she fine-tuned her plan so all that remained was which unfortunate drug baron would provide them with the cash that they needed to enact the vengeance on all who opposed Dark Seven.

CHAPTER THIRTY-FIVE

UPON ARRIVING IN BOGOTA, Geflin hired a car and made her way to the first place that her primary conduit was likely to be. And true to form, he was sitting at the bar drinking as he must have done for all those years.

He was totally flabbergasted when a beautiful forty-something woman sat beside him and offered him a drink, which he accepted, nevertheless. Geflin said a code word that sent him into panic mode. He thought he must be about to die as he had never seen his Principal before and the only time that happened was when you were about to die for somehow failing in what you were required to do.

However, she beckoned him over to a booth where she

explained that she needed information on drug barons—who was the biggest; where they were, as near to a river was essential; their security, guards, and plans for their facilities.

The contact said that was easy: "The biggest drug baron and head of the cartel is Enrico Jimenez who lives in a fortress underground on the Isla San Jose, on the Rio Magdalena. But it is impregnable. Even the laboratories are a hundred metres underground and nothing in the arsenal of America can penetrate that far underground should they have the inclination to take him out. The concrete that was used was state-of-the-art, the very latest, which the Americans use for their own deep bunkers, and which apparently can absorb a missile and render it harmless."

Geflin asked if Enrico had any proclivities that could be useful to her. The man replied, "Yes, he has a penchant for young western females, and in the west, he would be considered a paedophile but in Colombia, young girls come of age much earlier."

She thanked him for the information and warned him the conversation and its consequences would remain a secret between them or he'd be dead on the spot. His very real fear of her ensured his compliance and silence.

She gave him a thousand dollars and left him alive, but whether that was a mistake, only time would tell.

Geflin took a taxi to the Bogota Hilton and checked in, ordered room service, took a shower, then phoned her daughter in Florida, who told her that they had made a detour to Orlando and tried booking into a hotel with cash, but found out that the cash required was above a prescribed limit to prevent money laundering. The solution was to pay by card.

Geflin was angry with them for not going directly to the Keys, but far more worried about the money laundering restriction and its consequences on cash. During her time in the Americas, cash was king and could remove any obstacle or problem, but now, cash in large quantities had become poison, and as such, put the girls in danger.

"Damn!" she thought to herself, but she told her daughter to go to the Orlando Hilton and she would use her card to pay for them over the phone. She would meet them the following evening, and they would all travel to Key West together to find a suitable yacht.

The girls were overjoyed at the prospects of 24 hours in Orlando. She booked herself and them into the Hilton and told reception that the girls would arrive today, and she would be there a day later.

After that, she booked a direct flight to Orlando, which would get her in at 14:30 hrs. She had two hours before her room service meal would arrive, so she changed and went to the hotel gym, where several male trainers offered to assist her. Of course, she turned them down.

Her training regime left the trainers breathless despite just watching. She headed off to the pool and did fifty lengths, not even panting afterwards. She grabbed her robe and went up to her room where room service had just delivered her dinner, which she devoured before calling her friendly banker in the Cayman Islands. He had done many illegal transactions for her in the past, not so much for the money he was paid, but for the fantastic sex.

The phone call came as a complete surprise as he hadn't heard from her for over 20 years, but he knew who it was as soon as he heard her voice.

Geflin asked him about money laundering. "Give me the facts and tell me how the restrictions can be overcome."

"With great difficulty," he replied, "unless you know a dishonest banker!" at which they both laughed.

"How much cash are we talking about?" he asked.

"Ten million dollars plus," she replied.

"How are you getting it here?" he asked.

She replied, "By boat."

"Well, you realise that this is now the most policed part of the ocean, with navies from all over the world working together to stop drug trafficking. Your vessel would need to be carrying someone very special with sufficient standing that no Navy would even countenance boarding or without a doubt, you will be boarded, and you can't hide that much cash."

Her original plan was ruined. Geflin had a plan for obtaining the money, but it was a huge problem getting it to the Cayman Islands undetected. She could deal with a small patrol boat boarding party, but she could not deal with a tomahawk missile from a warship.

Enrique's drug empire on the island must have ways of circumventing all the barriers she now faced, so she would have to find out how he did it before she killed him. The honey trap she planned would ensure they were invited to Enrique's underground lair. It might be impregnable from the outside, but it would be so easy to take control once inside.

What remained was how difficult it might be to find out how the drugs went out and the cash came in on an island in a major river with satellite surveillance everywhere. At worst, it would take longer than she had planned, and she would have to allow whatever time proved necessary for a successful mission.

One positive would be that the remaining members of Dark Seven would be together and present a deadly force to be reckoned with.

CHAPTER THIRTY-SIX

IN SWITZERLAND, the sisters left finishing school. All had hired rental cars and their cards still seemed to work. Three went through Italy, two left from Germany and two from France, planned so that they would all arrive within three hours of each other and meet up at the airport.

It was the start of setting the honey trap. Geflin had told them all to look like models and to flaunt themselves while waiting for her to arrive with the younger girls. They would spend the night at the Hilton and travel to Barranquilla at lunchtime the next day.

She had received information on Enrico Jimenez from her conduit that his favourite nightclub was La Quinto, which he partly owned, and he went there most weekends.

They were very selective about who they allowed in whenever he was there. Geflin would have no problem getting in, and fifteen beautiful women would not be turned away, but to make sure she would ask the hotel reception to book tables at La Quinto.

The Prado was the most expensive hotel in Barranquilla and only the opulent stayed there.

The entire group took taxis to the Hilton, which was buzzing with anticipation of fifteen stunning women arriving to the party, as Geflin had casually mentioned that intention when she booked their rooms.

She instructed them to unpack and meet her in her suite.

Thirty minutes later, she was explaining to them that her original plan was to use a boat to get the cash to the Cayman Islands, but her sources there told her it would be impossible as the Caribbean Ocean was heavily policed and everything that floated got searched. "Our target is a drug dealer called Enrico Jimenez. He lives in an allegedly impregnable underground fortress on an island in the Magdalena River. He is the biggest drug dealer in Columbia and holds vast amounts of cash. Our mission is to part him from that cash and get it to the Cayman Islands. Our main priority is to find out how he gets his drugs out and cash in.

The island must be under surveillance 24/7, so he must have a system that eludes all conventional equipment. Now, we shall set up a simple honey trap, he is part-owner of a club called La Quinta, my sources say that he goes there most weekends, so we must be at the club and get ourselves invited back to his home, and once inside its imperative that we find where he keeps his cash and how the drugs are shipped. We will fly to Barranquilla tomorrow. I have booked us in to the Prado for five days. Once there, we will get the hotel to book tables at the nightclub. We have to party big time tonight, so all the clubbers of Bogota know we have arrived and believe that partying is what we are here for!"

The older girls had plenty of sexy clothes, whereas the younger girls had pretty but modest attires. They needed to look the same as the older sisters, who took them shopping to get them kitted out.

Dinner was booked for 10 pm. They all looked stunning, even the younger girls now looked like adults. Every male who saw this array of beauty was drooling, and as they entered the restaurant, the maître-d' rushed towards them and showed them to their table, and waiters appeared from all over the restaurant to pull out the chairs for these beautiful guests, to the neglect of all the other diners.

During the meal, Geflin told them their target had modified an old conquistador fortress that had been built on the island. She and the elder daughters had a great deal of information on the Spanish conquest as Dark Seven had funded most of the piracy, which relieved the Spanish of their riches from the New World.

She assumed Enrico would have some knowledge and possibly as much as her; she hoped their beauty would distract him from any gaps in their cover story, but just in case, during the flight, they would read up on the Spanish conquest of Columbia.

Geflin arrived back at the hotel in the early hours after leaving the Bogota night scene breathless and with a few broken bones on any men who had tried it on uninvited. Geflin ordered coffee in her suite. All the girls were buzzing, especially the younger ones; it was their first time for such excitement. Geflin told them to be down for breakfast at 09:30—they would be at the airport by 11:00 for the 13:00 flight, so they all went to their suite after the coffee.

CHAPTER THIRTY-SEVEN

THE OWNER OF THE NIGHTCLUB in Bogota phoned La Quinta. "Arriving tomorrow at the Prado are fifteen stunning women, total man-magnets! We had our best night ever. Every man tried to pull them, but none were successful, so the wealthy ones are going to try their luck again and follow them to Barranquilla. I suggest you get some complimentary tickets over to the Prado for them. It would be the best move you could make over the next five days!"

La Quinta phoned Enrico to let him know as well. He ordered, "Make sure this happens, and send limos for them; they will be my guests!"

The taxis arrived to take them to the airport, then they

had just over four hours to brush up on Columbian-Spanish history, which they did studiously during the flight.

When they arrived, customs and passport formalities were no problem, and they entered the Prado with aplomb befitting beautiful wealthy women, causing men to stop what they were doing just to get a closer look.

Geflin went to reception and booked them all in. She enquired about a nightclub and was told that La Quinta, possibly the best nightclub, had heard of their arrival and would send their own limousines to take her party there. There was proof that the exhibition they had put on in Bogota had paid off. How easy it was to fool men!

Up in their rooms, she told the girls the bait had worked, and they were going to be the guests of the owner of La Quinta. "Most importantly, whatever propositions are made to you, the group will not split up, so whoever wins the charms of the target must make sure we all go. He favours very young girls, but should he approach any of the young ones, you must point him in my direction as I am the matriarch of you all and I will ensure we get inside his place. Whoever he chooses, nothing can happen until he shows you where the money is, so once inside, we will use our charms and kill them gently. We don't want blood flowing, and we need to leave them as if they are asleep. You all know how to do that."

They all nodded. "We must play it by ear. The guards are not such a problem to take out, but we want to find the people who know how they get the money in and the drugs out. I would doubt the target has more than five people who know everything about his operation, so we need to find those people and we will use everything in our arsenal to ensure that we are successful. Is that clear? Now, let's get ready for tonight!"

Two limousines arrived to collect them and take them to the club.

As they left the hotel, every man nearby turned to look as they floated across reception to the waiting vehicles, where the drivers' eyes nearly popped from their sockets as they opened the doors. Even getting into the limos was done for effect, allowing the drivers to catching glimpses of thighs and thongs.

It took about 30 minutes to get to the club, arriving just after 11:30 p.m. to be eagerly ushered in and shown to their tables.

Enrico could not take his eyes off these stunningly beautiful women, totally mesmerised by them from the moment they had entered the club. He went over to his partner and asked what was known about them. He knew nothing except that the Prado had already booked tables for them at his behest.

He sent one of his bodyguards over to the Prado to check them out, and the guard came back with the information that they were from an exclusive finishing school in Zurich and were in Columbia as part of their History and Geography studies, studying the Spanish conquistadors and the legacy the Spanish left; they were from very wealthy families and were serious about their studies but also intent on having fun.

After they were seated, Enrico sent a message to Geflin, inviting them to join him at his tables. He made room for them by sending away most of his bodyguards, leaving four men only. All, including Enrico, were handsome.

Geflin read the note, and the waitress pointed out the sender. She went through the motions of conferring with the girls and them nodding their agreement, so they moved to join Enrico at his tables. He ordered champagne, and the party began.

As expected, Enrico's interest was mainly in the younger girls. Geflin would have killed him there and then, but the importance of the mission meant she would have to put up with everything until she could get her hands on his cash.

He boasted to them that he lived in a fort built by the Spanish in 1620; he had many artefacts from that period and found the women well informed, having tested their knowledge of the conquistadors, and was reassured that they posed no threat to him at all.

He relaxed in their company, and the allure of the young girls combined with the effects of the champagne dulled his judgement, and he invited three of them back to his fortress. They politely declined his offer, and Geflin interrupted, saying, "I cannot allow them to go. We must all stay together. As nice as you seem, I am responsible for their safety, so if you want them to go to your home either we must all come, or decline your invitation."

Enrico apologised and said they were all welcome to his home, so Geflin accepted his invitation and the party continued at the club. They danced until dawn, all being sufficiently provocative to leave the men in a state of eager anticipation made even worse when no amount of pleading by Enrico to continue was successful and Geflin ordered taxis to take them back to the Prado, telling him they needed their beauty sleep.

Enrico accepted defeat and promised to send vehicles to collect them later that day, about 4 pm. He would personally show them around, and he asked them to be his guests for dinner, an invitation Geflin accepted before they left.

The bait had been taken as she knew it would. "Men are the same all over the world. It doesn't matter how clever, cunning, or ruthless, when it comes to beautiful women, their brains sink below their trouser belts!"

CHAPTER THIRTY-EIGHT

BACK AT THE HOTEL, they went up to Geflin's suite, where she told them: "Go to bed but be ready for 2 pm. We will have lunch after the gym—only exercise and no martial art training routine, just limber up. As always, we will have an audience, so we will put on a show. When we are at the target's home, we must play it by ear. We know what we want, and you all will do whatever's necessary." She looked at the youngsters. "You are the main key to unlocking Enrico's secrets. I can see that he lusts after the three of you, and you must taunt and tantalise him much as I find that repellent and want to tear him apart. You have not had the education you would have received during your schooling in Zurich, none the less you have what he craves. How you do it is up to you, the other guys that were with him must be his closest and trusted friends so they may also have the information that we require, but you will do whatever is needed to get the pin numbers and passwords his cartel uses, while those of us not chosen by him will pick off his security one at a time and keep the bodies in our guest rooms. They must be clean kills, with no blood to be seen. Without a doubt, we will have to torture these men to get the information, and once we have the place secure, I will coordinate it myself, you will be able to watch and observe as none of you has had practical experience, then once we have obtained the information, checked its veracity and we completely understand his system, you will have the **privilege of killing them, are you all clear?"** They all concurred.

The cars arrived at the hotel, black Range Rovers with blacked-out windows. They left the hotel looking every bit like movie stars, each carrying a handbag matching their outfits. In each handbag, along with the expected contents, was a small canister of their all-in-one stealth outfit, disguised as a tampon carrier.

In all the years Geflin had gone through countless airports' security, and not once had any official completely opened the canister; women had understood and men ignored

it. Anyone inspecting more closely would be told it was another pair of tights, and it was unlikely they would probe further.

It took about 45 minutes to get to Enrico's home. They crossed the river on his private chain ferry, which seemed to be designed for those cars and it probably was.

Geflin exited her car and looked around during the five minutes it took to cross, observing eight well-armed men, the telltale sign of a bulge under their jackets indicating something other than small arms and most likely to be an Uzi automatic or something similar, assuredly with a rapid-fire facility that would provide cover for their principals to escape.

Looking towards the island, she saw ten more armed men patrolling and deduced that ten more would be on the other side. She noticed that the guards were out of sight for at least three minutes, but all connected through earpieces, so there had to be a central command station that needed to be neutralised before they could seize control. They needed to eliminate the guards but choose their timing and take them out first.

Geflin was not perturbed by the number of guards, just the threat they posed. Automatic weapons were lethal because of how fast they could spread bullets, whereas the women had the skill to dodge fire from a semi-automatic weapon.

They arrived at his fortress. Assuming that he had CCTV and everywhere would be bugged, as the others left the vehicles behaving like party animals, she made a discreet sign for silence.

The cars entered a large courtyard leading to few stairs. A massive door opened, and Enrico came bounding down the steps to greet the girls, followed closely by another four men.

Geflin knew that word would have gone round the security guards, and men being men, they would all try to get a view of the guests. She counted at least forty guards and surmised that was his total commitment to protect the outside. She also noticed the CCTV was homing in on the girls, instead of watching for threats from the outside.

Their host greeted them with natural Latin charm and escorted them through the massive door into what had been the old part of the fort. It was more like a museum inside—all the artefacts were from the Spanish conquest: suits of armour, swords, maps, coins, letters, bills, journals and diaries of the troops stationed at the fort.

There was also a large ancient map showing the area under the influence of the fort, which Geflin spent some time studying. It showed the territories of local indigenous tribes spread out over a 360-degree area, so whichever way the conquistadors left the island, they would have encountered hostile tribes.

This would have made the exploration of the new territory difficult; fighting the tribes on the way out, and then back, certainly would have taken its toll on the workforce available to them.

Having assimilated that information, Geflin was puzzled because only a few died from wounds received in fighting the natives and most of them died of tropical diseases or smallpox, as did the indigenous population eventually, so how did they keep the fatalities down? It would soon become apparent.

She followed the daughters around while they asked interesting questions. It seemed they were enjoying themselves.

A bell sounded. Enrico announced that dinner was ready and led them through double doors to a balcony overlooking the other side of the island, where a large table was laid with gold cutlery, crystal glasses, flowers.

It really was a banquet; he had ordered outside caterers to prepare and serve the meal of fruits de mer, chateaubriand and the most delicate meringue dessert.

An associate boasted that the beef came from their own Argentinian ranch; it was exported all over the world and they believed it was comparable to the Japanese Kobe beef. Certainly, all the women agreed it was probably the best steak they had ever eaten.

Geflin realised this had to be how the drugs were distributed, otherwise how did they get through customs?

The wine was definitely flowing, and the men were actually drinking twice as much as the guests appeared to be drinking since the flower vases were actually doing their drinking!

Following the sumptuous meal, they strolled to the poolroom and bar, where Enrico pressed a switch and a floor started to appear, covering the pool, turning the room into a ballroom.

Geflin could see that the barman was carrying some sort of small handgun, but he would be easy enough to take out.

After about an hour of pleasantries, the men were most

certainly drunk and had chosen which girls they preferred, so the others said they would like to look at his artefacts some more.

Enrico just waved them off, and they went about their deadly business. The communication centre had to be taken first—the CCTV was following their every move, possibly more for lustful reasons than for security!

The museum section was spread over the whole ground floor. The communication centre that they all had noticed must be in the west part of the fort as all the aerials and satellite dishes were there, but exactly where would be trial and error, and their pretence would be looking for the ladies' room.

Two of the older daughters settled on a large settee and started putting on a show, so then all the CCTV cameras homed in on them, giving the others precious time to discover the location of the communication centre.

There were three men inside and none heard the door open, as they were too busy watching a real-life tease. Two died instantly and one was paralysed, just in case they needed to understand the system. He would be out for at least an hour, but they knew how to work the cameras.

They counted forty-seven guards, returned to the other sisters, and they all changed into their stealth outfits, rendering them almost invisible in the dark, and in just 20 minutes, all the guards were dead.

The threat was always expected from the outside and never from inside, a mistake for which the guards paid the ultimate price.

It took longer to drag the bodies into a guest room before they rejoined the others in the ballroom and just 45 minutes in total had elapsed.

Enrico was drunk and so were his associates, who had been dancing and drinking constantly. Geflin saw the sisters return and give the sign for mission accomplished.

She sauntered up to the bar and in one smooth move pushed the nose of the barmen up into his brain, killing him instantly so fast that Enrico and his associates had no time to react, and before they could say or do anything afterwards, they had been rendered unconscious.

The torture Dark Seven practiced varied, but when they wanted information—and quickly—they got it by using their bodies and their victim's genitals. Men can withstand a lot of pain, but the thought of not being able to have sex makes them vulnerable.

The men were stripped and tied to pillars, where each one would see the agony of the others, but first, they would be unconscious for at least an hour, giving the women time to reconnoitre the fort.

The part of the museum to the left of where the communication centre was seemed slightly out of the symmetry of the rest of the walls. Upon closer scrutiny, they saw a join eight feet vertically from the floor which had to be a door of some kind, and they soon discovered a secret panel which they opened to find a simple "call" button, which one of them was going to press but stopped as they didn't know yet what was on the other side.

Having found the secret door, they went back to the

ballroom, and two of the older sisters went back to the communication centre.

The guy left alive was still out cold. They started to skip through all the cameras on the one console which all three had been watching, but all it showed was the outside and the inside, which they had already seen.

They powered up the other two consoles and almost immediately gained a vast amount of intelligence—most of what they were looking at was a subterranean cocaine factory.

The cameras were in real time, and as far as they could see, there was nobody there. Taking the cameras around in a full circle, they still showed nobody underground, so it seemed safe to press that call button they had found.

A lift door opened, and one sister got in, while the other went back to follow her progress in the communications room.

The cameras followed her sister from one room to the next, the laboratory and offices, then a really large room that must have been the manufacturing hub for distilling the cocaine. Still no sign of human presence.

She felt the vats, and they were cold. Despite the air purification system, the dust had settled on the surfaces of desktops so she concluded that at least a month had passed since they last produced cocaine, but not knowing the cycle, it would be a question to ask in interrogation.

She went back to the lift and descended to the next level, where the first thing she saw was six tunnels, three showing signs of recent use and of being well maintained, whereas the other three appeared completely disused and, on closer inspection, ancient, with timbers supporting the roof and sides. Something else to include in interrogation.

Back in the lift again, she descended to the last floor, where there was only one tunnel, which she followed to arrive at a large heavy metal door. She pushed a switch on the right of the door. Red lights flashed above the door, and after a couple of minutes, they stopped and a green light showed. The door slowly opened, and she went inside to find a submersible, something like a submarine.

She approached the vessel, clambered aboard, opened the hatch, climbed down the ladder and went forward towards the cockpit. She was surprised at the lack of instrumentation, as it probably had less than the glider she occasionally flew.

Intrigued, she started to investigate more closely, and it appeared that the vessel was controlled by a computer or computers, ran on batteries and when necessary, a diesel engine topped the batteries up. She started up the onboard computer, where all the commands were apps or similar; she touched one which told her there was enough air for 34 days, one told her the life left in the batteries, another requested a destination and gave a list of previous destinations by longitude and latitude which meant nothing to her but she memorised them, so when she got back above ground her phone would easily identify where this vessel was going regularly.

Further exploration of the vessel revealed a large empty cargo hold towards the stern with several ratchet straps to secure the load. It was either drugs or money and this vessel had been designed purely for that use.

Anyone able to use an android phone would be capable of taking the craft anywhere safely. She would ask Geflin if she could have it once Dark Seven had finished using it.

She left the vessel, went back to the lift and returned to the communications room, where her sister had been busy with the remaining operator.

Since he had given her all the information about the communication centre and was now superfluous, she despatched him to join the other victims, then both sisters made their way back to the ballroom where the "fun" had already started.

They took off their stealth suits as everybody else was already naked, with the men tied to the pillars. One by one, they parted with every detail which was required before they met their maker.

Enrico was left until last, and after giving the information, he died in extreme agony, as Geflin made sure that his death was long and lasting.

CHAPTER THIRTY-NINE

THE WAY ENRICO'S DRUG EMPIRE worked had slowly evolved because of losing over 50% of his drugs and money. At first, bribery had worked on some, but as time went by, incorruptible people took their place. He knew it had to stop, and there had to be a better way.

His sister had married an Argentinian cattle rancher, who had come to see Enrico with a business proposition. He wanted to breed the ultimate beef cattle into his herd to make the finest meat in the world, which would be sought worldwide. It would take about three years to bring his herd to this standard.

Enrico, attracted by the concept of a legitimate global

meat business, set up nominal companies to fund it with help from his bank in the Cayman Islands.

He funded a property company similarly and built three industrial estates in Barranquilla. One of the larger units on the estate had won an order from the Argentinian beef rancher to build eight hundred insulated shipping containers to a specific design, the insulation had to be a standard, which would allow the meat to hang and mature during shipping and must comply with worldwide food hygiene legislation, rather than variations for each country.

These containers would be very specialised due to the high requirements and would need expert cleaning in between shipments, so all over the world small, accredited units specifically designed to carry out the deep cleansing had been established, but only the manufacturer of the containers could recharge the cooling and heating elements to maintain the exact temperature for the hanging of meat.

Bureaucracy throughout the world required traceability, records, and conformance which

meant Enrico's brother-in-law was providing him with the means to supply cocaine across

the globe via the containers, knowing that they would come back to Barranquilla at some point.

It was easy to ensure that the insulation material specified was sourced locally—he had a company to do just that. This insulation had a tonne of pure cocaine inside it and was fabricated within the container's structure as a completely sealed part of it.

Over eight years, all the containers had a tonne of

cocaine inside. They were tagged and chipped and could be diverted anywhere in the world to a customer.

The meat would go to the wholesaler. Once unloaded, the container would go to the special cleansing unit to be swabbed and certified clean. The drivers always arrived at the units after business hours; these units were on call 24/7 so the rostered out of hours team would be summoned.

It took 40 minutes to get the drugs out, and the cash in, all high denomination notes. In the integral design, bolts held the roof, sides and floor; turning them anticlockwise would raise the roof and the sides so the internal panel could be removed to access the drugs and replace them with the cash

The problem with drugs was getting them into a country, whereas once in, the likelihood of being stopped was negligible. It had been over 12 years since the first container rolled off the production line and in all that time not one had been exposed or even searched because the cargo was checked by vets, customs, Argentinian meat agency and health officials, certified and then sealed by each, and every agency had their own seal. None of these could be broken without destroying the certified provenance of the meat, thus rendering the £750,000 cargo worthless, so even the most zealous customs official would think twice. If the sniffer dogs showed interest, it would be put down to the cargo and x- rays would only show the meat. It was the perfect smuggling operation.

Geflin had recorded all the interrogations, so nothing was missed. In Enrico's study, she started up his computer, entered his password and hit the container icon. A map of the world appeared, flashing red and green lights, red indicating drugs, and green for cash. Touching any of the lights would give you its exact position.

She then logged into his bank accounts, all offshore. His total cash reserve was $453 million.

$173 million was in the same Cayman Islands bank as she used, so she transferred one million into her bank account, checked her balance and it showed the transfer as complete.

Suddenly her mobile rang, startling her. It was her Cayman bank account manager who was coincidently also Enrico's. He advised her that a transfer had been made. "I know," she said. "I now have access to all his accounts. He no longer needs his money because he and his gang are all dead, and I have taken over his business. I know you looked after his interests. I will be transferring all his cash, including from his other accounts, into my account."

The bank manager had little doubt out about that, having just seen the transfer. "Just a word of advice," he said, "do not transfer large sums, as they stand out like boats on the Caribbean, little and often would be my advice."

"Understood," she replied, "we have his submersible and know it brought cash to you. Where was it delivered?"

"My boat house was built out of a natural cave. The waterside entrance is deep enough for the submersible. He operated the vessel himself. He did not trust anyone else enough to bring the funds, although he sometimes bought his associates with him," he explained.

"How did he find you, the Caribbean is large, and it's over a thousand miles to the Caymans?" Geflin wanted to know.

"I have a GPS beacon in the boat house, and the submersible locks on to it, it's put on autopilot, and it arrives 36 hours later," he told her. "It's an incredible vessel; it was purpose-built for him and cost him more than two hundred million dollars. There is no information on it since the factory where it was designed and built was destroyed in a fire and the owner and the designer were both killed trying to put the fire out. Apparently, it is invisible when running on its batteries under water, it only leaves a detectable signature when the diesel engine is running, and someone has to be really listening, which means the Navy, but currently, no submarines of any country are deployed looking for a submersible. In the five years he's had the submersible, it's never been close to being found yet alone stopped."

"How do you know all this?" she asked. "Enrico bragged at dinner that he had the perfect narcotics smuggling operation and hadn't lost a shipment or payment in five years, with all the containers he had, he only needed to produce drugs as and when the containers got back to Barranquilla," he explained.

Geflin had a decision to make, as Dark Seven, they would never be this close to a business end-user, she had taken out Enrico and his guards, but she would have to silence his employees, rather than trying to transfer their allegiance to her, and their families and friends must know what they did for a living, the risk was too great to her.

The alternative, which she chose, was to blow up and destroy the whole operation.

She had numbers of all the containers with either drugs or cash inside; most still had the drugs. There were thirty-seven containers, but only three containing three million dollars each were on their way back to Barranquilla. She would have to let that money go.

With over 50 dead bodies, she had to destroy the evidence, get away and leave the country quickly.

The daughters had painstakingly gone round the house and reported that the fort was full of very expensive goods and in his safe was over a million dollars in cash, but it would all have to be left because the death and destruction had to look like the work of the rival cartel or some kind of vengeance, not a robbery. The only thing she would take was the submersible, as it could come in very handy.

How to destroy any evidence and throw suspicion onto someone else was the next problem to be solved.

They had found his armoury, which included enough Semtex to blow up Colombia. She gathered the girls and instructed them: "We need to dress the bodies and get them down to the floor with the laboratory, together with the guards. Put bullet wounds in the corpses, shots to the head should do, then we will douse their bodies with heating oil, petrol or whatever combustible material we can find. I've changed my mind about leaving them undamaged and looking peacefully asleep, as you can tell from what we've done to Enrico and his friends! Make sure they have their genital area soaked and put any testicles inside their mouths back in their proper place just in case."

She asked the daughter who had been in the submersible if they would all fit in. She nodded confirmation but said air might be the only problem. "There is a gauge that monitors both oxygen and CO2 in the sub, and if we needed more, I am confident we could go close to the surface and recharge if it doesn't do it automatically." "Then we will use it to leave Columbia and get to the Caymans," declared Geflin, "let's get started."

It took a couple of hours to get all the bodies into the laboratory, then they hit a snag. Unnoticed in the original recce, there was a sprinkler system, but even with all their knowledge, no one had any idea how to disable it, all they were sure was that every eventuality was programmed into the system and would thwart their intention of incinerating the bodies.

Geflin took a walk into the manufacturing plant. The vats were cold, and she checked the contents to find two of the vats contained H2 SO4, pure sulphuric acid, which would do nicely if she could blow the tops off the vats so the bodies could be chucked in.

Some Semtex was bought to her, which she carefully made into spaghetti rope and placed it round the welds at the top of the vats.

Using a 60-second timer detonator, they were all able to move to safety before there was a muffled bang as expected. The tops of the vats were still on, but on closer observation, the welds had fractured, so one of the girls fetched a hammer, hit the top of the vat and it came away easily.

They constructed a makeshift ramp. Geflin had used this method before, but not with so many bodies. She knew the dangers and made them wear all the safety gear appropriate to handling dangerous chemicals.

The first bodies to be dumped in the vat were Enrico and his associates. Geflin wanted them to be immersed in the vat the longest so all the flesh would definitely be dissolved and would not show the torture they had suffered.

What she had forgotten was the smell that sulphuric acid and flesh made, and the more bodies thrown into the vats, the worse the acrid stench got. The younger girls were unaccustomed to this smell of rapidly decomposing bodies and were suffering from their first experience of it, but after their seven years of training, they braved it as expected by Dark Seven.

Geflin and the daughter who had been on the submersible went down a floor to check what they presumed must be pressurised doors, both quite relieved to escape the stench.

The daughter pushed the button, lights started flashing red; Geflin could hear massive pumps starting up, blowing the water out of the submarine pen.

Two minutes later, the door was opened, and they went through, but before entering the sub, Geflin had a detailed look at the door and found what she thought were the weakest points. She asked the daughter how far underground she thought they were, and she replied, "No more than a hundred feet."

"That's what I estimate too; the depth of the river must be about that—it's tidal, so there will be a rise and fall. So, if we blow both doors when the river is at its highest point, it will flood everywhere above here, only leaving the fort dry, as the water will find its own level."

It would be another three hours before the river would be in full flow again; staying another 11 hours for its next cycle was not an option. They needed to get away before normal daily life of Enrico's empire would resume.

After assuring herself that the daughter could pilot the sub, she went back up to Enrico's office and wrote a note to leave for anyone to find. She typed "The Avenger has rid the earth of a sinner in drugs and taken his women as payment, signed The Avenger", the sign of Dark Seven in an ancient hand with A G and R overlaid on the A, recognisable as it had been used for hundreds of years representing untold mayhem. It was on all police and intelligent services records, all files tagged "pending, unresolved".

This note would provide the reason Enrico's guests were spared from the carnage which took the lives of so many.

She would contact Jojhinda again, once in the Cayman Islands; new identities would be needed for the older daughters who would disperse to their designated countries, and the youngsters would go back to New York to school as it was assumed Zurich had been compromised.

CHAPTER FORTY

THERE WAS SCUBA EQUIPMENT in the submersible, and Geflin would need it to set the explosives, as she would have to dive to get them around the whole of the watertight doors. She tested the cylinder; it was full, and the air was good.

She told the daughter to go above and pick up four packs of plastic explosive, and two detonators and timers, and by the time she returned, Geflin was in her wetsuit and ready to go. She told the daughter, "Flood the chamber. It will take about 30 minutes to set the explosives. I have air for an hour. Empty the chamber in 40 minutes when I will have finished. Have all the girls assembled for embarkation. I will set the timers for three hours from now, which should coincide with high water. It will be down to you to get us away. The ferry to the fort has to be disabled too, see to it."

The chamber was flooded, and Geflin got on with setting the explosives, although it had been a long time since she had used plastic and she used rather more than she actually needed but better to be safe than sorry.

The chamber emptied again. Geflin got out of her wetsuit and stored it in the sub. Everyone was assembled, and she got the thumbs up for everything above having been done as she had ordered, but the stench was on all of them and would be utterly unbearable with 36 hours of close confinement ahead travelling in the sub.

She sent one of the daughters to go up and fetch the clothes they came in and told the others to strip, burn their body suits and take a dip in the sub-pen to wash the smell of death off them. The daughter returned with their clothes. They got washed until the smell had gone, got dressed and boarded the sub.

Geflin told the daughter to make ready the sub, and the others to spread about the loading bay and make themselves as comfortable as they could. They would have to take turns to sit in the comfortable chairs in the cockpit.

The hatch was locked, ready for departure. The daughter pushed a button that flooded the pen, and once the pressure had regularised, the outside door started to open; she punched the GPS co-ordinates into the computer, put the sub into drive. As it started to move, she steered it through the open door, where auto-control took over.

According to the depth gauge, they were 60 feet below

the surface, the sonar and GPS were in sync and steering the craft, avoiding any objects in the river, but not making maximum headway as they were going against the tide.

From the observation windows, you could see the marine life, it was like an aquarium. Those in the loading bay wanted to see too and started to move forward, when an alarm sounded on the bridge, because moving forward had altered the buoyancy. Geflin ordered them back to the loading bay, and to come forward one at a time, which stopped the alarm immediately.

It took two hours to clear the river and get them into the Caribbean Sea. Once out of the tidal pull, the speed gradually got up to cruising rate, causing a bow wake which eclipsed the view of any marine life and made it look like night; the depth gauge showed two hundred feet. The sub was working well, all signs were green, the daughter in charge was confident that in the event of an emergency, the craft and she could cope between them.

With 48 hours to go, everyone was tired, and to make the cramped conditions more tolerable, most managed to get some sleep by using a martial art technique to go into stasis.

Geflin would not sleep until she got to the Caymans, though. Her adrenalin was in full flow. All that was left of Dark Seven was on that sub, and if anything happened to it, everything would be lost without the possibility of revenge. Unthinkable.

CHAPTER FORTY-ONE

IT TRULY WAS AN INCREDIBLE CRAFT. When the air got low two-thirds of the way, it automatically rose to its snorkel depth and replenished the air tanks; similarly, the diesel engines fired up and recharged the batteries.

After 36 hours of travelling, the sub started to rise—they had reached their destination.

Geflin told them to wait below just in case and be ready for anything. She opened the hatch, and water splashed all over her dress.

She emerged from the sub to see her banker, who had been waiting for nearly an hour. It had been a long time since they were lovers, but what a welcome reminder he got since the material of her wet dress was transparent and she might as well have been naked! He helped her off the sub.

She called down to the others, who emerged one by one. He had never been so close to fifteen beautiful women dressed for partying!

Geflin went straight to business. "Who knows we're here?"

"Just me," he replied.

"Good, now, is your beach house empty?"

"We have no guests, and the servants only live in when we have guests. They are all gone by now and will be back first thing in the morning. All the rooms are made up, there's food in the fridge, a well-stocked bar, everything you need," he explained.

"Can you stop the servants coming back in the morning, give them a day off?" she asked. "No problem, it happens all the time."

They all walked up to the beach house together. He unlocked the door and handed her the key.

They went inside to find the kitchen to the right, lounge to the left, study straight ahead. Next to the study was the cinema room. Upstairs there were ten bedrooms and one master bedroom, all ensuite.

The girls dashed to the kitchen, as it had been a long time since that sumptuous meal
at Enrico's.

Geflin asked one of the daughters to make her something to eat and went into the study, although the banker was hoping it would have been the master bedroom.

"Tell me what the news is about Enrico," she demanded. "It has made international news, but mostly speculation, as there seems to be more or less a blackout on facts about the whole affair. The airwaves are full of hypotheses ranging from an American smart bomb, a hit from another cartel, to a massive explosion at the refining laboratory, but what is clear is that a massive explosion took place, water rushed in at such a force you can see the lift coming through the roof; it's causing an ecological disaster as bits of bodies are turning up and for some reason, the piranhas are dying by the thousands, that's about it," he reported.

"They must have improved the power of plastic explosive!" Geflin exclaimed. "It's been a long while since I had to use any before that."

"It's still making the news, so you can follow it on Sky," he suggested.

"The girls and I have several things to discuss and best you're not here, as what you don't know you can't repeat, but come back later and I shall reward you handsomely," she told him and winked. She accompanied him to the front door where he tried to kiss her, but she gently pushed him away, murmuring "Later..."

Geflin collected her food from the kitchen and took it back to the study, telling the others to search the house for wires and surveillance equipment and then meet her in the lounge.

She phoned Jojhinda and told him they needed fifteen new female identities, three US, two UK, four EU, two South African, two Hong Kong, two Australian, one of each for a

14-year-old and a 21-year-old, and one more American aged 42, which all must have a Cayman Islands entry stamp, predated at least by a week, but all different coinciding with flight arrivals from various countries. "How long will it take?" she asked.

"At least three weeks," he replied.

"When they're ready, I will tell you where to deliver them," she told him.

Geflin went into the lounge, where they were all waiting for her. "We will all have new identities, with which we will set up bank accounts with Chase Manhattan. They are global. Normally your sisters would help you settle into your territory, introduce you to their bankers, show you around real estate etc, but you are going to have to start from scratch. Opening bank accounts is difficult but transferring does not seem to invoke so many security questions. I will transfer 25 million dollars into your individual accounts with Chase; that should set you up with property and cars, etc. You must find a safe house that is secret and known only to you; it will need to be close to a tidal river or the coast, and most importantly, isolated. Older properties make good safe houses, as they tend to have a basement or cellars, which you will need. For the modifications which need to be done, use foreign workers who live in while the work is being carried out and once completed, dispose of them. It will be three weeks before the new identities arrive. We must split up because the whole world could be looking for fifteen females, and I think you should pair with your house sisters, so in that way, we can start again and rebuild our Houses to their former glory. I had booked you younger ones into Chapin's in New York to finish your education, but that is no longer an option as we are supposed to have all been kidnapped by The Avenger, so your education will have to be in your designated country. I really don't want you to use the identities that you have at the moment because of the traceability. Those identities need to have ended at Enrico's, so for the next three weeks, we must keep a low profile. Our banker will be back later. We need to use him to find places for you to stay without passport scrutiny. I am sure his bank could rent a few properties on Grand Cayman."

One of the daughters spoke up, "We are on Cayman Brac, 145 kilometres from Grand Cayman. There is an aerial photo on the wall in the kitchen showing the beach house."

Geflin replied, "That might be useful to see where everyone is if we have to disperse and disappear for three weeks. When he returns, I will find out before he gets me in the sack. I will make sure the servants don't return for another day, then we will have the whole of tomorrow to split up into pairs. I will phone him now and get him to bring some cash. Are the freezers full, or do you want a takeaway?" They opted for takeaway.

She phoned him and told him to bring a hundred thousand Cayman dollars and order a takeaway for fifteen people. "Sixteen!" he said, and they both laughed. "I need to split up the girls for security reasons. Can you rent six properties? Bring the keys with you and get us each a mobile phone.

"No problem, see you later," he replied. She turned to the girls and told them it would be a couple of hours before the food arrived, so they should make use of the beach house and enjoy themselves. She went up to her room, showered and slept soundly until the noise of the helicopter woke her—dinner had arrived.

CHAPTER FORTY-TWO

COLONELS GILL AND BERRY had separated their aircraft, and the solar craft was dousing the whole of Messapth with slumberland, every nook and cranny. It was just like crop spraying. They radioed mission complete, but Stephen responded that if they had any of the drug left, just carry on until it was all gone. The reply was affirmative, and for another 30 minutes, we watched in real time as, hopefully, they continued to prepare, putting the world's most evil organisation to sleep.

"We will know for sure in 20 hours, there will be constant satellite surveillance, and nothing will go unobserved. Deflin is the only mother normally outside

Messapth, but we know that she has made her weekly trip, so she is there and to the best of our intelligence, all the key players will have been affected, apart from the four daughters already accounted for, so in the next 48 hours we will have eradicated the evil of Dark Seven."

Deflin's daughter had been the only problem. After being exposed to the drug, she took the train from Cambridge to Kings Cross, which she did regularly to go to her flat in Pimlico.

We knew all the daughters' mobile numbers which we were using to track them as it was far too dangerous to follow them, anyone doing that would have been spotted and killed, so when the train arrived at Kings Cross, and the signal stayed there, Stephen realised that she had fallen asleep on the train and wouldn't be waking up, which would obviously cause concern at the station.

Within minutes, Stephen had a private ambulance at the station, contacted the station master and told him that he had a sick passenger on the train from Cambridge who had just discharged herself from Addenbrookes, after being heavily sedated for an operation. Although she had not had the second anaesthetic and would have retained mobility long enough to catch the train. It would have taken effect since, and she would be still on the train.

"There is an ambulance on its way, should be with you in minutes; I need the platform number to tell the emergency crew, and if you could get a staff member to find her on the train, it would save time."

The station manager agreed and told him to tell the

ambulance to drive straight onto the platform. This was all achieved without a problem. She was taken to Media Corps in the ambulance, and from there to Prague, having been rendered harmless and no longer evil. All being well when she woke up, she and all her sisters would be in Messapth.

The ease in which the remaining sisters were removed from their evil work was remarkable, they were now neutralised and would live the rest of their lives in Messapth, providing we could achieve the same for all its inhabitants, but it would be a way of living completely changed from total opulence to basic existence.

Dark Seven had been responsible for so much evil for over 7000 years.

Stephen said that they should all be despatched so they would no longer present a threat to civilisation.

If we took them all to trial, evidence would be essential; knowing what they had done, we could have made sure they would tell the truth about their atrocities, and they would be incarcerated for life, but with their beauty, I felt that they would easily find a comfortable existence in any prison hence they should be sentenced to a hard life exile in Messapth which we would monitor 24/7.

I hoped that none of the studs would stay once all the riches had been removed, so the gradual demise of Dark Seven would be inevitable, but we would not be sure until we controlled Messapth.

CHAPTER FORTY-THREE

IN THE HERMETICALLY SEALED LABORATORY in Messapth, Deflin and her sisters had been updating the programme stolen from her husband in Cambridge. The lab was a replica of the labs at the university and at their home and its first rule was it had to be sterile and use artificially produced oxygen, so they were all wearing suits plugged into that oxygen supply.

They were all tired. The computer programme was now running. According to her husband, it would be at least another year to achieve a replica of a male or female, but it would be worth the wait as the House of Deflin were going to replace wealthy men and women with clones and strip them of their wealth. For the last ten years, they had been following every move of their targets and knew them as well as themselves.

They went through the first vacuum chamber, waited for the green light and walked through it to the disrobing room, where they left their state-of-the-art oxygen suits and hung them up, walked naked through the next vacuum chamber to the sterilising showers, and on to the final chamber where they took normal showers and put on their outside clothes.

The clock showed 01:37. "No wonder we are hungry!" one sister said, as they went up the stairs.

Finding their other sisters asleep at this time of night would not be unusual, but when they rang for food, no servants came. They went searching for the servants, found them all asleep and no amount of shaking them would wake them.

They rushed to the other houses, but everyone everywhere was asleep and couldn't be woken.

All three felt it at once that something was attacking their senses and trying to neutralise their brains. They heard helicopters approaching, large ones, and instantly realised that Messapth was under attack.

Not knowing how many enemies were outside and using so much power to control the attack on their senses, they agreed rapidly that the best attack would be the lateral flailing manoeuvre which would wipe out everything in front of them. The speed of that discipline was such that bullets miss, and the shock of the speed at which they would approach their adversary was so daunting that they would be dead before they knew it. They would move forward to the next one as if on autopilot and anything standing in their way would be eradicated.

By the time they had descended the few steps from their house, they were ready, speeding forward to the first group of enemies—they would knock them down as if they were pins in a bowling alley. They were inches from the first strike...then nothing.

CHAPTER FORTY-FOUR

ROBERT SAXHAM AND STEPHEN had worked out all the logistics for the taking of Messapth and explained what was to happen. The Utopians who had helped neutralise the sisters in Prague would do the same to all of Dark Seven. It had taken a little under five minutes for each sister; Monk and I had shown them what to do, so they knew exactly what we wanted and were confident they could do it.

Aircraft and helicopters were chartered and ready to roll; we still could not take weapons on a verticular no matter how hard I tried to convince it they were necessary, so the weapons would be dropped by helicopter as soon as we had established that the inhabitants of Messapth were fast asleep.

Eight verticular would be used carrying four Utopians and four special forces and would materialise around the perimeter of Messapth. The Utopians would connect a neural net similar to the one we used at the General's dacha in Moscow.

Monk and I felt that it would control most of the inhabitants but Dark Seven could keep control of their own minds and fight off the neural net, so if any of them were awake we should abort the mission, we couldn't get enough men on the ground fast enough to prevent the deaths of any members of the team, so we would retreat rather engage in conflict.

CHAPTER FORTY-FIVE

WE HAD A PROBLEM. Sheflin had got us to where we were now, was madly in love with Pat Smith, and he with her, and knew what was about to happen to Messapth. She really didn't want any part of the new Messapth, and just wanted to be with Pat.

Could we make an exception for her? It was a dilemma left to me, I would have agreed, but Stephen was, as always, playing devil's advocate.

He told them both that Sheflin should go back to Messapth, because they all had to be punished for what they had done, and remorse was not enough. "Then I will return with her," Pat announced. "I just could not live without her."

Stephen knew from Pat's medical records that he had had a vasectomy, so both would finish their days in Messapth without adding to the numbers. It would also allow him to have an insider in Messapth and should anything untoward happen, his bracelet would allow communication with the outside.

Stephen knew that Pat might be driven by his hormones, but that evil was repellent to him, and he would never assist in any wrongdoing. I thought that lust and love would soon wither when faced with hard toil to simply exist.

Without the luxuries of the 21st century, Messapth would revert to the dark ages and slowly cease to exist. We would not have erased in their minds the memories of their former lives, just the part of their brain which caused the evil they perpetrate, as the need for punishing them had to be the primary objective.

I asked Stephen to step outside where I told him I disagreed with him on this; we needed to make an exception with Sheflin. Pat would for a month or so be driven by the love he had for her, though he could have been the only male left there, so all the hard work would be left to him. Despite some sex as compensation, he would be induced to try to find a way out for him and Sheflin.

"So, they will be my guests at Assington until when, and if we can, find a solution for Sheflin's punishment," I declared. He was full of ifs and buts, but I told him to take it on board and live with it.

We went back inside, and I told the couple that I didn't want them in Messapth, rather that I wanted them both to be my guests at my home and be part of my security team.

Robert had produced a virtual 3D image of Messapth on his laptop, using satellite surveillance. Sheflin was detailing all the buildings, and we had the information to finalise our plans.

It was Sheflin's idea to keep her sisters sedated until they were returned to Messapth because they were extremely dangerous when conscious, so they would be travelling in the verticular with us and placed into their own houses.

It was past midnight in Messapth when the heat signals showing on the satellite surveillance had become stationary, but we would wait another hour to be sure and then go to rid the world of this evil machine.

I entered a verticular and told it what we were trying to do and why. We could not save the planet if our people had to worry about their own safety. By preventing Dark Seven's funding of orchestrated crime and evil, the perpetrators would start to disappear as their funding dried up. We aimed to be successful in bringing the third world out of poverty and introducing real democracy for all. The truce we negotiated with the leaders of all terrorist groups appeared to be holding. All that would help us in the task that lay ahead, but I was concerned that what we were about to do was jeopardised if even one of the women was not asleep and could kill any member of the team.

As if this wasn't enough to worry about, Infinity entered my mind and told me what Oblivion had done at earth's core. The details were lost on me, but sufficient to leave me extremely concerned. They could not reverse what he had done, but they could slow its progress up to the earth's crust and change its trajectory but it would still reach it in a little under three months.

I left the verticular and contacted Professor Dave Mac with my bracelet and relayed all the information Infinity had given me, and he perfectly understood the full implications.

"Oh, my God! We are talking about a ball of hydrogen-enriched magma ninety thousand cubic miles. The size compared with earth would be like a golf ball inside a basketball, which would not such be a problem if we directed it to the Pacific; I will have to run some computations, but my first assessment is that it would displace four times the amount of magma on its upward journey, and if that hits North America, it's goodbye Earth!" he exclaimed.

"We have very powerful allies who don't want this to happen, so come up with a solution!" I urged him. "I will leave my team in Utopia and get back to Flint. Everything I need is there," he assured me. I asked him to keep me informed and returned to the team.

CHAPTER FORTY-SIX

STEPHEN WAS STILL SCRUTINISING the satellite information. All the heat signals were dormant and had been for two hours. Nothing had moved at all.

As I came back in, he said, "We're green to go!" "Let's do it!" I replied. Monk, two fellow Utopians, Stephen, and four of his very special forces entered the verticular with me.

I read their minds to discover they had been told their only objective was to protect me and were to sacrifice themselves to give me time to get back to the verticular if necessary, and nothing else mattered except my survival.

It took just over ten minutes to arrive at Messapth. The special forces were the first to leave the verticular in order to protect the Utopians while they established the neural net, once that was done, we would move forward, our transport would put us two hundred metres from the main buildings, meaning we would be the closest to potential danger about which Stephen had argued during the planning stage. He wanted us to be the furthest away, but my reasoning was how could I decide to abort from so far away, so it was my call.

When the neural net had been established, we started to amble towards the buildings, when suddenly, from out of the House of Deflin, burst three spinning women, approaching us so rapidly we only had only seconds and disabling their minds would take longer than we had.

"Abort!" I shouted out, but they were nearly on us, and I could feel the power emanating from them. The special forces and Stephen surrounded Monk and me to get us back to the verticular, but I knew there would not be enough time. I felt death approaching; they were so close now you could smell them, and Stephen made to sacrifice himself, inches from certain death when they just vanished.

I turned around and saw the soft glow of a beam aimed directly at where our adversaries had been. Stephen also turned round to see it as the colour slowly came back to his face, he hadn't been that close to death for a long time, and he remarked, "I must get one of those!" and we laughed. What a huge relief and boost to our confidence—that was the second time the verticular had saved our skin.

We didn't see those women again until the verticular deposited them back, suitably changed in their minds, just before we left Messapth for the last time.

We heard the helicopters and saw them land. Over a hundred heavily armed special forces leapt out, only to find that all their weaponry disappeared in front of their own eyes. That soft beam from our transport was glowing again. Apparently, weapons would never be needed while we were under the protection of the verticular.

Our confidence increased hugely. We were free to accomplish our mission without fear and complete it by ridding the world of Dark Seven's evil.

Where the attackers had sprung from was the first house we entered. The opulence was staggering—it was as if we had entered a Pharaoh's tomb. Everywhere we went, people were fast asleep, most naked or barely clothed.

It was so easy to work out which were family—anyone stunningly beautiful had to be part of Dark Seven and would be first to have their mindset changed. Stephen wanted to find out how three of them had been unaffected by slumberland, which soon became apparent when we found the laboratory and realised it was hermetically sealed.

He could see the air locks and said we would need a special team to go further, as they could be housing deadly live viruses. I said that Deflin was married to Professor Roger Bane, and he dealt only in cloning, "Pick him up and have him flown directly here from Cambridge, and he will be able to decide what's in those labs."

Stephen made the call, which ensured that he would arrive in six hours.

The Utopians started to alter the minds of Dark Seven, while Stephen's men started crating up everything of value in all the houses.

We left the men's house till last as they posed the least threat to us. There were no doors apart from the large entrance doors and there must have been at least fifty bedrooms, each occupied by a young, mostly naked sleeping male, but in one room there was someone in pyjamas.

We approached the bed and were shocked to find it was Bruce Kennett. Stephen's men had been searching for him since he gave them the slip in Prague. I said, "You can call off the search now, he's going to the States to stand trial for ordering the deaths of several people, it was a condition of bail that he stayed at his ranch, and he broke that condition, so his next stop is jail. Put him on the first plane out of Messapth. He is to be guarded until he can be handed over to the FBI. His crimes took place in many states, so they can have the problem of where he is to stand trial."

Stephen called for two of his men to carry him out, instructing them, "This guy is to go on the first plane; he is not to wake up until he is in New York and in custody, so sedate him if necessary."

I contacted Felbrig using my bracelet to inform him that Kennett was on his way to America via Zurich. "Can you get the FBI to meet him at Anders Airfield, he will be there in a little over ten hours; he will be asleep, and I want him to wake up in a cell."

"Consider it done!" was the reply.

We started waking the men up, starting with the ones who looked European. Stephen said he thought he recognised two of them. Monk and I took one each and reversed the effects of slumberland.

As they slowly came round, it was as if they were just waking up, their eyes opened, and they were startled to see people they did not recognise. "What the heck is going on?" they wanted to know. We told them we were there to neutralise the evil of Dark Seven and rescue them if they wanted that.

Stephen recognised their Australian accents and remembered who they were. In desperation, the parents of these guys had employed his company to find them after the police had stopped looking, as they were both presumed dead. His company had spent many hours, nearly two million Australian dollars, which he knew was more than both sets of parents combined could raise even by selling everything they owned. He had sent them a bill for five thousand, split between the families, disappointed not to have found them, but he reassured them his gut feeling was that they were alive and didn't want to be found, making it harder for anyone searching.

They were now fully awake and got dressed. Stephen introduced himself. They were reassured by his accent as a fellow Aussie. "We need to sort out who's who of the guys in here, but before we start, do you want to send a message to your folks to say you're safe and will be returning soon?" he suggested.

"When you said you're neutralising this place, does that

mean you're taking the women away?" they asked.

"No, everything will remain the same except Messapth will be an open prison where there will be no wealth or outside communications and from now on, life here will be very austere subsistence living, and any men will doubtless be doing most of the work. It will be completely isolated but monitored constantly via satellites. The women are still capable of killing at will. We have just altered the need to do so in their mindset and placed a remorse file in all their minds should they contemplate reverting to their old ways," he explained.

"Well, that's a bugger. We were going to leave in a couple of years. You would not believe what the older sheilas have given us. They're so bloody grateful for a good bonking," they told us, indicating the gifts they had received.

Stephen said, "You seriously think they would have allowed you to leave this place? Either of you tries anything, they would kill you both. You must have been here for nearly two years. How many people have left?"

"Several - as they get older and can't keep it up to their standard, they get retired and leave with all their gifts," they said. "And you believe this?" Stephen challenged them. "Well, we did until now..."

"So, are you coming back with us, you can keep your gifts, or are you staying?" was Stephen's ultimatum, and it didn't take long for them to decide they were coming with us, in exchange for telling us everything they knew about Messapth and its people. It was a deal.

The men's house was mostly home to studs, but in a separate part, we found the servants, both male and female, who looked after the house.

When we woke them, they took us on a tour of the Houses, pointing out who was family and when we got to the House of Geflin, I queried why there was an empty room, "She left at the end of July with the children to go to somewhere in Tibet, to start their martial arts training, and take the older children who have finished their training from there to Zurich to a finishing school. I suppose those leaving finishing school go on to take up the roles of the sisters who will come back here to have children," they told us.

"So, what you're saying is that, in theory, we have seven children in Tibet, seven adolescent females trained to kill and on their way from Tibet to Zurich, seven more young adults leaving Zurich, and an adult," I said.

"Who are all going to be well pissed off by what we are doing here," interjected Stephen.

"The seven in Tibet aren't going to be such a problem. We can take care of them later. Herr Hoffman will close all their known bank accounts, but these are very clever, dangerous, and now very angry ladies who will surely have access to other identities and cash and cards or use their looks to get what they need. We are going to have to find them as top priority now, or none of us are safe," I pondered.

"I will find them. Rest assured there will be a trail to follow; no matter how clever, they leave signs," Stephen assured me.

We moved outside the Houses and were shown all the other areas.

There was a great deal of activity; everything of value was being carefully packed in crates and loaded into helicopters and onto aircraft to be taken directly to a secure warehouse in Zurich where it would be itemised and valued.

The guys took us to a cave, and we didn't need to say, "Open Sesame". Stephen and I had never seen such treasure—pallets of gold and platinum, and so much paper currency as far as the eye could see, we couldn't even estimate the quantity and we wouldn't know until Herr Hoffman and his team had taken stock of the hoard.

They showed us to the communication centre, which was already being dismantled, and further on we approached what they said was the garbage disposal.

Stephen realised it was a large quick-lime pit that would get rid of all the waste for sure! Using a rake propped up nearby, he fished around the base of the pit and when he brought it to the surface, there was a large bone on it.

"That, guys, is a human fibula; no man ever left this place, they were killed and disposed of here," he announced.

We went back to the men's house, where they had all been woken up, given a choice and all opted to leave. Like the other two, they had received rewards for their work, which we told them they could take, but nothing else.

"We need more people or it's going to take weeks! How many men can you spare?" I asked Stephen.

"Possibly twenty without compromising security," he

replied, then an idea sprang into my mind.

"What about the Swiss army? I am sure Herr Hoffman could organise it!"

Within minutes, he could confirm that a hundred and fifty men from the Swiss army special response force would be with us within five hours.

The first plane left for Zurich with Bruce Kennett on board and the C-130 was full of items from the houses. Kennett would be in jail before he woke up, even if he had to be sedated to make sure of that.

CHAPTER FORTY-SEVEN

FIVE HOURS INTO THE CONFISCATION of Messapth's wealth, Stephen's plane had arrived containing a rather dishevelled, tired, and furious Professor Roger Bane. On the way to the laboratory in the House of Deflin, he thought he saw his wife in her room, but Stephen took a firm hold of his arm and led him on.

We approached the first airlock and entered the chamber. We took off our clothes and changed into greens that were in sealed bags, through another airlock into a chamber where he pushed a button and decontamination took place. We could now enter the laboratory.

The professor was shocked and surprised to discover what seemed to be a replica of his own lab, but actually even better as there were no constraints on funding. He was further stunned to find at least twelve cabinets holding created beings or clones.

I said it had to be completely dismantled as fast as possible and asked him how long that would take. "The lab itself is a simple self-assembly, but the problem is the living tissue in those cabinets. It needs life support if we want it to survive. At the university, I have a portable support system which could be adapted, and all the other things I need are there, including some of my staff to assist in the transfer," Bane replied.

"Contact your staff and ensure everything can be made ready. I will have them picked up and brought here directly," I told him. "How big is the life support unit? It will need to fit into the hold of a Learjet."

He made the call and told them to adapt the unit for twelve cabinets and get it all to Cambridge Airport as soon as possible. I contacted David and asked him to get my plane to Cambridge to pick up people and scientific equipment which we needed urgently, telling him "When you're at the airport, Stephen will send the information and flight plan and codes that Turkish and Iranian air traffic control will recognise so you won't be shot down."

The professor demanded to see his wife, but I had to explain to him that the woman he saw was not his wife. "It was a sister or daughter; your wife and two others tried to kill us and were removed to somewhere they can do us no harm."

He asked if she was still alive. "Of course, they are, but I don't know where, and it's the least of my concerns. This is hard for you to hear, but your wife was only using you for your knowledge. The House of Deflin were going to replace prominent businesspeople with your clones. However genuine your motivation was for cloning, they would have used it for evil. What you have achieved is a giant leap for science, but she only wanted you for your knowledge and used the oldest trick in the book as she and her daughter obliged you with the sex that you craved, putty in their hands, and they played you like a violin as a means to their end. Once they had obtained all your knowledge, you would have been expendable, and while it's just possible, they may have let you live in case they encountered any problems they needed you to fix, you can be sure that these women would have had no further use for you."

"But she loved me!" he protested.

"They don't love anybody. You're a fool if you think they do," I retorted. "They love sex. You must have seen all these handsome men here for one purpose only, and if they couldn't perform, they were killed. We have found bones in a lime pit. Your wife and the rest of the women here were pure evil and would kill anyone who stood in their way. Your scientific expertise was your only attraction, and you were just a pawn in the scheme they were enacting. Now, it will be at least six hours before your equipment arrives so you can take a nap in the men's house if you want to or help us move all the valuables to the helicopters."

"I would rather have a look around this place. The buildings seem most interesting," he decided. I said that was ok as long as he didn't get in the way.

When we got back out of the lab, the Swiss army had radioed that they were 30 minutes away. Once they arrived, we would have over three hundred people on the ground.

Stephen's logistics chief was coordinating the removal. It was just over six hours since the operation began, and we went to find out from him how everything was going.

"All seven houses have been emptied of anything of value, 80% is in the air and the remainder waiting for returning aircraft, all men wanting to be repatriated are in the air, but only 10% of the cave vault contents have been removed and the vault is the big issue because there are tonnes of precious metal, which is slowing us down," he summarised.

"Well, there are another hundred and fifty soldiers just 30 minutes away, so that should help the heavy side of the operation," I told him, then asked, "Bearing that in mind, how long before this place is completely emptied?"

"With the extra men crating it up ready for shipment, ten hours, we have enough helicopters, but insufficient cargo planes is what is really holding up the operation," he replied.

"There will be two more aircraft on the ground shortly which we can utilise, so how many more cargo planes do you need?" I asked.

"We really need them now, our first shipment has arrived at Zurich and will be back here in five hours but what we need are planes on the ground now to take up the lead time, then we could complete in the ten hours, we would need another nine which would take up the slack, although if the two that are carrying the troops are C-130 or similar, we would only need seven but they need to be within an hour away and arrive every 30 minutes from then until our first aircraft arrives back," he told me.

I said I would see what we could do, and I told Stephen I had an idea, and he walked with me to my verticular. I told it of our problem and asked if it could do to seven much larger non-threatening aircraft exactly what it had done to the stealth fighters.

It seemed it could and would assist; however, it would not break the security shield and summoned an additional verticular.

I communicated to the British Prime Minister that we needed seven C-130 and crews to be immediately available, and he told me that Brize Norton was always on standby. I told him to make the call and we would be there in 15 minutes. The planes should have their engines running so we would know which ones were designated for the mission, and to clear the control tower as it would not be needed.

"The fewer the people who might see what happens to the aircraft, the better, but I need them now and I can't wait the six hours flight time. I'll use my special transport, so they will just disappear and reappear on their own. It's just logistics, not dangerous. We had no idea of the extent of the riches in Messapth, it's going to run into billions, and I'll let you and the President know how much as soon as I have an accurate value, although it's going to take weeks to value the antiques."

"The trial of the Cabinet and the ex-prime minister starts a week on Monday in our new Supreme Court. No jury; just three judges, and it will be heard at the same time as the American trial. Their defence lawyers are pulling their hair out because they're unable to keep their mouths shut and they are answering questions truthfully, making it nigh on impossible to defend them, so I have a feeling they might plead guilty and try some plea bargaining; we will see," he told me.

We ended the communication with him, agreeing to keep me informed.

CHAPTER FORTY-EIGHT

I ENTERED THE VERTICULAR, and we were at the aerodrome in under ten minutes. The monitor showed seven C-130s ready to roll, and one by one they disappeared, which took five minutes, then another ten to return to Messapth.

The verticular materialised on the Messapth airfield, where the Swiss army aircraft were on the ground. I told it I was ready for the aircraft, and one by one they started to reappear.

I entered the minds of all the crew and told them all not to worry, I would explain everything; they could leave their aircraft as they wouldn't be needed for at least an hour, and I would show them all around.

I contacted Stephen and told him to tell his logistics man that the extra transport had arrived so we could get the job done without hindrance.

I met the crew, who had by then figured out that they had travelled six hours flight time in ten minutes, so to reassure them, I told them we had used a top-secret machine which shifted through differing time dimensions to get them there so quickly; they accepted the explanation in order not to look foolish for not having realised.

We hitched a lift in a helicopter back into Messapth. Intense and continuous activity was what I could see. No sooner had we left the craft than it was being loaded, and by the time we got to the men's house, the loading was complete, and that helicopter was up and away.

On the way over, I explained what Messapth was and what we were doing. "This place has caused the deaths of countless thousands, possibly millions, just driven by greed and evil. This house is where they kept the men used as studs. When they became of no more use, they were killed. They were all lied to about being allowed to leave and take their gifts, and everyone ended up in the lime pit," I explained.

We went on to the nearest women's house where they had all been neutralised but were still asleep and showing no signs of waking. The crew were astonished by the sheer beauty of these women, but, reading their minds, I saw that they just couldn't believe anyone so lovely could be so evil.

"We have rendered them harmless. They are condemned to stay here without their wealth, and hopefully without their slaves since they can choose to stay or go; the life here is going to be austere, to say the least, and if they want to survive, they are going to have to toil for what they need. We will leave them with the basics, and the rest will be up to them," I told them.

Next, I showed them the cave vault, where I was impressed with progress as two thirds of the contents had gone thanks to the Swiss army who had made all the difference, but wherever we went, we always seemed to be in the way.

Eventually, Stephen caught up with us and said they were ready to load the first of the RAF C-130s, so the first crew went back on the next helicopter, the other crews followed in successive flights so it was all was going to plan, and the logistics guy informed us that we should have the site cleared in another 4 hours.

We were going to leave some people on the ground and the Utopians as observers reporting directly to me until the women all had woken up, and to be sure that the neutralising of evil had worked. "I shall leave the verticular in place to ensure their safe exit. Dark Seven's physical abilities are still working. We've just erased the will to kill and replaced it with remorse for their crimes, so they will realise how wicked they were. We have had to modify it a bit as when we did this to Sheflin she nearly went suicidal over the extent of her own evil past," I declared.

The servants had all been woken up and were offered the chance to leave and when we explained that life there would be more like an open prison with subsistence living, all but three wanted to leave, which gave us another problem. Unlike the studs who could go back to their former lives and take a small fortune with them, the servants' only home was Messapth. They had been born there.

We had to do something. It was unfair for them to be punished, and their only skill was to be servants to their mistresses. We would retrain them and give them proper identities, similar to the witness protection programme, then they could decide themselves what to do with the rest of their lives. The good thing was that English was their second language, so any transition would be easier.

CHAPTER FORTY-NINE

STEPHEN AND HIS BEST PEOPLE were now looking for Geflin and the daughters. It hadn't taken long to find their arrival in Tibet, the records at Lhasa airport clearly showed the arrival of eight females, seven of which were minors, and a check through four weeks either side of that arrival date conclusively proved that these were the targets.

Sheflin had told us the trek took nearly three weeks to get to the temple, and a few days less on the return, as the daughters who had finished their training there were superbly fit.

Taking no chances, they started to check departures from three weeks after the arrival date and found eight females departing Lhasa to Delhi, all under different names from those on the arrival, but which had to be Geflin and the girls leaving the monastery.

It should have been straightforward to find those names next on a flight to Zurich, but in the event, it was not Zurich but JFK, New York!

"Geflin must have found out what had happened at Messapth. It's around that time that the seven daughters in Zurich just disappeared before we had a chance to tag them. It was simple to find the hotels Geflin had booked as it was on their entry visa. We checked the hotels, and they were still showing as guests, but detailed examination of the room bills showed that no food had been ordered for three days, nothing there except the daily room charge," Stephen told me. "From then on, tracing them is going to be difficult, because she would have known we would be after her and she's not going to make it easy."

We had to approach it from a different angle. We knew she would want revenge, but even with all their deadly skills they still needed money, and a large amount at that, and depending on how much, it was unlikely that Geflin had sufficiently hidden away.

Stephen thought she would have a safe house only known to her. "...and a safety deposit with cash, high-value notes to a maximum of two million dollars, although that's too much dead money, so about a million I would say," he said.

"To exact vengeance on us with the protection we have, she will need a lot more than that, so where would she get it, and quickly? Bank robbery—there have been no big robberies in the States. Fraud takes too long to set up, and so does blackmail, so it has to be drugs," I pondered aloud.

"No!" exclaimed one of Stephen's people. "Take out a drug dealer, better still, a drug baron. Remember a few days back, one of the wealthiest Columbian drug barons had his whole operation taken out and fifteen of his women were kidnapped, but some of the girlfriends and wives have turned up subsequently and have no idea who the females were. The police are keeping a tight lid on it."

Stephen called the Columbian secret service, who confirmed that fifteen female tourists were believed to have been the kidnap victims, feared dead as they had disappeared without a trace, and he told him about the note and the significance of the signature.

Stephen thanked him, then rang his contact in the DEA to find out what they knew about Enrico; apparently, they estimated his drug wealth was over $1.2 billion, mostly cash, but they had not been able to catch any of his drug rings or find any of his cash over the last few years. "We know he's refining but how he's distributing and laundering his money we are clueless, we're bloody glad that he's been taken out, as the other barons are still making mistakes and we're able to catch them."

It was not quite the news we wanted, and $1.2 billion in cash could wreak a lot of revenge.

CHAPTER FIFTY

THE DEMISE OF ENRICO bore all the hallmarks of Dark Seven; it would have been easy for them to get the information needed to take control of his money and find out how and where he was getting his cash laundered. It had to be offshore.

The Caymans were the closest but would be the hardest to get the information we needed. Herr Hoffman had already warned us of the difficulty. The banks' computers would be highly encrypted to prevent the security services from being using their massive resources to get the information they could not get through legitimate means, and they had not been able to break their security. But we knew a man who could.

I communicated with Court Leiston and asked him to join us as we had a problem, and 30 minutes later, he walked through the door. There were rather a lot of banks in the Caymans, but with the help of Herr Hoffman we ruled out all the global banks as the pressure could be exerted in their home countries to obtain information and what we had was only speculation.

The Independent Bank of Cayman Brac had far bigger cash reserves than their size of business warranted, so we would start with them. It was the early hours of the morning in Cayman, so no one would know of our activity until business opened in the morning.

It took less than two minutes to get into the computer but trying to find our way around its system was proving hard, so Herr Hoffman took over remotely and started looking for large cash deposits.

A regular monthly deposit of 30 million dollars stood out. He accessed the account for these transactions. It showed a zero balance, but a week ago, it had over $450 million before it was all transferred to another account within the same bank.

We were now looking at that bank account, showing transfers into it, all of which were under £12 million, and one transfer of £1.5 million going out.

It didn't take long to find out the recipient was Jojhinda Ravagit, and a few seconds later, we were into his account, where he had the princely sum of just over 40 million, but the account showed multiple transactions in and out and it would take a long time to trace all the other parties.

I asked if we could get names to the two original accounts, and after some time he confirmed one account belonged to Enrico and that all his funds were transferred to 'Shannon Gray'.

I then asked if he could transfer the money out of her account and into Earth Corp's, and I had hardly finished speaking before the funds were in our account.

"Make sure our 'Shannon' knows who has it. I want her so angry that she is concentrating more on revenge than being careful," I declared.

We checked over the last month for her name in arrival manifests by sea and air on all islands, but nothing turned up, nor with her other known alias; we checked the CCTV in both customs, and at the yacht clubs, still nothing.

If they were on the Caymans, they came in secretly, in which case someone was shielding them and that someone must know where they were, which must surely be a person very high up at the bank. It would take some time, but Stephen and Herr Hoffman would find him, of that, they were sure.

CHAPTER FIFTY-ONE

JOJHINDA WAS WELL PLEASED with his efforts. Coming up with fifteen new identities was a tall order, but his extended family had always come up with the goods. He took out the hard drive from his computer containing all the information for the identities and smashed it into pieces. He used a new hard drive for each commission he received, and he also could forget everything about the commission and the identities once the job was done.

He booked a private charter plane to Cayman Brac, then he phoned Geflin and told her that the package would be with her the following day since it was nearly 15 hours flight and would need to refuel at Northolt Airport in London before the last hop to Cayman Brac.

He booked a taxi and then retrieved from his safe a necklace. He was by profession a jewellery maker and took commissions, which he delivered all over the world, providing him with ideal cover for the clandestine operations.

With a £1.87 million necklace in the attaché case disclosed to customs and paying whatever import duty was required, they never checked for anything else, and if the client rejected it, he simply took it back to customs on leaving and got the duty back.

He had a customer for this one in Cayman as well as the package for Geflin, so the cost of a private jet was justifiable.

The taxi arrived and took him to the executive charter lounge where he was well known and within 20 minutes, he was aboard his Learjet, with the whole plane to himself apart from the crew, two pilots and two hostesses, so much more personal and luxurious than even first and business class.

He had his first drink after take-off and several more before, as well as an excellent meal a few hours into the flight. After that, he felt a bit light-headed and used the cabin to sleep,

completely missing the refuelling stop in England and waking up four hours from Cayman to a welcome breakfast and fresh orange juice.

Relaxing in his seat, he mused how simple it was to create false identities. His family had been good at forging them for as long as documents had been required to travel.

Centuries ago, that meant only an official letter of

introduction: "the bearer of this letter should be afforded protection," and all the pleasantries, easy to forge, but now with electronic checks, it should have been much harder, although quite the reverse in his case, it was actually simpler.

Since India was colonised by the British, they needed Indians to assist in the bureaucracy of ruling a country. The Ravagit family excelled in any post given them and they soon became the backbone of the civil service, and quite indispensable. From then they spread their expertise throughout the post-colonial world and acquired important positions throughout the Civil Services of the world.

Jojhinda's extended family contained some fourth-generation nationals of their chosen countries, more national than Indian, but still providing the family bond facilitating his business. The money he paid for their efforts ensured the next generation were sufficiently well educated to continue to fill such important positions, which would allow him to continue his real business.

It wouldn't be long before he had people in the world's secret services, adding another aspect to his business. "God blesses the family and its sense of duty to its benefactors, life can only continue to get even better," he thought to himself.

The captain put the safety belt sign on and announced they were 20 minutes from Cayman Brac, so Jojhinda phoned his client, who ordered the necklace, telling him he would be at the airport in 20 minutes and to send a car for him.

It was 10:30 in the evening. He was glad to have spent

most of the 15 hours asleep, so he felt well.

It was a short distance to the terminal and customs, where he declared the necklace and paid the duty and as always it went like clockwork. He had no luggage except his attaché case, which he would never let anyone else carry, so he declined the chauffeur's offer to carry it for him.

It was just a ten-minute drive to the client's house, where he was shown to the study before the client joined him. He took the necklace out of its box—it was a work of art, a truly amazing, unique piece of jewellery. The client was suitably impressed but hesitated over the price. Jojhinda would never negotiate and started to put the necklace away and told the client, "We agreed on a price over the phone, providing you liked it. The stones in it are worth over a million pounds. It took three years to make, and that's the price, so unless you pay it, we are wasting each other's time."

The necklace was for a very special person as a surprise, so the client agreed to the price plus the duty, then transferred the money while Jojhinda wrote his receipt. They shook hands, both satisfied with the deal.

Jojhinda asked, "Could you order me a taxi, please? I have someone else to see on the island"

"No," he replied. "You can have use of the Rolls. Just tell Charlie where you want to go, and he will take you." To decline the offer would have looked suspicious, so he accepted and when in the car, he rang Geflin to tell her he was about an hour away and described the vehicle. "I will be expecting you," she replied.

He gave Charlie the address, asking if he knew where it was. "I should do, it's the boss's beach house, although I haven't been there recently as the boss usually takes his helicopter," the chauffeur responded. Jojhinda stifled the shock.

He phoned Geflin again. "Apparently, the beach house where you're staying belongs to my jewellery client! Is this going to compromise our situation? I am ok to go along with it but how is it for you?". "Fine," she assured him "he is a really good friend of mine and we will have no problems. see you soon," and hung up.

Geflin rang her girls and told them to be back at the beach house within the hour. They dutifully obeyed. Jojhinda arrived soon after them and went through their new identity, with each one supplying them with the history which they needed to learn to ensure they were convincing as those other people.

He was to stay the night since, due to the length of the flight, the crew had to rest before they could fly him back to Delhi. They ate together and relaxed, then he was shown to his room, where he promptly fell asleep.

The rest of them took the scripts of their identity back to their rooms and booked flights to their allotted countries. They would all be gone from the island within the next 72 hours.

CHAPTER FIFTY-TWO

STEPHEN MUSED, "They must be on the Caymans. How they got there is irrelevant for now; finding them is the priority. The transfer of money to Delhi was interesting."

He contacted his office there to check it out; they ascertained that owner was away on business but would be back at the weekend, so they returned later to search the business premises, but all they could report was it was a bespoke jeweller and there was a smashed up hard drive in the trash can which they had retrieved for an IT forensic lab to see what was on it but the lab had said it could take a long to decipher - probably months, possibly a year.

"We checked all flights out of Delhi over the last three

days and he was not on any scheduled flight, but we found him on a private charter to Cayman Brac via Northolt for refuelling, arrived 10.30 pm two days ago and left again the following day," he informed us.

Accessing the airport communication centre, we scanned the CCTV and saw him picked up by a chauffeur, then getting into a Rolls Royce in the VIP parking area. They captured the number plate and within minutes, discovered the vehicle belonged to the President of the Independent Bank of Cayman Brac. "Now there's a coincidence!" Stephen said, "Let's get into his bank account."

From that, they learned that he was one seriously wealthy man. The most recent large transaction was for £1.87 million, timed 23:05 and to Jojhinda, which looked like a straightforward deal.

"Where did he go from there, then? He didn't go back to the airport, none of the airport hotels had him staying there." Stephen phoned Pat Smith, asking, "Can you ask Sheflin whether the name of Jojhinda means anything to her?"

She sent back the information that he was a master jeweller but also a brilliant forger, used by all the houses. The odds were if we found out where he went, we would also find the elusive women.

"We need to start thinking outside the box. The President of the bank would know all his large depositors and if it was drug money, he would surely be aware of it. What do we know about him?" I asked.

Herr Hoffman looked him up, "Well educated, first-class honours in economics, started the bank in 1963, married and has been now divorced for a long time, a keen sailor and helicopter pilot."

I said "If he is a keen sailor why is he not living by the ocean? With all his money, it would be the logical thing to do so perhaps he has more than one home and uses his helicopter to commute between them. If he has, there must be some record of that."

It didn't take long for us to discover that the bank had several properties, but one at the top of the island was in his own name—it had all the facilities for a sailing man. We used Google Earth to locate the place in real time and although there was some time lapse, you could just see a female lying by the pool and a head bobbing in the pool, but the resolution was not good enough to focus.

Stephen phoned his American military contacts and asked them to scan Cayman Brac, which they said would take three hours to set up, so that would have to do.

I suggested, "Let's go there and find out for ourselves. We could be there in half an hour." "You are not coming. It's far too dangerous, and that's final," he declared. I was about to argue, but seeing his expression, I accepted that I wouldn't be putting my shorts on.

He would go via Australia and pick up his best scuba divers Shane Simpson and James Baker. They were in the Australian SBS before joining Shefford Securities, who he told to get all their gear ready. "We will take it on the verticular, and if it doesn't allow the gear inside, we will ask to beam it like the C-130s."

"I will continue on to Flint, Texas, to see how the professor is doing and then go on to see the President at Anders," I announced. We had enough information. I thanked Herr Hoffman. Court turned the computer off and said he would come with me.

Thirty-five minutes later we were in Sydney Harbour, picked up the divers and their kit, their incredulous faces watching as the boat was disappeared in front of them to be beamed across.

Fifteen minutes later, we were on Cayman Brac. The beach was deserted, as dawn had just broken. Our divers, still gob smacked, saw their boat appear on the ocean. I said, "Welcome to the Cayman Islands!" and left Stephen and the divers, telling them "It's reconnaissance only, do not engage with the women, we only want to know how they got there."

By the time they would have completed all the checks on the equipment and motored round to the beach house, it would be just after 9:00 a.m. Cayman time.

CHAPTER FIFTY-THREE

JOJHINDA HAD STAYED THE NIGHT, partly to see whether there were any queries on the new identities; all the information was on fact sheets for them to learn, and there were no questions, so Charlie came back and took him to the airport.

He left the Caymans a lot wealthier and feeling very pleased with himself.

Geflin climbed out of the pool and relaxed on the lounger. Looking out over the sea, she saw a huge cruise ship. It must have just left Grand Cayman with a flotilla of small boats following in the wake; as always, they were making for the headland to dive for shells and sponges. At first, she was concerned that they came too close but was reassured by her friendly banker there was nothing to worry about.

It had been nearly three weeks since they had arrived there. The new identities were excellent and some of the girls had to leave that day; they wanted to get on with finding a secure base in their territory, from which to plan revenge. They would have to start from scratch in their countries without the help of their predecessors to improve their field-craft skills and introduce them to the contacts they would need, but it would all become easier in time. With more or less unlimited funds, once again they would reign supreme.

Geflin was pleased with how things had turned out. The need for a quick revenge attack on those who had desecrated Messapth was not so important as a slow, lingering, painful death for all of them.

Two daughters came outside with fresh orange juice and croissants that they devoured eagerly. They were going to make the most of their last day before returning to the States the following afternoon.

The banker would be back after close of business and was going to take them all out for a sumptuous meal. It had been enjoyable renewing an old acquaintance, and he was still good in the sack.

It was a great evening. The necklace was just beautiful, and she had worn it at dinner. He had booked the best restaurant for them. The whole evening was rounded off with an energetic session in bed. He left just after midnight.

He tried pleading with her to stay but to no avail; she would be leaving that afternoon but said she would come back soon.

She heard a helicopter—strangely, the banker was returning unexpectedly. She went to meet him, and it was plain to see his anxiety. "What's wrong?" she demanded. "Let's sit down," he replied. "Overnight, we have had a cyber-attack on our main computer. The only accounts which have been compromised are Enrico's and yours. Everything in your account has been transferred to a Swiss bank and is in a suspense account held by Earth Corp!"

"What does that mean?"

"It means that the money is now inaccessible to you. Your bank balance is now zero! We have placed an objection to this transfer as an unauthorised electronic transaction, but it could take months, possibly years, to resolve. We have the most secure security system; even the CIA are unable to get into it and I can assure you they have tried. All cyber-attacks are monitored and we are able to trace them, and my first thought was an internal attack and specific to both accounts, but our head of digital securities has ruled this out, there has been no attack from any employee of the bank, so someone has got into our computer - how, we don't know but we are working on it. "

"So, Earth Corp have my money; it's all gone, and I am left with nothing again?" Geflin exploded.

"Well, not quite. It was an illegal transaction that you didn't authorise, so the bank is culpable to the extent that it should not have happened. The amount taken exceeds our normal procedures, and therefore your compensation or the recovery of the money will have to go to the board. As both you and Enrico were my personal accounts, it will be difficult to explain illegal laundering of Enrico's fortune and it then appearing in your account, and it could bring the bank down. As for where the money went to and how easy it was to trace, it's my belief that they want you to know they have it, more importantly, they want to see the face behind the numbered account. In a nutshell, they want to draw you out by forcing you to challenge them about the legality of the transactions. Meanwhile, our security systems failed you, but if we replace the funds, I'm positive they will just take them again until we have found how they're getting into the system and can stop them, so what I am proposing is to give each of you a debit card that has a limit up to the total funds taken from your account, it will be activated using a pin only, although you may wish to put some additional security on the cards, but it's not necessary as all transactions will go through my desk, and if I find any unusual activity, I will get in touch."

"Some of the girls have already left. I will have to get in touch and tell them to come back, and I will postpone leaving for another day. I don't trust having these cards posted to them," concluded Geflin.

She made the calls. Some of them hadn't reached their destination and others had just arrived, but dutifully they started the long journey back.

There was nothing else to do but wait. The Caymans are probably the best place to do so. The banker left to organise the cards and would return later. She went back to the sun lounger and looked out to sea; with all the boats bobbing about on the ocean. She hadn't noticed a new boat with three divers on board and it just blended into the scene.

CHAPTER FIFTY-FOUR

STEPHEN AND HIS DIVERS NAVIGATED their boat into the middle of all the others. It would be at least a half-a-mile swim to the boat house, taking an indirect route using the cliff to hide the oxygen bubbles, whereby to see them you would have to be hanging off the cliff. The water was so clear it required special precautions.

They approached the bottom of the cliff and followed the outline until they reached the entrance to the boat house, which was unusually deep.

The reason was soon apparent, as a large submersible was moored there. Staying underwater, Shane took out a miniature pinhole camera and extended it above the water to scan the surface, but everything was clear, and no one was about. From the seaward side, they used suckers to climb up the outside of the submersible, reached the top and climbed in through the hatch.

Stephen's guys rapidly assessed the capabilities of the submersible. It would have been cramped, but fifteen females would fit. They started fitting tracking devices on the inside and on the outside and left the way they came. If the women used that route to get away, we'd got it covered.

The verticular dropped off Stephen's guys and their gear back in Sydney, then he rejoined the team, trying to uncover the identities of the fifteen women.

He told them how they had got to the Caymans and about the submersible, "So they will not appear on any arrivals by sea or air. If we then compare arrival and departure lists and discount any names which appear on both, we will be left with a list of names of people who just arrived or just departed. We check these lists with the electoral roll and eliminate all residents, leaving us a much shorter list of names for women who departed without being matched to an arrival and those will need checking out thoroughly."

I arrived in Flint, Texas, at the home of Professor Dave Mac. His wife and daughter had also been working on the magma bubble problem and were so engrossed in what they were doing they didn't notice my arrival, and it seemed rude to interrupt them.

I went across to the computer and saw a picture of a hollow Earth the size of a basketball and inside the Earth was something the size of a golf ball.

He looked up and saw me, and suggested I went to the fridge and fetched some beers for us all. With that priority out of the way, he began telling me what he had done, with the model showing the size and scale of the problem.

"Well," I said, "it really doesn't look such a big problem. Surely the earth could stand it. The golf ball looks pretty small compared with the size of the earth." "It's not so much the size but where it will hit the earth's crust, you already know how weak the crust is in North America, and if it hits there, it will be 'goodnight civilisation', the scenario we have been contemplating will happen, but with an explosive force far greater than we first envisaged," he told me.

I replied, "I have been told that we can slow its momentum and alter its direction, but not prevent it altogether."

"That's what we are working on. The Utopian tunnel we are building will dissipate possibly a third of the bubble. The normal magma control could cope with another 20%, leaving us with over half still to diffuse. We do not have detailed maps of the Pacific seabed, although we know there are active volcanoes that cause the earthquakes and tsunami which devastate the Pacific land area, but if we had the detailed maps we could, in theory, organise these volcanoes to vent the remaining 50% in such a way that the tsunami would crash into each other instead of hitting any land mass," the professor told me.

"That's an amazing theory. Who would have these maps, or how long would it take to make some?" I wondered.

He replied, "I am sure some of the Pacific is mapped but

how much I don't know, our Navy would know, and the rest of the world's submarine fleets would have charts, but whether that encompasses the whole Pacific, we would have to ask."

"I am about to see the President, so I'll ask the question. You will have all the information America holds within the next hour, the rest of the world may take a bit longer, but you will get it, I guarantee," I assured him and asked for a copy of what was on the computer, which he put onto a flash drive.

I finished my beer, and five minutes later I was at Anders with Rodbridge, showing him the scenario. He called Admiral Steven Greaves, head of the US Navy, and told him to send all the Pacific Ocean charts they had to the professor, dismissing his objection that most of the charts were classified. "That's an executive order, just do it. Which other countries would have charts? Get me a list as I will need them as well."

"Yes Sir!" replied Greaves, and hung up, the list appearing just 15 minutes later.

"I had better get back to the White House and make those calls. We might need a bit of diplomacy or a nudge or two," said Rodbridge, and we both laughed.

"I could give you a lift, be there in seconds," I offered.

"You create too many problems when you just appear, so I will use my helicopter, thanks," he replied.

I asked how preparations for the trials were progressing. "Quite well, despite the defence trying to stall and asking for more time quoting this and that precedent, but it's falling on deaf ears; as most of the Supreme Court Judges were appointed by the late President, my honest opinion is that they will put in a guilty plea with mitigation and not let them testify as they would incriminate themselves," he told me.

CHAPTER FIFTY-FIVE

I ARRIVED BACK AT BASE and was brought up to speed. The list of females leaving the island but not arriving was getting smaller; checking their names against residency was a little time-consuming, but we were getting there.

Stephen showed me the photos of the submersible, "If that leaves, we will be able to trace it anywhere in the world, my guys estimate it has the capability of travelling two thousand miles submerged before having to get to the surface for air and recharging batteries. That would be enough to get them to the States." I asked if he thought it was used to transport drugs, but Stephen said he thought not, "Just to get his cash there and another system for supplying drugs. We won't dwell too much on that, but no doubt the women know how he did it and there is still over seven hundred million dollars unaccounted for, and if they are able to get their hands on, it will mean trouble for us."

Eventually, the list came down to twenty women who had left the island without arriving and who were not residents. We had all the departure flight details, and we identified them on the airport's CCTV as they were checking in. It was like a beauty show and easy to pick out the right number of beautiful women and teenagers and, most importantly, obtain their new identities and destinations.

Stephen rang his offices in Paris, Pretoria, Hong Kong, and Sydney, giving them the details and instructions to tag them, if possible, but not to engage with them. "Do not get close. Tag every hire vehicle at the airports from a safe distance. Ascertain which vehicles they use and then de-commission all the other tags, so we are able to trace where they go. These women are extremely dangerous. I want them to be lulled into a false sense of security to continue with whatever their plans are, but I need the highest level of electronic and CCTV surveillance from a distance. Is that clear?" Stephen's company had the contract for security at nearly every major airport.

Paris was the first to report that they had landed and then promptly departed straight back to the Caymans, without even leaving the airport, and would arrive back in about 30 hours. Over the next ten hours, the others were also reported as having returned to Cayman Brac.

We agreed the only reason would be money; by now Geflin would have realised that we had diverted her funds and were likely to do the same again if any more money was put into her account, so they must be coming back for alternative provisions. "The bank will have to do something as they were at fault and carrying suitcases full of cash would not be a good idea, so they must be coming back to pick up credit or charge cards. Getting the details of those would be a big help as we could track them electronically through their spending," I observed.

Court got us back into the bank's computer and Herr Hoffman started a remote search for the cards from the myriad details. It didn't take long to discover that the President of the bank had ordered fifteen additional cards from his own account, with no limit on the amount that could be drawn or spent. We now had details of the cards and Stephen had them electronically tagged, so we would know when and—most importantly—where they were used.

Stephen and I were now a lot less apprehensive. The danger was still looming, but we had the edge now. If they came for us, we would know they were coming. Neutralising Messapth meant that for the remaining women, whatever they did, they must start out without the benefit of any network behind them.

"All except Geflin, but surely even her contacts and conduits will be wary of hearing from someone they have had no contact with for years? But she is the real danger. Her field-craft may be rusty, but her deadliness isn't. If we could get her, then the daughters are still deadly but will find things a lot harder as novices. How to neutralise her is the problem. Slumberland would be the answer, it's been so successful, but how to get to her with it... we can't really KO the whole of Cayman Brac and put the entire island to sleep!" we debated.

"She has only three ways off the island, the submersible, a boat or to fly. Her friendly bank President has an ocean-going yacht which they could use, and the submersible is good to get to the US mainland although it might have to come up for air, but both of these options would be time-consuming. My best guess is that as soon as they have got their cards, they will fly back to start whatever they are planning to do in their respective areas. Cayman Brac uses Miami as its forwarding hub, so if we book all the first and business class seats for the next 72 hours, they will have no option but to charter, the only plane available could one be of our Lear Jets, flown by our very own Colonels Gill and Berry. We could dose them half an hour before landing at Miami so they would be unlikely to fall asleep until they're on the long-haul part of their flight, but even if they did, the US is very amenable to assisting us in our mission and an executive order from the President would soon sort that out."

The security team booked all the flights and charter aircraft for the next four days, leaving just one charter plane available, our own. Stephen contacted his SBS guys again and told them to make ready as we were going to employ a special motion sensor that would deliver a drug to facilitate the safe capture of the targets, so the devices were to be planted on the yacht and the submersible. "We will pick you up the same way as before, it's night-time, so if you use an underwater motion unit of some kind you can go straight from the beach and place the devices on both vessels."

I found out where the Colonels were and told them to get a Learjet to the island. They were in London and would take 11 hours to get to the island, so I decided we would pick them up and get them to Los Angeles. "You can take Court Leiston's company jet. It's only a three-hour flight from there and you will be here before sunrise ready to take a charter of fifteen evil women to get them to Miami as you will be their only option.

We're going to use what you did at Messapth and put them to sleep with slumberland, which you will put into the cabin 30 minutes before you land at Miami," adding "If you should succumb to it yourselves, I will pay you double time while you're asleep," at which they both laughed.

Everything went like clockwork. All devices had been planted, and we had the only charter aircraft available on Cayman Brac. Our military satellites were now in position and gave minute by minute live coverage of the beach house and most of Cayman Brac. All of Dark Seven were now back on the island, or at least at the airport. A helicopter left the beach house and was tracked to the airport.

CHAPTER FIFTY-SIX

GEFLIN HAD MADE CALLS to a few of her old contacts in different parts of the States, telling them to arrange a meeting with the key players in the cocaine trade. Like the guy in Columbia, they were terrified by the implications that she had contacted them again after 14 years.

She had decided to sell the drugs racket that Enrico had masterminded to the highest bidder. She had all the information she needed, and for the right price, she could avoid all the work of maintaining a major drug operation, concentrate on revenge and reinstating Messapth and its riches from whoever had ruined her sacred place. It would take a great deal of money to get Messapth back to its former wealth, but with three tonnes of pure cocaine in over seven hundred containers scattered across the globe, it should be attractive enough to any criminal gang to pay the price. Unfortunate that she couldn't make this available worldwide, but she had to play it safer by keeping it within the Americas.

Travelling in the helicopter to the airport, she received a phone call from her New York contact telling her a meeting had been arranged for 10:00 the following morning in the Crowne Plaza's Presidential Suite, giving no more details but the wording as he signed off meant that he would leave details in the dead letter box they used, so to anyone hacking either party's phone it would appear just a simple business call. She would need to be in New York that evening, to ensure all was well and not a trap; normally she would be there at least 24 hours before any meeting, but her daughter and niece could provide backup if necessary.

On reaching the airport, they all went to the charter VIP lounge. Geflin went over to the desk and told them she needed to extend the charter to New York after the first stop at Miami. The receptionist said that would necessitate another flight plan and she would talk to the charter pilots.

Fifteen minutes later, the receptionist returned with the pilots, saying there was a problem with going on to New York. It was impossible as after getting to Miami, the plane had to go to Houston for a regular trip to Caracas to take some oil people to their investments. "I will double the price!" Geflin said, "I need to be in New York this evening."

Colonel Gill spoke up, "You don't understand, the flight is a contract for thrice weekly, forty- eight weeks a year, this one contract pays for the aircraft and to renege on it would seriously damage the business -their legal people would tear us to shreds. It's impossible to do as you ask. We will get you to Miami and that's as far as we can take you."

Her anger was mounting, but her bank manager said that they had a small six-seater Learjet on Grand Cayman, which a quick call ascertained was available and could take them to New York.

Geflin said goodbye to the main group and left them at the airport before she and the two others got back in the helicopter for the trip of just under an hour to Grand Cayman. They would be in New York by 21:00, giving them enough time to do the reconnaissance, establish emergency escape routes and equip the Presidential Suite with a few mundane items which could turn into lethal weapons in their hands. Dark Seven were always thorough in what they did, which is why none had ever been caught.

When they arrived at Grand Cayman airport, the bank manager was so besotted with Geflin he wanted to go on to the States with them, but Geflin told him it could be dangerous. "You're safer here and more useful to me on the island; rest assured I will be back as soon as this business is over and we will spend some serious time together," she promised. He looked so forlorn but accepted her decision, watching as his Learjet taxied and took off for New York.

CHAPTER FIFTY-SEVEN

COLONEL GILL COMMUNICATED to Stephen and me through his bracelet, saying they would only be taking twelve passengers as three needed to go to New York urgently. "They bought the excuse I gave them, but her banker friend offered the bank's small Learjet on Grand Cayman, which is going to take them to New York. We will be leaving in about 15 minutes for Miami where they will catch connecting flights, but by the look of them, some won't even make it off our aircraft as they have been travelling for nearly 48 hours. If we administer slumberland 30 minutes before landing, those who have fallen asleep will not wake up, the others will try to wake them and when they find it impossible, they will know something has happened."

Stephen replied, "Administer the drug when taxiing at Miami airport ensuring they are all awake and take your time in getting to the jetway to make sure they all get dosed even if it means you will both be taking a nap for a day or two. We can cover any eventuality in Miami. I have very close links with their security. Book yourselves into the Radisson hotel and take a nap. If we need you urgently, we will come and restore you to consciousness."

They altered the timing of the slumberland device on the aircraft and moving it by 30 minutes they would ensure they would be on the ground before they were exposed to the drug. Colonel Berry would ensure that all the passengers were awake for landing to maximise the exposure to the drug.

Their passengers embarked, and the flight got underway, duration just under three hours. There were no cabin staff, but they could help themselves to whatever was in the galley. It didn't take long before most were asleep.

Gill had an idea about 45 minutes from landing and made the announcement: "Miami air traffic control have warned of the possibility of poor weather conditions and that our landing there may be difficult but well within the permitted safety margins of this aircraft, so we might have a bumpy landing, that's all. My co-pilot will ensure that you are all awake and in the brace position for landing just in case."

It was the perfect scenario and certainly got the

passengers' attention; everyone was awake and a little apprehensive at their first experience of not being in control, their fate potentially in the hand of the pilots. Berry came forward, checked they were all awake and showed them the brace position. He introduced the drug now since no one would be going back to sleep with the threat of a possible dangerous landing and the resulting adrenalin levels.

The drug was released in the cabin over the next 30 minutes. As they touched down safely, they emptied the aircraft of drugged, recycled air and dragged in Miami filtered air. The pilots thought that with luck they would be unaffected by the drug, although only time would tell. They were hoping to see their families as it had been nearly a month, I'd given their families the chance to join them but taking kids out of education and resettling somewhere else was not an option, even for a month, so they had only stayed a couple of days. The families of USAF pilots were used to long periods without their husbands, and only when a tour of duty was greater than two years would their wives even countenance moving to be closer to their husbands.

The much-relieved passengers were taken to the VIP transfer suite to wait for their connecting flights. Stephen had his people there keeping a close eye on them by CCTV, following their every movement. Apart from the flight to Sydney, which was delayed by three hours, all the others were on time, so within the next hour and a half, all except two would be on a flight. Stephen's people would ensure that no one fell asleep before flying except the two remaining for the Sydney flight. If they fell asleep in the lounge after their cousins had departed, they would be scooped up and taken to Prague, as would the ones who fell asleep during their flights.

We were in a waiting game where only time would dictate our next actions, apart from Geflin and the two with her—they were a ticking time bomb on their way to New York. We knew the flight plan to JFK, any deviation to the flight plan not agreed with American air traffic would have two F16s up and escorting them back onto the path, and if they continued and did not cooperate, they would be taken out with a couple of Stingers. Once they arrived at JFK, the whole CCTV camera network would monitor their every move.

CHAPTER FIFTY-EIGHT

THE LEARJET HAD MADE SUPERB TIME, thanks to a strong tail wind. They were on the ground at JFK just after 20:00, cleared customs and were at the Avis rental desk to hire two compact cars with sat-nav. They would need a third but would get that in New York City.

Geflin and her daughter drove in one and her niece followed in the other, making their way to the Crowne Plaza. It had been decided that they would stay there because as guests it would give them more time to reconnoitre the meeting place and they would not be challenged by security, especially as they had hired the Broadway Suite which was on the same floor as the President's Suite. The bell boy showed them to their suite. Geflin gave him a ten-dollar tip which was gratefully received and asked him if the President's Suite was occupied. He said, "No, but it's booked for all day tomorrow, which is why you were unable to hire it tonight, but I think the Broadway Suite is nicer as it has better views." She thanked him and he left.

They quickly changed and went shopping for ordinary items which would not look out of place in the hotel suite but which in their hands could become deadly weapons in case the meeting turned nasty. Each of them bought three sets of different clothes and wigs, hired another car and parked it on the ground floor of a multi-storey about four hundred yards from the Crowne Plaza, making their way back to the hotel after hiding their spare clothes—basic field-craft, so much CCTV everywhere but changing appearance several times in a short distance would stop them being identified and allow them to get to their hire car undetected.

They arrived back at the hotel, headed to the Brassiere for something to eat; it was 11:30 pm when they got back to their suite. Geflin put the electronic door key into the door and from her handbag she pulled out a gadget which she fixed to the door lock, duplicating onto it the electronic signal produced by the key. Experience had taught her that the signal should be similar for all the locks on the same floor. She kept close to the wall to evade the security cameras and reaching the President's Suite, she placed the device on the lock and was in. She went to the control panel, closed the drapes and turned the lights on, then placed a set of Parker pens on the desk and another set on the coffee table, before going over to the bar where she left an ice pick and hammer which crushes the ice.

After that, she turned the lights off and opened the drapes again, carefully making her way back to her suite, satisfied that should it be necessary she had plenty of weapons to employ to buy them time to escape from any danger, and with everything set, she would sleep well.

CHAPTER FIFTY-NINE

ALBERTO MARTINI WAS THE GODFATHER of the east coast Mafia, and he was annoyed that he had to go personally to this meeting and could not delegate to one of his subordinates. Geflin's contact had told his Mafia contact that it had to be the boss if he wanted to know where Enrico's drugs were. The price of cocaine had tripled since Enrico's death. There was not enough supply, and everyone was hurting in the drug business.

Alberto left his mansion. It would take 30 minutes to get to the Plaza, and as was the norm, three vehicles were involved, and his was in the middle for extra protection. Arriving at the hotel, his men swiftly escorted him inside, two men went to the reception for the key to the President's

Suite and took the lift, going into the suite first to sweep for bugs and check all the rooms, having closed the drapes. They sent word down that everything was clear, so the rest of them came up. Two men were stationed at the lift, two **outside the suite, and Alberto's personal bodyguards went** inside. Then all they had to do was wait.

Geflin had slept well. Her daughter and niece were already up and heading to the gym for a workout, so she joined them. She was hoping the gym would be empty so early in the morning, but it was too busy for them to follow their full routine. Back in their suite, they showered, and the girls put on track suits while Geflin wore a sexy designer dress which accentuated the shape of her body, an outfit in which she was guaranteed full attention, verified by the heads turning as they walked into the restaurant when they went for a light breakfast. Her phone rang. It was her conduit to inform her that Alberto had left and would be at the hotel in half an hour. She and the girls returned to the suite to wait.

Geflin and the girls left their suite just before 10 a.m. The girls called the lift, looking as if they were going for a jog and Alberto's men took no notice of them as they could not take their eyes off Geflin, who walked straight past them towards the President's Suite. The men outside the door were stunned by the vision of beauty that stood before them but told her she and her laptop case would have to be searched.

She consented, handing the case to one man while the other searched her, but he took his time and turned it into more of a grope than a search. Like lightning, her fist came up and broke his jaw. His pleasure turned instantly into pain, whereupon the other man dropped the laptop and went for his gun. Geflin caught the laptop and at the same time kneed the man in his solar plexus, leaving him gasping for air, and his gun didn't make it out of the holster.

She stepped over the two men and walked into the suite to inform Alberto: "Being searched is one thing, being groped is another. Your man needs hospital treatment for a broken jaw. The other is just winded and will recover in about 30 minutes. Are we here to talk business or not?"

Alberto beckoned her to the chair in front of the desk where he was seated and told a bodyguard to see the men outside. He asked, "What do you have for me that is so dammed important I had to come myself?"

Easing herself into the chair and crossing her legs to give a deliberate sight up her skirt, she replied, "How would you like to own the whole of Enrico's drug empire? It is worth around seven hundred million dollars and it could be yours; it's all on this laptop."

"How did you get hold of it?" he wanted to know. "Enrico told me everything before I killed him and his entire gang. Are you interested or not?" she asked him.

"$700 million is a large amount of money. You will have to show me that my investment will be secure," he replied. She opened up the laptop and in great detail, she went through the whole drug operation.

Alberto was hooked; the price of the cocaine was at last month's and it had now trebled, and the smuggling operation could also be used for other illegal commodities. He warned her, "Such a vast amount of money will take time to organise."

"You have 20 minutes to get the funds into my nominated account or I walk out and offer the deal to someone else," she retorted.

"It just can't be done that quickly," he objected.

"Have you got the money or not?" she taunted him.

"Of course, I have, but it's spread across the banking world and will take time to organise!" he exclaimed.

"Have you got the passwords and security codes for these accounts? If so, we can do the deal right now," she informed him.

He replied, "Of course I have, but I need to use my computer as access is limited to that computer only, any other will be seen as a threat and will be barred, so I can only transfer funds using my own computer."

"That's fine, you go off and organise the transfers," she told him. "Here is the number for my banker, and when he calls me to say it is all set, we will reconvene to complete the exchange, do you agree?"

"Can I not take the laptop now?" he asked.

"No. It stays with me until the money is paid," she stated.

"My men could just simply take it from you," he said.

"Which one of them wants to die first, and you will be the second? I have already hospitalised one of your men, another is still trying to breathe, and I can assure you I am able to kill you all should I need to, but we are trying to do a deal and show good faith; so you leave, arrange the transfer and I will bring the laptop to you, now are we agreed?"

He said "Yes," and they shook hands.

On the way out of the suite, Alberto asked her, "Could you really have killed us all?" and in one movement she had picked up a pen and thrown it at the bodyguard furthest away, parting his hair and ending with it stuck in the wall, and all in the blink of an eye. "I could have killed you all within three seconds, should it have been necessary," she answered.

Geflin phoned her bank manager and told him that a huge sum of money would be transferred to her account shortly, but he advised her that would be foolish as his bank still had no idea how the transfer to Earth Corp had happened on her account so it could happen again. "So, what do you recommend?" she asked.

"Ask him for a banker's draft. I will come over and collect it. We can then give a credit line for that amount but from the bank's resources and not from any particular account; you ring me anytime 24/7 and my bank will put the money into another account of your choice. We already have your security protocol in place. The chances of it being diverted to Switzerland would be nominal unless someone is continuously hacking our computer, in which case our security team would know straight away."

"I will have to get back to him fast," she concluded and promptly phoned Alberto to tell him that the electronic transfer was unsafe and a banker's draft made payable to the Independent Bank of Cayman Brac was required, to which he agreed and said he would contact her when it was ready and the transfer could take place over dinner at his favourite Italian restaurant. She said she would bring her girls, and he replied the more the merrier and he would send a car for them.

263

CHAPTER SIXTY

GEFLIN SPOKE TO HER CONDUIT to find out where Alberto's favourite restaurant was. She looked it up on the net and from the outside, it looked shabby and was in an undesirable area of the Bronx which even the cops were hesitant to enter, however, the food reviews were outstanding. It could still be a trap, so she decided to check it out.

At the reception, she extended their stay for another two nights, which flagged up on the FBI computer, showing the occupants were a priority and this information reached us in minutes.

It was early afternoon when they left the hotel and hailed a cab. The driver was totally surprised by the address he was given and asked if they were sure, but Geflin just smiled, and the taxi drove off. The driver knew of the restaurant's reputation, so when Geflin told him to drive past it and drop them off a couple of blocks away, he thought they were mad. She paid the fare, and the three of them started to walk back to the restaurant; they needed to get real information about the area.

Sure enough, five men emerged from an alley brandishing knives, demanding they hand over their valuables but the "or else" was never reached. They were knocked out and dragged back into the alley, ignored by people passing. They trussed them up with their own clothes so that any movement on their part would cause acute pain.

The one who had spoken and who Geflin assumed was the leader she viciously slapped back into consciousness, threatening him "You are going to tell me all I want to know!" "Go fuck yourself!" he retorted despite the pain he was enduring, which despite having been shot and stabbed a few times was never anything like this with every nerve ending in agony. She released the pressure and relief flooded through his body, as she demanded, "Now are you going to answer my questions?" but he remained silent. She picked up a knife, rolled one of the still unconscious men onto his stomach, pulled his head up by the hair and cut his throat, making sure no blood came close to her clothes. That convinced him to talk and within 30 minutes Geflin knew all she needed to be safe on these streets. To avoid any problems if the attackers were left alive, they were all despatched to their maker after collecting up all their weapons.

Geflin and the girls left the alley and walked towards the restaurant. There was still a block to go, but they had no more confrontations. By now it was closed after the lunch session and would not re-open until 20:00.

The kitchen was at the rear of the building with an alley leading to it by which the deliveries came in, and the dustbins were opposite the kitchen door, underneath a fire escape. The weapons they had taken from the muggers, which included three loaded guns and five knives, three of which were throwing knives, they stashed in and around the alley hidden but easily accessible if they needed them. They continued along the alley until they found the fire escape from the second-floor flat of the dead muggers, which would give them an exit on the street behind the restaurant and a clear and safe way out. Geflin went through his wardrobe and they each chose some of his clothes, leaving their own hidden in the flat, before going out dressed as men with their hair tied up under baseball caps.

CHAPTER SIXTY-ONE

HIGH ABOVE THE BRONX were two unmarked helicopters. There was no CCTV coverage in that part of the Bronx. As fast as a camera was put up, it was vandalised.

The helicopters had picked up the taxi as it entered the Bronx and followed it until the passengers got out. It continued the surveillance of the three women, and everything was being filmed. Five males confronted them. Seconds later, they saw the men being dragged into the alley, where the helicopters lost sight of them. Switching to infra-red, they picked up eight heat signatures and knew they were still there but couldn't make out what was happening.

After about 30 minutes, the women emerged from the alley and continued along the street another block before disappearing into another alley, but as they went further in, the heat signal weakened and finally disappeared altogether. They radioed in to report that they had lost the subjects.

CHAPTER SIXTY-TWO

GEFLIN AND THE GIRLS HAD TO WALK another five blocks before they could hail a cab that got them to one of their clothes stashes where they changed again, before making their way back to the Crowne Plaza.

Inside the hotel she spotted the bodyguard whose hair she had parted, throwing the fountain pen. She rapidly assessed whether there were any other potential threats, but he was on his own and waiting for her. He had brought a message from Alberto that the drafts would be ready the following day and that a car would pick them up at 20:00.

She asked why Alberto hadn't phoned himself as he had said, to be told that the line was tapped. It didn't worry her as she had a supply of sim cards, regularly changing and destroying them. "Until tomorrow then," she said, getting into the lift and going to their suite.

While the others changed into their gym gear, she spoke with her banker and told him that she would have the drafts the following evening. He said, "I will fly up late tomorrow evening but I have to leave again early to get back for a board meeting in the afternoon." "Fine, we should be back by midnight, all being well," she replied, and they agreed whoever was there first would wait in the bar.

She joined the others for an intensive workout in the gym before they went back to their suite to shower and change for dinner, intending to see a show afterwards, since they were on Broadway.

By the morning, it was well over 72 hours since the other girls had started travelling to their respective countries. Geflin had changed the protocol for contact. In the past, important information was shared at council and then disseminated down through the individual houses, but with Messapth and the council gone, the only way was direct communication creating problems that should be overcome by using once-only techniques. She had told them all to phone as soon as they were settled, and she was getting concerned about the lack of contact. She had all the flight numbers, so she checked online to discover that all the flights had taken off on time except for the Qantas flight which had been delayed for three hours.

She soon hacked into the Miami International Airport camera system, found the VIP lounge and called up the tapes for their departure date, watching as all of them were in the lounge, and left as their flights were called, except for the delayed flight. She fast-forwarded it and could see that the girls had fallen asleep, but when a stewardess tried to wake them for their flight, it appeared they were out cold.

She continued to watch as paramedics with stretchers arrived and carried them out of the lounge. Zooming in on the back of a paramedic, she read "Atlas Air Ambulance Services" but if they were ill, why not a normal Miami ambulance? She soon discovered why—Atlas had four air ambulances, and all had been charted by Shefford Securities.

She got the aircraft registration numbers and learned that all four had flown to Prague, leaving to coincide with the arrival of all the daughters in their respective countries. All the girls must have been drugged or they would have caused carnage in the process of being taken, an instinctive reaction to threat in all of them. But how could anyone get close enough to drug them all except Geflin herself and the two with her? The answer had to be on the plane from Cayman Brac to Miami.

She phoned her bank manager there, who investigated and didn't take long to get back to her with the news that Earth Corp had charted every aircraft, leaving only one that she could use, and then even the pilots were from Earth Corps.

To confirm her suspicions, she contacted her conduit she had used to arrange the meeting with Alberto, and set him the task, giving him a list of names. "Find out whether these people have entered the UK, Paris, South Africa and Hong Kong by air in the last seventy-two hours. The UK may be a problem, but the other countries will not be."

He was back within an hour to confirm that none of those names appeared as entering those countries, although he said it would take more time to get the UK information. She hadn't really doubted her instincts, but here was the proof she was right.

There was a knot of anxiety in her gut. Things were happening which she could not control; people knew of their existence. The speed at which this was happening was not normal. It was as if they knew every step she took. Things had changed so much since her time controlling the Americas.

One thing she would do was ensure that her enemies would not live long to savour their defeat of the Houses of Messapth. She contacted a company previously used by all the Houses with a 100% success rate, arranging with them for the elimination of certain targets, names to be forthcoming, and even better if it involved a high degree of suffering, in exchange for 20 million paid now by her bank manager, and another 20 on completion of the task. That done, she felt a little more relaxed, knowing whatever transpired next she had covered all bases.

CHAPTER SIXTY-THREE

BACK ONLINE, she linked up with an intelligence satellite and put in the map co-ordinates for Messapth, where it was the middle of the afternoon, and saw that only women were busy working in the gardens—no men, no servants!

Inspecting the footage more closely, she saw the two who should have gone to Australia, but to make doubly sure, she freeze-framed the shot and superimposed it onto the VIP lounge shot achieving a perfect match. How on earth could they have reached Messapth from Prague, where she knew they had been taken?

She went through the history of the last 72 hours, observing at 14:30 the previous day a sparkling—no, more of a shimmering—before twelve sleeping bodies appeared out of nowhere to be placed on the ground. For a split second the men carrying the girls were visible, and she captured a screenshot of them. She knew for sure now there were only three of them left from Dark Seven to regain control of all that was Messapth. One of the men she recognised as Stephen Shefford; the others she did not know but would make it her business to find out.

She was interrupted by a knock on the door of their suite. One of the girls opened it to find three porters, each almost totally hidden by a huge bouquet of stunning flowers. The girls ripped off the cellophane and arranged the flowers around the lounge. The card said they were from Alberto: "a little token for a successful deal." Even Geflin was impressed.

She returned to her laptop and sent the photo to her conduit to get names for faces. He reported back that four of the men were unknown, probably bodyguards, while the one on the left was Robin Witney, head of Earth Corps. Shefford, she already knew, and the other guy was still unknown despite appearing in every photo taken of the head of Earth Corp. as if they were joined at the hip. Since he looked too small for a bodyguard, he must be extremely important to them in some other way.

She thanked and dismissed him, then sent another encrypted email with that photo, specifying everyone in the photo as people she wanted dead.

CHAPTER SIXTY-FOUR

I SPOKE TO THE PRESIDENT and explained the situation; he already knew how dangerous these women were and pledged that the FBI and CIA would cooperate with us; they would call us back directly.

Ten minutes later, we had a conference call with the directors of the FBI and CIA. Stephen brought them up to speed, and it was agreed that, from the moment they landed at JFK, the three women would be under surveillance 24/7. "Do not try to arrest them. They are deadly. One of these ladies hospitalised ten of my best men before we could subdue her, despite being tasered, blinded by white light and having enough sedative to knock out an elephant. They have incredible mental control and can close down their pain receptors at will, and our only success has been using slumberland on them. We have most of them under our control and had plans to take out the remaining 15 together, but these three changed plans at the last minute as for some reason they needed to be in New York, so unlike the others, they will not have been subjected to slumberland. The other twelve will be picked up as soon as they go to sleep whether it's on the plane or wherever they go if they last until they get off, their luggage has been tagged so we can follow them electronically again, except the three flying into New York."

Stephen asked for a direct link to the surveillance so he and his men could follow it as well. We just had to wait for an opportunity to administer the drug and we were sure one would present itself eventually.

The FBI had Alberto's house under permanent surveillance, his phones were tapped, and anything which happened in his house was recorded. Alberto was aware of this and maintained the appearance of a normal blameless life at home, hoping one day they would give up on the surveillance; however, there was a tunnel from his cellar leading to a subterranean room where he conducted his nefarious business without being observed.

Ordering flowers for a lady friend was normal enough, and he did it all the time. Having them delivered to the Crowne Plaza Broadway Suite should not cause any problems in itself, he thought, but what he didn't realise was the Crowne Plaza and the occupants of the Broadway Suite were flagged, so no sooner had he ordered the flowers, we were aware of it.

All we needed to do was to intercept the flowers, spray them with slumberland, and wait until the women slept. The decision was where and how—ideally at the hotel, but not easy as the flowers would be sealed, so maybe we needed to switch them for some already treated.

We would have to prepare some similar to those we knew he had ordered, expose them to slumberland, seal them so that anybody coming into contact with the flowers would be protected until the cellophane was removed, and switch them for the original flowers. A minor traffic accident would have to happen involving the florist's van and a police car, with the police car at fault, and the exchange would take place under cover of that and taking witness statements.

All the remaining 12 Dark Seven had been picked up. Those on the delayed flight to Sydney never made it out of Miami airport. They were quickly put on an air ambulance and flown directly to Prague; the others succumbed during their flights, were picked up at arrivals and also taken there.

Monk and I travelled to Prague to decommission their minds and make them safe while sleeping, then return them to Messapth before they woke. It only took three hours to complete the task. Afterwards, Monk and I met up with Stephen, who had gone directly to New York, at the FBI's office in Manhattan. We were given badges and shown up to the communications room where they were watching live the movements of the remaining three.

Stephen told us the plan to switch the flowers, and that the FBI planned to capture Alberto and get something that would stick in court; the head of the District Attorney's office was

to ensure every legal aspect of the arrest was watertight so that Alberto's lawyers could not find loopholes as they had done in the past.

"The problem is what to put on the arrest warrant. Dinner with a beautiful woman is not a crime, and we know there will be a trade-off, but what? It has to be Enrico's drug empire she's selling; she needs money and lots of it. She had ample time to get all the information before she destroyed him and the fort. She must have Enrico's laptop or something with details of the whole smuggling operation. The DEA have already told us that his empire was worth over a billion. We were able to get just a third of it, so the remainder in cash or drugs will still be out there. Let's look at the CCTV footage of Geflin arriving at JFK."

Sure enough, she was carrying a laptop, and in every part of the footage she had the laptop with her, it never left her side; fast-forwarding: "It was the reason those guys confronted her today to their peril. Five bodies have been found, one with his throat cut and four with broken necks. They all had form, and none will be missed, but no weapons were found. We lost them soon after they went into the alley and we did not pick them up until they changed their clothes from men's back into women's wear—we were looking in the Bronx for women and not men, but the telltale sign of the laptop was there all the time. The hotel's

CCTV of them shows the laptop with her at all times, it has to be the trade."

. We all agreed, and Alberto's arrest warrant was made out for drug smuggling. I asked, "Do we know which restaurant he uses?" and was told his favourite was Rosanna's in the Bronx. "Can you show me?" I requested, so they produced a map of New York and pointed it out. "Is that not the alley you lost them in?" I pointed out, and sure enough, it was.

"They were casing the restaurant, and should anything go wrong, they would have an exit in mind, somewhere the weapons taken from the muggers would be hidden for them to find if necessary. We have just under 24 hours, so let's be patient. We don't have to do anything yet. We know the slumberland on the flowers will work; switching the bouquets really shouldn't be a problem."

"Arresting Alberto at the restaurant is not the best option, but once he has the laptop in his possession, we could arrest him on his way back. He expects to be stopped sometimes, as we have done in the past, which he puts down to an occupational hazard. He has tried unsuccessfully to sue the NYPD for harassment because we've never found anything incriminating."

"This time you will, and he will know it and might not be so accommodating. He will have just parted with three quarters of a billion dollars for this laptop; without the laptop, he will have a large black hole in his finances, so big it might ruin the whole east coast Mafia," I pointed out.

It was agreed that reinforcements would be required as

it could end up in a bloody battle and he would be intercepted near his home. Where he was normally stopped, most of the property was owned by the Mafia and the occupants stayed inside with their heads down and eyes closed, seeing and hearing nothing.

Stephen said he would stay, but Monk and I left and returned to Assington.

It was one o'clock in the morning, and only security was up to greet us. We made our way to the kitchen. I felt tired. It was over two days since I had slept. I made a sandwich for us both. Monk had coffee, and I washed mine down with a beer. Monk was going back to Utopia and meeting me at eight for breakfast in just under seven hours.

I went to my office to check my email—147 were marked priority, however, my priority was sleep. I would deal with the mail in the morning. I got undressed in my changing room and crept into bed. I thought I had managed not to wake Sue but was greeted with "Hello, stranger!". I laughed but told her I was too tired to talk, and I would bring her up to date in the morning. Within minutes, I was fast asleep.

CHAPTER SIXTY-FIVE

A WELCOMING CUP OF TEA greeted my return from the sleeping world. I recounted everything which had happened in the last 48 hours and what was about to happen in New York.

I showered, dressed and went down for breakfast, which I took to my office. I got through the emails quickly. Most were asking me to confirm committing funds to projects around the world, and I replied to them all tersely.

The CEOs had been appointed to each project with the brief and funds to carry out the work. I didn't have to confirm their decisions. Any anomalies would be sorted out at monthly reviews, or quarterly budget reviews, and I told them, "Only contact me if what you're trying to do is being delayed by bureaucracy, political pressure or threat." Hopefully, after that, my inbox would only contain genuinely important mail!

Herr Hoffman had sent me an update on the treasure from Messapth. "So far, the running total has reached £3.95 billion. Several stolen works of art have been given back to the owners or the insurance company that paid out. Several have already been sold at auction. The price for works of art has increased tenfold and the insurance companies, after costs, will donate the balance to the United Nations. So far, they have sent over a hundred million, and that is expected to rise."

I phoned him and told him to give them the £3.95 billion as well. "I will be in New York this afternoon. See if you can arrange a meeting. How much more do you expect to realise from their assets?"

"Double what we already have certainly, and probably half as much again the way the artworks have gone, so we are looking at a conservative total value of 14 to 15 billion pounds although it could still be much more, as some of these artefacts have never been catalogued. According to my specialists, they are original Assyrian and over seven thousand years old, predating the pyramids, unique examples of a long-lost dynasty and exceptionally rare throughout the world. We've got enough exhibits in pristine condition from that period to fill five museums. The books are equally exceptional and ancient, requiring specialist knowledge, and we have asked the Vatican to help.

A team is currently about to start analysing twenty of what resemble dead sea scrolls."

Alarm bells sounded. "I will be with you in 30 minutes," I told him. Monk had arrived for breakfast with us, but I informed him we had a job to do in Switzerland first.

We arrived at Herr Hoffman's house where I told him of my concerns, so he took us directly to the warehouse where the deciphering was being undertaken.

The team from the Vatican had just arrived, but before they started, I needed to know what their intentions were, should the contents of these scrolls differ from the Christian doctrine.

The cardinal in charge of the team came to meet me first, seemingly very pleasant, but Monk and I entered his mind. Sure enough, there was a plan to either buy the scrolls or destroy them should they contradict traditional religious teachings, ordered not by the Pontiff but by the head of Doctrine and Divinity. One by one we changed their mindset so they would decipher the scrolls accurately, whatever the consequences to their religion, and we instructed security that any further team members must be scrutinised personally by us before getting access to the scrolls.

I spoke to Stephen and told him, "I want everything intercepted in terms of communications in and reports out. The misinterpretation of religion has caused too many deaths and continues to do so. The truth will be told, and if it turns the religious world upside down, so be it."

Monk was hungry, having missed his breakfast, so I

suggested he could have a continental breakfast there or we could go back to Assington, where they would surely still be cooking before we carried on to America. He practically ran to the verticular, having discovered food on the surface excited his taste buds compared to Utopian food, bland and tasteless despite looking spectacular at times.

CHAPTER SIXTY-SIX

LUIGI CALIGARI was the fourth-generation owner and master chef of Rosanna's restaurant; it was opened by his great-grandparents at the turn of the 20th century after they had to flee Sicily.

His great-grandmother Rosanna was the illegitimate child of a Mafia clan godfather. At her wedding his wife found out who she was and was so incensed she went to see her father who was the supreme godfather to tell him about the infidelity of her husband and that she wanted Rosanna dead, she did not want a living reminder of her husband's misdeeds. Her father asked if she still loved him. She said yes, more than anything, so he agreed to do as she had asked.

He summoned his son-in-law, for whom he had great admiration, and to whom he would eventually hand over his role as head of all Mafia clans. He asked, "What is all this Rosanna business? Your wife has come to me and wants her dead."

"During her pregnancy with my second son, she would not let me into her bed even once, so I had to sleep with other women during that period just to satisfy my sexual urges. I didn't love them, but one had a child, Rosanna, and I love her as much as my sons," he explained.

"Well, I have told my daughter that I would do as she asked, so that couple had better disappear and never be seen in Sicily again!" declared the godfather.

"They will leave today," promised the son-in-law.

He rushed back and told the couple that staying in Sicily meant certain death and they had to leave immediately, no packing, nothing. "I will fake your deaths and wrap your bodies in chains and take you out in a boat supposedly to drop you in the sea past the horizon, but we will meet another boat which will take you to Capri where you will be given papers to travel to Naples and then on to the States. My cousin will meet you and assist you through immigration and to start a new life there. Never come back while my wife is alive!" he told them, giving them a thousand dollars.

The plan went like clockwork, and not long after, the couple found themselves in New York in an apartment in the Bronx, with most of their money still unspent. They decided to open a shop that would sell Italian bread and pizza for people to take away.

It became very popular, so they expanded and turned the shop into a restaurant. The protecting hand of the Mafia was always over this couple; any teething problems the restaurant had were soon sorted, the Mafia saw to that with their customary violence, ensuring that there would be no repeated attempts to rob the restaurant or extort money.

At the turn of the 20th century, it was not particularly a bad area where the restaurant was established, but as its reputation for fine food increased so the surrounding area deteriorated. If the restaurant had been anywhere else, it would have had a three-year waiting list to dine, but the neighbourhood ensured that only the bravest of gourmets went there to eat.

The restaurant itself was safe but getting there was a problem. The few taxis willing to go there had to pay protection for the vehicle and occupants at $25 per person, passed on to the diners willing to pay for the eating experience, and more importantly, safe passage in and out of the area.

CHAPTER SIXTY-SEVEN

ALBERTO WAS THE UNCLE of the current generation of master chefs, with his own table giving him and his bodyguards a view of all doors and exits so no one could enter without being seen. Luigi, his nephew, took his booking for a table at 8 o'clock the following day and asked if anything special was required. "Plenty of Maine lobster, and I will be finalising a deal, so I don't want people close enough to overhear my business," Alberto stated. Luigi replied that would not be a problem, as they did not have too many other bookings.

The cars came to the Crowne Plaza hotel to collect Geflin and the girls. They travelled downtown to the restaurant where they would meet Alberto, taking a little over 30 minutes to arrive. Alberto was already at his table with two companions, and they all stood up as the ladies arrived and everyone was introduced. With the pleasantries completed, Alberto asked them, "If you like lobster, will you allow me to order?" They agreed, and he introduced his nephew as the owner and chef who was to create something spectacular, which would delight their taste buds and be remembered forever.

After that, it was down to business. Geflin switched on her laptop. Alberto and an aide started to look at the screen while Geflin explained what they were looking at while he handed over an envelope with bankers' drafts for seven hundred million dollars, completing the deal.

The aide, more interested in the laptop, took it to another table and started to get his head around what it was telling him, such that he missed the first two courses. When he returned to the table, it was to tell Alberto he had struck gold, "If these trailers exist, and I am sure they do, we have over three hundred million in cash to collect in some and 70 tonnes of pure cocaine in the others, which we can send anywhere in the world! We just have to pick up the pieces of Enrico's empire."

"We will talk about it later. Let's enjoy the meal," Alberto replied.

He turned to Geflin. "If I can be of help to you in the future, I can pull strings anywhere in the fabric of this country. Police and judges are on my payroll so I can turn black into white. You are now a very wealthy lady and may need my help."

Geflin acknowledged what he said; it would be good to have him as a close friend, one that she could depend on. A real connection was forged, albeit motivated by pure lust on Alberto's side and by the need for connections on Geflin's, but he was not that bad looking, and she knew she had him in the bag.

At the end of the meal, they parted, and a car took them back to the Plaza. Good food and a lot of wine had taken their toll on the youngsters, and they went off to bed.

Geflin met with her bank manager as arranged and she handed him the drafts. He had taken a room at the hotel that he said she might like to share for a couple of hours before he had to leave.

Later, they both showered and left; he was on his way back to Cayman and she went back to the Broadway Suite. She needed to wake her daughter to find out where the pills were to stop an unwanted pregnancy, but neither of the girls could be woken.

"How the fuck have they been got at? We have been together apart for the last two hours. We must have been drugged!" she exploded. "I have not slept yet, but if I do, presumably I shall end up the same as them!" No way was she going to sleep there and risk waking up in Messapth.

She changed into her body suit and forced the fire exit. By the time security got there, she would be on the ground and have disappeared. She did not go to any of the multi-storey car parks where her rental cars were since they would probably have been compromised; instead, she went to a private car park for residents only. By checking each car in turn, she found one with a magnetic key safe housing a spare key under the offside rear wing. She smashed it against the wall and the key popped out.

Two minutes later, she was heading to her secret safe house in Kingston. It would take two hours, but then she could sleep without the risk of being captured.

To keep her awake, she listened to the radio. Alberto had been arrested, according to the news. No charges had been stated, but it was rumoured to be connected to drug trafficking. She had her own problems of staying safe until whatever drug has been used on her had left her bloodstream.

When she arrived at Wood Lane, she put the car into the garage, not bothering to put the generator on, went indoors straight to bed.

CHAPTER SIXTY-EIGHT

ALBERTO'S CAR STOPPED at a predetermined position, a contingency for such an event as they anticipated. A secret switch was pushed and silently the floor opened, a manhole cover was quickly lifted and the IT man with the laptop disappeared down it, the floor closing again before the police even arrived.

The police would not know how many people had been in the car as the windows were blacked out; he knew there would be no CCTV coverage at the restaurant unless it was from the air, and he was pretty sure there had been no helicopters or he would have heard them. Without the laptop, the police would have nothing, but the next few hours would be tedious.

When the police pulled them over, he called his lawyer as he opened the car window so that as he asked where he would be taken, his lawyer was already listening and would continue to do so during the arrest procedure. They were read their rights, and the cars were impounded. Everyone was transferred to police vans for the journey to NYPD headquarters.

The laptop needed to be found—the warrant and the whole arrest depended on establishing drug trafficking, but it was nowhere to be found. They all denied the existence of it, and without it, they could not be held much longer.

Stephen, Monk and I were watching and listening from a two-way mirror and said we could help, but the DA said, "As you're not part of the NYPD, DEA or FBI, whatever your evidence, it would be inadmissible."

Stephen said, "We know he had the laptop. It's worth a fortune, so someone he trusts must have it and got out of the car before the arrest." He fired up his laptop, got into the CIA surveillance satellites, asked for and entered the co-ordinates for Rosanna's restaurant.

Going back over the last four hours, we could see nine images entering the restaurant from three vehicles, and another two vehicles arriving soon after the first ones with five images, of which three were definitely females. On closer examination, one was carrying something which had to be the laptop. Later, the nine in the first cars left, and sure enough, one of them was now carrying it. "How many have you arrested?" Stephen asked. "Eight" was the answer.

"Well, if you find who's missing, he will have the laptop,

but you better be quick!" After that, we couldn't do much more, so we left.

Underground, Alberto's consigliere and IT man headed for the secret office. He would need to download everything quickly, then replace the hard drive and the ram on the laptop with Alberto's own legitimate business affairs.

When he had done that, he continued underground until clear of the surveillance team on the surface, popping up in the garage of one of the no-seeing neighbours whose car he took to his office just off 42nd Street. He had a legitimate and successful accountancy practice in his own right and had an apartment in the same block, close to Broadway. Alberto and he thought they would have about an hour before the police realised that he was missing; as it turned out, it was closer to two hours later when he too was arrested, and the laptop confiscated.

The President of the Independent Bank of Cayman Brac took a limo to JFK airport, where his plane was ready to take off. VIPs are not normally screened let alone searched, but on this occasion he was. Inside his attaché case was an envelope containing bankers' drafts drawn on several American banks totalling seven hundred million dollars. When asked what those were for, he claimed they were the balance of business reimbursements and other services. We had expected the drafts would be made out to Shannon Gray/alias Geflin so we could link him with her and to the laptop to make a case, but under the circumstances, we could do nothing, so the banker went on his way.

Alberto's lawyers had them all released by 5 in the morning. The police knew the laptop had been doctored but could not prove it. They reclaimed their cars and went back to Alberto's, well pleased with themselves that the NYPD would be off their backs for some time. The Mayor and the Police Commissioner were furious. All those resources spent and nothing to show for it AND having to personally apologise to a known criminal.

CHAPTER SIXTY-NINE

THE HOUSEKEEPING STAFF ENTERED the Broadway Suite at 9 o'clock, by which time the guests were always up, but to their surprise, the girls were still asleep and would not wake up. They phoned reception to call an ambulance, the call we had been waiting for, and we sent our own to gather up the remaining three evil women, but there were only two—what had happened to the eldest?

Stephen went down to hotel security and checked the tapes. Geflin and the girls came in, the girls went to their suite, Geflin met her bank manager and gave him an envelope. He finished his drink, and they went to his room. Two hours later, they came out. He settled his account and left. Geflin went to her suite. About ten minutes later, the door of her room opened and shut quickly. It was a blur, but something or someone had left that room. The fire exit alarm had then sounded on that floor according to the log. Freezing the image, it was definitely a person and had to be Geflin, making her escape. Presumably, she must have tried to wake the girls, and when she couldn't, she realised the same fate would befall her if she slept there.

When Geflin woke up, it was still dark, but she soon found out that she had been asleep for 48 hours. She started the generator and fired up her computer. She googled the New York times and looked for reports on the arrest of Alberto. He had been released without charge with a possible lawsuit for harassment pending, and all surveillance stopped by order of the mayor for the foreseeable future.

He still had the laptop, so she thought he would help her. She needed a completely new identity. "Shannon Gray" must have been compromised, as the Crowne Plaza had those details. America was getting too small and uncomfortable; it seemed they knew what she was going to do before she actually did it.

"The power this Earth Corp. has seems infinite, whole governments defer to them. Their power base is in Europe, so that's where I have to be," she decided.

Everybody would be looking for a woman, so it was time for a gender disguise. So, from the resources within the safe house, she gave herself the appearance of a man.

She had over $100,000 cash but decided to walk to the interstate, to find en route a private sale for a vehicle where cash would not be a problem. She could have taken a train to New York, but CCTV would record a trail of her new identity. If necessary, she would walk, but by the time she got to the end of Wood Lane, there were three cars for sale, an old VW Beetle, a Volvo Estate and a 3-Series BMW. To suit her new image, it had to be the Volvo.

She rang the doorbell, a forty-something mum appeared, "I am interested in the Volvo, can you tell me something about it?" The woman said they had owned it from new, it had a full-service history and was bought to take her children to school, and they were now grown up. "It's too big for me, and I want the totally restored Beetle across the road, it's just so pretty!"

"Do you have the pink slip for the Volvo?"

"Of course!"

"How much will you take?"

"Eight thousand dollars."

"It's a deal!" announced Geflin, as she groped around in her rucksack, peeled off the money and handed it over.

She was now the legal owner of a privately owned vehicle, and it would be weeks before everything was cross-checked, if it ever was, so as a male in New York in a clean vehicle, all she had to worry about was being picked up for traffic violations, as long as she stayed squeaky clean.

CHAPTER SEVENTY

WE WERE BACK AT NYPD HEADQUARTERS, having dealt with the two girls who would subsequently wake up in Messapth.

The search for Geflin intensified. She knew that if she went asleep, she would be captured, so it stood to reason that she would find a way out of the city, trains planes and buses were out of the question, and we knew she had used none of her hire cars as they had not moved. Cars are stolen all the time in New York, and the odds were she would have stolen a car from a residential car park so it would not be missed until the vehicle was required by the owner.

There were three residential car parks within a few

blocks of the Crowne Plaza. None had yet reported anything stolen. I asked, "Is parking at a premium in New York as it is in London?" they told me "Worse! We have had people killed for a parking space!"

"So, all the spaces in these three car parks would be filled, send some patrol cars to make a note of the empty spaces, get the licence plates and then check with the owners if a car should be in there," I suggested.

It took about two hours and a list of seventy-five licence plates to check, and 90 minutes later we had just one car missing presumed stolen and almost certainly the vehicle Geflin used to flee.

We were taken to the car park and went through the CCTV footage. The camera caught the car leaving 03:23, and though we tried to get a picture of the driver, it was just a blur. Back at headquarters, we tracked it to the interstate. Once on the interstate, the coverage was only at main junctions, known bottlenecks, and we lost it between two junctions, leaving an impossible amount of territory to check. We had to rely on "have you seen this car?" on national news and wait; for now, the vehicle, like Geflin, had disappeared.

If the owner had put a tracker in the car, we would have found it easily. If only all manufacturers fitted them as standard, it would make finding stolen cars so much easier.

CHAPTER SEVENTY-ONE

WE HAD LOST GEFLIN. How much damage she could do on her own was still quite a lot, but she would have to show herself in order to take revenge on us in person, and I was pretty sure we could handle anything she did, so our priorities could revert to focussing on the science to save the planet. We would return to England after my meeting with the UN Secretary General that afternoon.

In the meantime, I contacted Professor Dave Mac, who was in Flint, Texas, from where he continually commuted to Utopia and back. I told him we would be with him in just over ten minutes.

I needed to understand the magnitude of the problem

and gauge his confidence in overcoming the threat the magma bubble would cause. Reports don't reveal concern and anxiety. We were welcomed with a beer straight from the freezer, or so it seemed, as it was a mighty hot Texas day. His wife was rustling up some food as we made our way together to his lab.

The tunnelling by the drones had nearly finished, so we had the potential to channel the bubble through a mile-wide tunnel directly into the Mariana Trench, the deepest part of the Pacific Ocean. All his calculations had been checked and confirmed that his assessment was correct, but still, reading his mind showed his anxiety. The future of the whole of mankind depended on him being correct. "Dave, you are worried that you may have got it wrong, but what else can we do?" I asked him.

"The size of the tunnel should be more than enough to dissipate the known pressure the magma bubble can cause, but if it's not, then Utopia will fill up with the magma, their defences against it could not sustain the pressure, their doors would just collapse and there would be nothing left," he replied.

"What you are saying is that Utopia will be utterly destroyed if the pressure the bubble exerts exceeds your calculations?" I queried.

"Correct," he confirmed.

"So, we might be inadvertently sacrificing Utopia to save the surface population; that is not an option. Isn't there another way of relieving the pressure?" I mused.

"There are several dormant volcanoes around the

trench. If their volcanic caps were exploded, they would become active and give us the extra potential to relieve all the excess pressure, but it would have a cost. Several tsunamis would hit China, Japan, the Philippines and Indonesia, even Australia," he explained.

"But we would be aware when the tsunamis would happen and people could be moved to higher ground perhaps, we could make businesses and energy companies ensure they are tsunami proof, they have weeks possibly months to prepare, far better than the destruction of Utopia," I pondered. "Are these dormant volcanoes in International waters?"

He replied, "Most of them, except for the ones around Java which are the important ones."

"Are we talking about nuclear explosions to uncap them?" I asked.

"Possibly, but explosives are not my science. You will need to talk to the Navy," he said.

"How many of these volcanoes do you think we would need?" I wanted to know.

"All of them in the Pacific basin and around the trench. We don't have to blow the caps off unless the pressure builds up underground and we will have time to do it in stages and only use it as the last resort," he said. I said I would talk to the President, but not before we had eaten the light lunch his wife had prepared.

The President was at home and still at the airfield, so we joined up with him there. His security people were getting used to our comings and goings, a lot different to at the

White House. I told him what the professor had said. "We need to be able to uncap the dormant volcanoes in the Pacific if it's necessary; if the pressure builds up underground, they will act as safety valves. They would cause tsunamis, but in a controlled way so that warnings could be given to those counties which would be affected. You need to talk to your Navy and find out what we would need to use, ballistic missiles or something similar?"

"I will get right on it as soon as I am back in the White House," he promised and headed for his waiting helicopter.

We walked to the verticular, arriving in New York in seconds, and making our way to the restaurant in the UN building. Monk gave the impression that he wanted to run; he always seemed to be hungry when there was surface food to be had.

We had a delightful meal and then made our way to the Secretary General's office, where his aide ushered us in to be greeted with a beaming smile and a friendly but vigorous handshake.

I started by asking him, "Have you received some funds from Herr Hoffman? At this time, we are unsure what the total amount will be, but we anticipate at least 14 billion dollars, probably more. This money has no strings attached but must be used for the benefit of all mankind."

I continued, "The main purpose for this meeting is to bring you up to speed on the negotiations with most of the terrorist organisations. As you know, the truce has been extended for another 30 days and we are at a critical point in the negotiations. We will need a UN security force acceptable to all parties, which will exclude American and European forces as their actions are deemed to have caused turmoil and threatened the fabric of society. We are at a stage where agreement has been achieved on the holding of elections and allowing the people to decide because all sides have said that they will abide by the results. The UN must now work on contingency plans to redraft the boundaries of the countries in question, taking into account all ethnic and religious differences and giving each new country a sustainable income in order for them to be able to support their citizens. In the interim and until they can support themselves, a carbon tax will be applied to all polluting and oil-producing countries, which will be short term as there is no long-term future for fossil fuel burning. The UN must get the support it needs from its members; I can guarantee that America and the UK will follow your lead, and now you have the financial resources regardless, whether any country might withhold their subscription in protest at being fundamentally opposed to what will be a consensus opinion of the rest of your members."

It was 09:30 in the evening when we got back to Assington. Lunch in New York was only a couple of hours ago, but Monk still managed some dinner. I just wanted to collect my thoughts and plan the following day, and with that sorted, I intended to have an early night. Monk said he would be back for breakfast. I smiled.

CHAPTER SEVENTY-TWO

GEFLIN ARRIVED BACK IN NEW YORK, where she rented a one-bedroom apartment in Queens; she had to pay three months up front, which pleased her new landlord. If she was going to be a man for a while, she would need a lot more clothes. She would visit Alberto this evening. She was sure he could get her a new male identity, and quickly.

After shopping, she turned on the news, nothing much was happening in the world today. The biggest news story was a press release that the UN had been asked to assist in the redrawing of national boundaries, putting right the wrongs done during the world's colonial period. Little did she realise that the funds being used were the proceeds from the treasures of Messapth.

She hadn't bought any food, so she went out to a diner close by—a simple chicken salad would do. She had a fairly busy night ahead of her and needed to be alert. She knew Alberto would have elaborate security, and guards she should not harm, so she would use her spider grips which enabled her to hang from a ceiling or wall if she wished. The only hindrance was not knowing the precise layout of his house.

After dinner, she went back to her apartment, showered and put on her stealth suit under her male disguise, packing everything she needed in her rucksack. Over dinner the other night Alberto had told her all about his fine house, his bedroom was south facing, and he had the sun on his terrace all day where he enjoyed having his breakfast as most Italians do, or so he imagined since he had only visited Sicily a handful of times in his life. Apart from having Italian genes and a Mafia connection, he was a New Yorker through and through. She took the subway most of the way, then got a cab to take her the rest.

Geflin had used Google's satellite maps to locate Alberto's house and to see all that she needed to. As she approached his house, she made for the dark spot between the two streetlights.

In seconds, she had removed the male garments, leaving her almost invisible in her stealth suit. She put on her spider pads, turned the rucksack inside out, and placed the male clothes inside it. The lining was made of the same material as her suit, so this way round, it too became virtually invisible.

She swiftly scaled the ten-foot wall with the pads, silently slid over and worked her way along the inside wall, resting in the dark shadows left by the lights inside the grounds. By staying on the wall, she only had to worry about timing her moves to avoid detection by the fixed cameras.

There was an arched gate between the wall and the house, from the arch she could get directly onto the house roof, where the cameras were less of a risk, and she made the 30-foot climb easily, then made her way to the south side of the house.

She anticipated that while Alberto might have sophisticated alarm systems in the grounds and the house, he would not want such elaborate systems in and around his bedroom in the interests of his privacy, and she was right. Bypassing the intruder alarms, she silently opened the door and entered his bedroom.

She closed the door and reached his bedside, where she placed her hand over his mouth and woke him. She said softly, "Alberto, it's Shannon Gray. I need your help!" A totally startled Alberto started to come round. After the initial shock, he demanded, "How the fuck did you get in here?"

"I told you I was very good," she replied, turning on his bedside light.

"What have you done to your hair? And you need a shave!" he exclaimed.

"That's why I need your help! My enemies seem to be one move ahead of me; they have captured my girls at the

Crowne Plaza. They were drugged and I could not wake them; I just don't know how, but I have lost fifteen of my team to them! It was sheer luck that I didn't go straight back to my suite, I had to meet with my banker, and when I couldn't wake them, I fled New York for my safe house and slept for two days!" she told him.

"So, what do you want from me?" he asked.

"I need a completely new identity as a man and fast. They will be looking for a female and it will give me the head start I need to get my revenge. It's now a vendetta and you know very well what that means," she said.

"Of course, but a completely new identity is expensive," he told her.

"As well, you know, I can afford it!" she said, and he laughed. "There could be a bonus if you say yes", she murmured as her hand deftly slid between the sheets, and she began to pleasure him. Alberto was ecstatic, so she chose that moment to stop and ask him what his answer was. "Yes! Yes!" he cried, so she went back down on him and minutes later, he reached ecstatic bliss.

She knew that this guy would now give his life for her; he was putty in her hands. And although she had got what she came for, there was something else she wanted badly— pleasure, and he was well-endowed to provide it. She stripped off her stealth suit, slipped into bed, and got him excited again.

Thirty minutes later, both lay exhausted side by side. She knew he was totally hooked and removed from the rucksack photos she had taken of herself as a male. Then she started to dress in her stealth suit. He begged her to stay, saying it would take at least three days to get her new identity. A tempting offer, but she had so much to do, so she said she would come back when her papers were ready and promised him another bonus.

Dressed and ready, she made for the French windows, but Alberto stopped her. "You don't need to go the way you came."

"I don't want to be seen," she said.

"I will show you a much safer way to get in and out," he told her.

He put on his dressing-gown and took her to a walk-in wardrobe, where he pushed a button on top of a full-length mirror. A door opened, revealing stairs. She followed him down into the basement, where it came to an apparent dead-end. He pushed one of the bricks into the wall and a gap opened with another set of stairs leading to what seemed like a storm drain.

From the distance they had covered, she realised they were well away from his house when he finally stopped and indicated various metal ladders, explaining that they came out in the garages of other houses which all had vehicles she could use.

She climbed a ladder and pushed the manhole cover off to find herself between two rather ordinary cars, both with keys in the ignition. She put on gloves and opened the door of one of the cars, finding on the seat a remote control for the garage door, which started to open when she clicked it. She typed her apartment address in the sat-nav, started the ignition and was immediately out on the road, following the directions.

She left the car in a long-term car park close to her apartment and walked home. She would use the car again to go back and collect her new identity when it was ready.

Like everyone Geflin used in the same way, Alberto was bewitched by her, and he pulled out all the stops, so within three days, her—or rather: his—new identity was ready. He sent a message to her that everything was ready; he would hand over the documents personally, as she had insisted that involvement was limited to him and the forger of the new identity.

She retrieved the car from where she had parked it and drove back to the place where she had obtained it, retraced her steps, and in no time, she was back in Alberto's bedroom, where she would wait until he came to bed.

She had decided not to kill him or the forger. She had him wrapped round her little finger and the forger would not dare go against the Mafia. Although leaving loose ends went across the grain, she was on her own now with a tremendous task ahead of her, so a devoted and tame Mafia boss with connections around the world might be very useful and could assist her in wreaking her revenge.

Over two hours later Alberto was preparing for bed by having a shower, totally unaware of Geflin's naked presence until she opened the shower door, the sound masked by the noise of the water, and slipped her hand round his manhood, telling him, "Bonus time!"

An hour later, as they relaxed on the bed, Alberto got

up and removed from the safe a large manila envelope, which he handed to her. She tore it open to find there was not just one passport but three, Canadian, American and British, all three had different names but each was supported with bank, credit cards and utility bills and a history going back forty-plus years. Expertly done; you would really have to dig extremely deep to find out the identities were fake.

"What are you going to do now?" he asked.

She replied, "I am going to be someone's worst nightmare! He will wish he had never got involved! I don't care how wealthy he is and what security he has, I am going to kill him, and everyone he holds dear."

Alberto wrote on a piece of paper a name, a phone number and a password, telling her "If you need any help in Europe, this guy's an uncle and he will help without any questions asked. We have a reciprocal arrangement."

She was about to get dressed, but Alberto started kissing her neck and another bout of energetic sex took place. Leaving Alberto exhausted and soon asleep, she finally got dressed and left the way she came.

Back at her apartment and with her American identity, she booked a first-class ticket to London. The Cayman bank President had told her that they were still no closer to finding out how the bank's computer had been hacked and he would post bankers' drafts to her, so she would contact him with the name and address to which a draft should be made payable.

First, she had to establish a base in the UK. Her

American credit card had a thirty-thousand-dollar limit, and she had about ninety thousand in cash, more than enough to get settled. She packed, ordered a taxi for the morning, and fell asleep plotting her revenge.

CHAPTER SEVENTY-THREE

THE TAXI ARRIVED, four suitcases were put in the car, and it took her to JFK airport where she went straight to the first-class lounge and ate a light breakfast. Her flight was on time and in just under seven hours it was night when she landed at Heathrow.

She stayed at the Heathrow Hilton and BA ordered a limo to take her/him to the hotel. Walking to the limo, she noticed a large advertisement for apartments to rent or buy called Canary Wharf, which looked suitably impressive, so she made a note of the developer and phone number to call them in the morning.

The developer sent a car to pick up the man who was really Geflin. The journey into London was a nightmare. "If you think this is bad, you should try the rush hour!" the driver said.

It took over an hour and a half to do the fifteen or so miles to their office, where she met one of the senior associates, who went into great detail about all the pros and cons of renting or buying without giving her time to speak.

She raised his hand to interrupt him and stated, "What I want is a penthouse with at least three bedrooms all ensuite, its own fully equipped gym, kitchen, car parking and mooring, with excellent security. Do you have such a unit?"

"Renting or buying?" the associate asked.

"Buying," she replied.

"How big is your budget?"

"Up to 20 million pounds," she told him.

The associate called his secretary to bring the details on the remaining penthouses. They were beautiful and ticked all the boxes apart from the private gym. There was a shared gym in the basement, which was not acceptable for obvious reasons.

One penthouse had five bedrooms, on the market for 12 million and had nearly been sold several times, but it was just too big and cost two and a half million per bedroom.

"How quickly can you get things done in this city?" she wanted to know.

"What do you mean?" asked the associate.

"Knocking the fourth and fifth bedroom into a gym, then all my criteria would be satisfied, and you would have a deal," she replied.

"I will have to go and see the CEO. He would need to sanction the alterations," he said and left just as his secretary brought in some coffee.

The CEO came back with the associate, introduced himself and asked what business he—Geflin—was in. Geflin told him "he" was a venture capitalist and felt the UK was a place "he" could do business but had to have a base.

"How soon could you complete?" the CEO asked.

"I have no banking facilities set up here. I only arrived yesterday, so it will take about 21 days," Geflin replied, offering him the letter of introduction from the Cayman bank, which impressed him.

They shook hands on the deal which was done before she had even seen the penthouse, soon remedied when they accompanied her there, but again a two-mile journey took three quarters of an hour, prompting her to ask if the traffic ever got any better.

"After midnight and until dawn," they told her.

"Then I think I will need a boat as well as a helicopter. I just can't spend this amount of time in traffic. Time is money!" she declared.

The penthouse was even better than the photos. "How soon can you have this ready?" she asked, and they said in about a week. "Fine, I will be back in a week. Got to get some serious flying hours in as my pilot's licence has now lapsed. Is there anywhere I can rent until next week? I must have a base."

"The ground floor of this building has a two-bedroom apartment, which you can have with our compliments until yours is ready," the CEO offered. She said that would be fine; they got the key from the caretaker who would bring a trolley and take her luggage in when she returned with it later. Everyone was pleased with the outcome; they said their goodbyes and left.

The nearest flying school was Biggin Hill, so she booked lessons on the spot and ordered a cab to take her there as she needed to fill in forms. When the black cab arrived and she asked to go to Biggin Hill, the cabby initially was hesitant about going 12 miles south of the river. He was prevaricating and making excuses, but he changed his mind when his customer produced two hundred pounds. He slipped through London traffic and got to the flying club in 40 minutes.

Geflin asked him to do the same every day for the next week, getting her there for 08:00 at 200 a day with a further thousand at the end of the week if he was on time every day.

The flying school informed "him" that getting a commercial pilot's licence would take 150 hours. "There are no shortcuts, another 20 hours to get instrument rating which you will need to fly a Learjet on your own, and a further 45 hours for a helicopter licence. That's two hundred and 15 hours in total, providing you pass each test the first time. That's going to take a good 18 months."

"I need to be flying within a month. Nine hours a day, seven days a week. At 63 hours a week, it would take less than a month to get all those hours in!" Geflin protested. "We haven't got the flight training slots to do this," he replied.

"Have you got the aircraft and instructors to do it?" she asked.

"No" he replied.

"Who is the best instructor with the highest pass rate?" she asked. He said it was him.

"Ok, I have a proposition for you: I will pay you three hundred thousand to get me my CPL in a month," she said.

"But I do not have the aircraft!" he objected.

"So, lease everything we need at my expense! I just need your expertise to get my CPL quickly. You will find I am a good learner." Finally, he agreed.

They went up in a small aircraft, an old Cherokee similar to her first flight while at the Swiss finishing school, before her turn overseeing the Americas where she continued her training to CPL standard. The instructor realised within the first hour lesson that his pupil had a feel for flying when, after the first circuit, she landed without assistance. This was going to be easy money for him. All he had to do was sit alongside while the hours ticked away.

Inside four weeks, she had passed all the tests and now possessed her CPL/Helicopter with IR licence, and she was now much better equipped to get revenge. Sceptre seemed to have reneged on the contract to take out her enemies so she would have to do it herself and deal with them later.

CHAPTER SEVENTY-FOUR

THE TRIAL OF ELLIOT COOMBS had taken place for the murders of Connor Lynch and Caroline Dunedin, which had proceeded as a charge of manslaughter on the basis of a tragic accident since the prosecution could not prove the link for a murder charge. His defence played on his terminal illness and had most of the jury in tears.

He did not take the stand as he would not have resisted telling the truth and would have been found guilty of murder. I couldn't give evidence. Who would believe me? I'd have looked like a magician or showman if I'd had to prove my ability to read minds and I had no time for all that, anyway.

Conrad's evidence was risky because he had been an alcoholic at the time of the tragic accident and the prosecution would just not take the chance, so had reduced the charge to manslaughter. His defence team wanted the charges dropped due to the length of life left for their client, but the prosecution was adamant about the case going to court.

The trial had just finished, and he was found not guilty on a majority verdict. His barrister handed him a letter from Stephen Shefford, which told him to leave England immediately with his family and resume his life in Australia, which he proceeded to do.

Bruce Kennett's trial was over quickly. Without financial resources and no likelihood of reclaiming Media Corp., he got an inexperienced state defence attorney straight out of law school.

He was found guilty and sentenced to death by lethal injection, which, of course, was immediately appealed. Bruce Kennett would be on death row for years, waiting for the outcome of the appeal process, giving him plenty of time to dwell on his sins.

CHAPTER SEVENTY-FIVE

THE MAIN REASON the terrorist organisations were still keeping the peace was the fact that those responsible for Operation Wipeout were being brought to justice. Robert Saxham and the two stealth fighter pilots, Gill and Berry, had made sworn affidavits presented to the trial judge and accepted by the prosecution, and were acquitted as they were only following orders, Robert Saxham included.

Not so for the CIA director and the late President's National Security Advisor. Their attorneys had tried to delay the trial, but it had backfired. Their clients had been convicted, the three Supreme Court judges had unanimously found them guilty of the attempted murder of an American citizen, and misuse of governmental power and resources. The attorneys produced the "get out of jail" letter signed by the late President, whose suicide might have been triggered by these letters being entered as evidence.

All the Supreme Court judges had been appointed by the late President on merit and for their expertise in law, and rather than the letters keeping them out of jail, they induced the judges to add a further three years to the eight-year sentence already imposed. The defendants had been tried by America's highest court, so there was no recourse to an appeal, and their sentences could only be amended by Congress and the Senate agreeing and the President having the final say.

We were now approaching 90 days of the agreed ceasefire. The slaughter of innocents had as good as stopped, and in the trouble spots around the world, all troops were back to barracks and none in any conflict zone. Special Forces were still on the ground but had blended into the local populations enough that they were no longer noticed. They would remain until the elections to help in the democratic process and implement the will of the people.

The only problem was that of the Histealam sect, whose leader Alim would not agree to anything. He claimed that he was God, not just a follower, a belief shared by his equally mad followers. He was holding up the discussions, which had stalled and were adjourned until early the next week. Two of the largest terrorist groups indicated that they would deal with Alim before the next meeting.

Within 48 hours, the problem of the contentious sect had been sorted. Alim Histealam was arrested under their religious law and given one chance of renouncing all that he stood for, which he rejected because he thought he was God so he also thought he would be indestructible, but as his head was severed and fell to the ground, his followers found their faith started to fail them. Some thought they were immortal, and they would come back too, but they lost their heads as well. The others pledged to follow the old faith and were spared.

The conference resumed and could reach a unanimous agreement whereby they would allow free elections for all and would send delegates to the United Nations to help redraw the map of the world. Some delegates were amongst the most wanted in the world, but I insisted they should have diplomatic immunity, and I told Stephen that I wanted his company to ensure their safety. For him, this was a very bitter pill; those people were responsible for the deaths of many of his men over the years and he would have rather killed them than protect them, but sometimes to move forward you have to forget the past.

CHAPTER SEVENTY-SIX

IT WAS WELL OVER A MONTH since we had lost trace of Geflin. Tosh, the boss of Spectre, had been transformed in the shimmering and had told Stephen about the hit contract he had been offered. He had put the whole advance payment into his widows' pension fund because in his line of work, plenty of his men got killed and those pensions helped their dependents to manage financially without their men.

We tried to find out who sent it, but it was an encrypted transfer and would take months to discover the bank and the sender. Our money was on Geflin and her bank, so we set Court Leiston and his unique way into computers onto it, but he found nothing conclusive that we could use against the bank. Her money had been well hidden amongst the bank's accounts.

We stopped the 24/7 surveillance of her bank manager as it was becoming a waste of resources and left it to a detective agency to continue monitoring and photographing any females he met outside of the bank. We were checking those against our actual photos of Geflin. Certain parts of a face can't be disguised, the distance between eyes and nose, for instance, but no leads turned up. She really had gone to ground, despite all major airports and ports being on alert.

CHAPTER SEVENTY-SEVEN

GEFLIN WAS READY to get even. Her expertise at hacking was still not sufficient to get her into Shefford Securities and Earth Corp, so she needed help.

She had read in a computer magazine an article about a company that for a fee would hack into your computer to test its security, and so confident were they that the fee would be refunded if they failed. They had an impressive list of UK companies that had used their services, but they wanted to expand, which was unaffordable despite them being very profitable. Geflin, in her disguise as a male venture capitalist, made an appointment to see whether a deal could be struck.

The first thing she saw was how young they were, all

between mid-teens and twenty. All twelve partners had an equal share and say in the business, which had been going for three years already, a remarkable testament to the young geniuses. Turnover was approaching three million this year and would make the partnership relatively wealthy, but for them to move forward and expand, they needed hard cash, and Geflin had lots of that, so a deal was struck.

Each partner would be paid in shares of the new limited company. Geflin would put in a hundred million in share capital, which would give them the funds required to expand globally. She would hold 52% of the stock with the remainder spread equally between the partners, now directors.

The new directors were now worth four million each and delighted with the outcome. A meeting was planned for the following week when the inaugural board meeting would take place. Geflin, or Ben Martin as they knew her, had made it clear that he was just the money man and did not want any part in running the business, all he wanted was access to the accounts to see how his investment was doing, and apart from that, he would leave them alone, although he would always be available to assist or mentor them.

The first board meeting took place, and it was unanimously agreed that the converted industrial unit was not in keeping with a hundred-million-pound business.

When "Ben Martin" arrived at the new offices at Cambridge Science Park, he found them all in awe of their new surroundings. They each had their own parking space, the offices were fully serviced, and all they had to do was phone to have anything they needed brought to them. Academic excellence was flourishing in Cambridge as always, and the directors were a suitable age to blend well into the student society. The new company wanted to expand rapidly and was in the best place to find and recruit the best talent in hackers.

"Ben" needed them to hack into Shefford Securities and Earth Corps so he had to come up with a convincing reason to get him access to those corporations and their most sensitive information on the movements of the people he badly wanted dead, and which would help him achieve that goal.

He fed them a story about what had happened during the previous week. He said that trying to get more companies on board, he had attended a charity ball where he was introduced to the CEOs of Shefford Securities and Earth Corp.

"I told them that I had invested in a company which is able to hack into any computer, find its weak points and access its sensitive information, and which so far had never failed. The CEO of Shefford Securities declared that their computer system was impregnable, and the same was used at Earth Corp, so no one would be able to hack into their computers or even try without being detected. I asked him whether he was a betting man and staked ten million which said you could. He accepted. I will take care of liaison between you and them, and all your results will be channelled through me. If you crack their system and win the bet, the money is yours."

He knew that amount would focus their minds and was quite confident they would break into the computer systems, but as for how long that would take, he would have to wait to find out.

Back at Canary Wharf, Geflin needed updated information on her enemies. It was easy to get plans for Media Corps. buildings as they were public records, but it was much harder to get any information on individuals. She tried Facebook, Twitter, Friends Reunited and came up blank.

She went onto the website of Shefford Securities, a massive global security business. As she scrolled through the site, she saw several photos of aircraft and helicopters, which she enlarged until she could get the registration numbers, assuming the helicopters were likely to be used to ferry the top brass to meetings from the airport.

Next, she hacked into the Civil Aviation Authority, which had a similar security system to the one used in the States. She entered the registration numbers and printed off all their movements over the last three months. It was a painstaking job highlighting all relevant journeys and destinations, but without doubt, the aircraft had been used to fly her girls to Prague from Cayman Brac and Miami, and another plane had flown from New York JFK to Prague about a month ago. What she could not understand was that they did not fly from Prague to Messapth, so how did the girls get there?

She studied the flight logs of the helicopters. The most

frequent places they went to or from were Assington in Essex, Cheltenham, and Central London. She put the co-ordinates from the flight logs in to Google Earth and found Cheltenham Manor Hotel, Assington Priory, and Media Corps offices off Park Lane. She needed up-to-date intelligence, which she could get using her helicopter to take photos of Cheltenham and Assington, then start preparing her revenge.

She filed her first flight plan to Cheltenham Racecourse because it would take her directly over the hotel, but the computer rejected it and adjusted it to bypass her target. She tried again and got the same result.

She hit a marker on the computer, and it informed her that there was a 50-mile air exclusion over the south of Cheltenham, and to get to the racecourse the computer flight plan gave her routes via Bristol or Birmingham. There was a similar air exclusion zone over Assington, directing her via Sudbury or Colchester.

She spoke to Biggin Hill and asked what the implications of flying into an air exclusion zone were. They told her, "Air Traffic would muster the nearest RAF typhoon, which would go airborne immediately. Air Traffic would ask you to follow the flight plan, and if you ignored this, the typhoon would reach you in minutes to either escort you to the nearest airport or blow you out of the sky." She asked if there were many air exclusion zones and who could apply for one over their property. The reply was that there were hundreds, mostly over sensitive military installations and Royal Households, but if you wanted one, no matter how wealthy you were, it was unlikely to be even considered unless you were a pal of the Prime Minister and even then, only during a visit from him.

She was going to have to get the information the hard way. She would have to drive, but all her driving had been done in the States, where she had no problem. She had only taken cabs in London and the sheer volume of traffic horrified her, as well as driving on the wrong side of the road, and roundabouts confounded her as accidents waiting to happen. She could not afford to have an accident and risk her identity being discovered; so far, she had no problems as a man, and it needed to stay that way for the foreseeable future. She could use a driver, which would solve one problem but create another because he or she would know everywhere she went.

This problem was making her angry, so she worked out for a couple of hours in her gym,

Showered, and then ordered a pizza for delivery. As she looked out for it arriving, she saw a little blue moped with a large white box on the back pull up and realised there was the solution—get a motorbike, not a car! She had not ridden a motorbike since she was 18, but she thought she would fare much better on two wheels than four, as well as avoiding the traffic congestion.

CHAPTER SEVENTY-EIGHT

IN THE MORNING, Geflin got a cab to the Kawasaki dealer in the city and purchased a Ninja XS10 and then came up against another problem. "Ben Martin's" American driving licence was only in the car and small van categories, and in the UK, she needed to have a full licence to include motorcycles.

She tried to explain that she was an experienced rider and said she must have forgotten to renew that part of the licence, but it was no good and once again she would have to start from the very beginning and take a test.

The dealer advised that he could organise the instruction, but if she wanted to try out the bike, she could do it at Brands Hatch, where they were having a promotion the following day, and the people they used for the test would also be there. He said he would send a car at 9 a.m. to take her to the circuit.

The car arrived on time. She had bought full leathers, helmet and boots, and had opted to be dressed ready for the ride instead of changing at the circuit. The journey was less than 22 miles, but it took close to two hours.

It was just after 11:00 when "Ben" arrived and was introduced to the instructors who were told that this customer could ride but did not have a valid licence and needed one quickly.

The instructors had made a practice area around the pit lane. They explained the circuit to "him" and showed him to a 125cc bike. "He" put on his helmet and gloves, got on and hit the ignition, put it in gear and was off. Geflin was quite astonished at how fast the bike was and she wobbled a bit at first but soon had full control and whizzed through the practice course easily. The instructors' assessment was "OK, we can see you can ride, but do the circuit again and this time, use the correct signals, as in your first practice you didn't show any."

The second was better, and the third was fine. They then put "him" on the 250cc bike. Wary of wobbling as on the smaller bike, she let the power engage gradually and it was a smooth take off. She did the circuit three times and then moved up to a 500cc bike, taking to it like a duck to water.

Both instructors agreed here was an accomplished rider and there should be no problem getting the licence, but "he" would still have to ride on a real road before passing the test. The dealership manager was equally impressed, so "Ben" asked if he could do the club circuit on a Ninja, to which he agreed. The dealership had its own Superbike team and "Ben" was introduced to one of the professional riders who explained the circuit in great detail and told "him" to follow him onto the track.

She took the first lap carefully but had no problems keeping up; the next lap was a lot faster and on the third lap she was waved past to do circuits on her own. Geflin was now really getting the feel of the machine. Her adrenaline was pumping, and she was getting faster with each lap. She was signalled in after her tenth lap and she hadn't had so much fun in years.

Back in the pits, she asked how she had done. The ninth lap was her fastest, "Just two seconds off the Superbike lap record and the fastest so far today. If it remains that way you will win the magnum of champagne, it's as good as yours already. The other riders bottle out on the bends, which you didn't," said the professional rider. "You followed exactly what I was doing, and you showed no fear at the bends. With a lot more practice, you could turn professional. You're a natural."

"Ben" thanked him for his compliments.

The instructors agreed and suggested that "he" follows them back on their 125cc to get the road training done on the way back to the office, and if it all went well, they could write out the ticket for a full licence without "him" having to go through all the stages for learners.

This was successfully accomplished, and three days later, Geflin's black and green Ninja was delivered. She was more excited about that than her jet and helicopter. She took it for a little ride around Canary Wharf, weaving in and out of the traffic with ease and returning to her apartment. She could progress to the next stage of her plans for the destruction of her enemies.

CHAPTER SEVENTY-NINE

IT ONLY TOOK TWO DAYS for "Ben's" team to hack into Earth Corps and Shefford Securities. She instructed them to send her the encryption codes so that she could try them herself. Once she was able to get access to the whole of the sites, she would go to see those top men who were so sure that they had an entirely secure system, show them, collect the wager and send it on to the team. "You really are incredible, guys. I thought it would take you weeks," she told them.

The encryption codes duly arrived, and "Ben" could navigate easily around both sites; however, the security in use at Cheltenham and Assington was state-of-the-art and new to her. She looked closely for a weakness, something overlooked as there always was, but as hard as she tried, she could not find any flaw in either place.

She had never come across a three-level digital security system. More worryingly it was unique to Shefford Securities, having been designed by them. Everyone had a digital signature unique to the individual; copying a signature must be possible, but she had no idea how. She was in the wrong country—all her contacts were in the States; there she could get help, but she would not be going back until she had succeeded in getting her revenge. Although in theory, she had all the information about Cheltenham and Assington at her fingertips it still wasn't enough without getting to see and reconnoitre the places personally, the only way she might find a chink in the armour of a most impressive security system.

With cash, she bought a camera drone, wearing a hat with the brim pulled down to shade her face and making sure that the security cameras in the shop could not get a good clear view of her. The shop assistant showed her how to operate it. She took it back to Canary Wharf and practiced until she was confident with the controls. Cheltenham would be her first stop and then on to Assington.

Her Ninja motorcycle was a racing bike with minimal room to carry anything, fortunately, she really only needed to take her male make-up and the drone, anything else she could buy. The drone was small but still too big for her rucksack, and she had to tie the transmitter to the fuel tank and take the rotors off, marking the blades so they would go back in the same position. Her sat-nav said the journey would take three hours.

She had a light breakfast and left Canary Wharf just after 10:00, when the worst turmoil of London traffic had abated and, with just the normal surge of traffic, she was soon on the M4 heading west. She refuelled at Melton Mowbray when she had been on the bike for over an hour and a half and the constant buffeting had made her hands numb, so she took a coffee break and then proceeded on to Cheltenham. She had booked into the Strozzi Palace hotel in the town centre, which had its own parking.

She had made good progress and arrived about 12.30, only to be told there was no check-in before 14:00. This annoyed her, but outwardly she remained cool. At least it would give her time to shop for the things she had not been able to fit in her rucksack. She returned to her bike to put the padlock through the helmet and went shopping.

She went from the car park into the street and observed what people were wearing. She would need clothes to blend in, probably two or three different outfits. She would certainly need clothes to dress convincingly as a rambler if she was going to get into Cheltenham Manor. An estate of that size must have dozens of public footpaths going across it, so she would need Ordnance Survey maps of the area.

The first shop she went into was called Stepping Out, which had everything she needed to pass as a rambler. She paid and asked to leave her purchases while she did other shopping. Across the road was a menswear shop where she bought smart casual clothes before going on to a shoe shop and purchasing a couple of pairs of smart shoes.

With the shopping done and everything collected, she made her way back to the hotel loaded down with her bags, checked in and went to her room where she unpacked, showered, and got dressed in her new rambling outfit.

She took out the maps and studied them. She was right, there were footpaths going through the Manor's grounds, but not as many as she had expected. Still, she only needed one to do her reconnaissance.

It was just after 3 o'clock when she set out to take the footpath from the town centre which led to Cheltenham Manor, roughly a three-mile walk that would take about 40 minutes, so there was plenty of daylight left. Leaving the hotel, she looked quite the part as a male rambler, powerful binoculars, maps in a clear plastic satchel.

About twenty other ramblers were heading in the same direction. A couple of miles into the walk, the footpath forked where the right went to the racecourse and left was signposted to Cheltenham Manor, and to her surprise, they all went towards the racecourse, not one went towards the Manor.

She picked up the pace and came to a major road that had to be crossed before the footpath continued round three quarters of the estate. According to her map, the entrance to the forestry part of the grounds should be directly ahead, but all she could see was a new brick wall in its place. She crossed the road and read a sign next to the former entrance:

"FOOTPATH CLOSED - NO ACCESS TO CHELTENHAM MANOR. FOOTPATH REROUTED. 24/7 CCTV COVERAGE. PRIVATE PROPERTY.

SHEFFORD SECURITIES PLC. 08001501507."

CHAPTER EIGHTY

GEFLIN COULD FEEL HER ANGER rising again. Her plan had been to fly the drone from the woods to get the information she needed, and now she would have to do it from a distance.

The rerouted footpath followed the outside perimeter wall of the estate. The wall itself presented no problem, but the security on the other side was the major setback. Following the arrows indicating the new route, the path took her past the main entrance, which formed a junction between the town centre road and the one which ran around the estate.

From the opposite side of the road, she would have a

better view. She spotted a bench that faced the main entrance, offering an ideal position to observe the security there. She took off her rucksack and sat down on the bench, pretending to look at her maps out but actually looking directly over them.

The first thing she observed was a dozen of concrete blocks, six on each side. No vehicle could burst through. All traffic had to slow to a walking pace. Inside the entrance, she could see at least four armed security guards, with every appearance of deadly professionalism. According to the information she had gleaned from Shefford Securities' computer system, there were always a hundred on duty on a three-shift rotation system with a one-hour overlap, so if she picked the wrong time, she could be up against as many as two hundred guards.

A baker's van arrived, negotiated the chicane, and stopped at security, where the driver got out and was taken into the office. Another guard came out with two dogs, walked them twice round the van, and then both dogs got in the cab. Then the back doors were opened, but the dogs were not allowed in, all clear so far; another security guard got into the van and drove slowly over cameras hidden in the road. The guard was given the signal to proceed and he, not the van driver, drove to the kitchens. She couldn't be sure, but presumably, the armed guard would watch over the van being unloaded.

This whole episode showed how thorough the security was. The van driver might be regular and known to them, but there were no exceptions to the elaborate checks. The delivery took 20 minutes to complete before the driver navigated back through the concrete blocks and out onto the main road.

Another delivery van turned up as the baker's van left. She realised that all deliveries must be given a time slot to avoid the potential chaos if they turned up randomly.

She had been there for nearly 40 minutes by then, which she realised had been too long when a guard started to cross the road towards the bench. She began to fold her maps up and put them casually back into the plastic satchel. She could have taken him out easily, but he was being covered by at least two other guards from the main entrance.

As an accustomed liar, she had already thought of a reason for her lengthy stay. The guard approached and observed. "Excuse me, sir, you seem to have been here for a long time."

She replied, "Well, I have just walked 30 miles in new boots! The shop assistant said I should go for the next size, but I knew best, insisted on my regular shoe size and I have been suitably punished for my arrogance!"—to which he smiled—"Now I have missed the bus and the next is another 20 minutes."

"I could call you a cab," the guard offered.

"Thank you! That would be great. I can't wait to get these boots off and soak my feet," she replied.

The taxi took longer than the bus to arrive, so she got a bonus, 30 minutes of extra intelligence gathering. She justified waiting for the taxi as it would mean less distance to walk when the guard told her of the delay.

Back at the hotel, she lay soaking in the bath, deliberating on what she had seen. It would be impossible to go through the main entrance; even what she deduced were staff were bussed to the main entrance to collect their onward transport. They all had to go into the security building for what she imagined must be checking their chip implants, as clearly clocking in and out was nowhere near secure enough.

There were slight possibilities gleaned from that first reconnaissance mission, for instance, the dogs were not allowed into the baker's van only to sniff with the doors open, so it would be easy enough to disguise her scent from them, take out the unsuspecting guard, and disappear, but the infra-red or CCTV would pinpoint her location.

Tomorrow she would take the bike around the Manor. She had seen on the map that where the main road went right, there was a bridle path and a green lane that went directly north, then the bridle path went north-west following the perimeter of the Manor, and the green lane went north-east. Where the two parted was a coppice from which she could get her drone in the air to get an accurate look at the terrain she desperately needed to know about getting out alive after her attack on her enemies who had decimated Messapth.

With that planned, she went down to the restaurant and was impressed with the excellent meal she had ordered. After that, she went to the bar and had three large gin and tonics. The barman was a very good-looking guy, and she was tempted, but she couldn't afford to indulge herself and impede her vendetta, so she would have to satisfy herself.

345

CHAPTER EIGHTY-ONE

THE FOLLOWING MORNING, Geflin was awake before the sunrise. It had been over 24 hours since she worked out, so she decided to take a run through the town for a couple of hours. There was little traffic at that time of the morning, but to her surprise, several joggers were going the same way as her, so she upped her pace and they soon stopped trying to keep up.

She was cruising, and she felt good, feeling the adrenalin starting to flow as she ran faster and faster. It had been a while since she reached this peak, not since Columbia when she wiped out the cartel, but that was a high from killing, not from exercise.

By the time she got back to the hotel, she felt invincible.

After breakfast, she checked out her drone; it was easy to reassemble so she would not have any problems at the Manor.

She took the direct route there on her Ninja, passed the main entrance and arrived at the green lane and bridle path. The Ninja was a road bike, and the suspension was suffering so much so she felt it might break, so she took it extremely carefully into the coppice. At that point, she was about six hundred metres from the wall, behind which was the wooded area of the Manor and some distance to the main buildings, but the drone would easily cope with that.

She reassembled and launched the drone, which reached about 500 feet altitude with the cameras filming and downloading to her laptop. As it entered Cheltenham Manor, she heard a helicopter but thought nothing of it until her drone was caught in a net that the chopper dragged underneath it.

At that point, she had captured nothing of consequence that she needed, and she wasn't willing to take the risk that they would be able to track her controller back to her position, so she got back on the bike praying the suspension would hold up, and she got back to the main road as fast as she could. Once on it, she threw the controller into a river and put in as much distance as she could. She rode back to the hotel and checked out. Using the new, bigger rucksack, she was able to take some of her purchases, but the rest went into the hotel skip.

CHAPTER EIGHTY-TWO

BACK AT CANARY WHARF, she had time to pick out the main points from the failed mission at Cheltenham. Their security was excellent apart from the dogs not being allowed inside food vehicles, but it was one thing to get inside to do harm to her enemies and another to achieve it without being taken herself. Without backup from her sisters and the daughters, it would be suicide on her own, so Cheltenham was ruled out.

A different tactic needed to be found for Assington, where the security would be the same—if not better—as it was the home of her enemy. Moreover, Shefford, himself, coordinated the security there. In all probability, they would both be there at some time, and she could easily find out when as she now had complete access to Shefford's computer system.

She needed to know about the surrounding area and what better way than being shown round properties in the area? She found the names of the villages nearest to Assington and then phoned several estate agents in Colchester and Sudbury telling them she was interested in moving into the area and needed a substantial home and grounds around ten million but for the right place, she would go as far as twenty million, if necessary, cash purchase.

It didn't take long for an estate agent to call her back with the news that although they had nothing on their books that fitted the bill exactly; they had a few large farms with substantial farmhouses where there could be the possibility of building a mansion. The agent suggested that they meet up and spend a couple of days looking at the area in detail.

Geflin said that sounded like a good plan. When asked where she would be staying, she replied "I don't rightly know."

"Well, you leave that to me. Are you driving or coming by train?"

"Train."

"Great, I will pick you up at Colchester station if you text me when leaving Liverpool Street. I will book a hotel for you and take you there," said the agent.

Geflin responded "That's very kind of you, I'll see you tomorrow," and they exchanged numbers before she ended the call.

Perfect, she thought. Now let's find out what Colchester is all about. By the middle of the afternoon, she had found out everything important, including that it had a garrison containing all the sophisticated weaponry of a modern parachute regiment. She planned to check out the security of the garrison, figuring it would be impossible for it to be as good as Shefford's, on the basis that the army wouldn't have the funds to afford it.

CHAPTER EIGHTY-THREE

THE FOLLOWING MORNING, Geflin took the tube to Liverpool Street where she caught the 0900 train to Norwich; the second stop was Colchester, and the train was relatively empty. She sent a text to the estate agent advising him that the train should arrive at Colchester 09:40, which he acknowledged.

She got off the train and headed towards the exit where a guy on the other side of the barrier was holding a clip board with "Ben Martin" written on it. They shook hands. The agent handed "Ben" his card and ushered "him" to his car.

Leaving the station car park they took the Sudbury

Road, and as they drove "Ben" explained he was a venture capitalist and his first venture was just established in a science park in Cambridge, and although the city was good the surrounding countryside was rather featureless. "That's why I am looking around the Essex/ Suffolk border. I can keep my plane at Cambridge, and it would be a short helicopter flight to Cambridge Airport from the part of the county I am looking at."

They turned off the road at Leavenheath and headed towards Sackers Green, which was where the first farm was. "It's 900 hectares," he said.

"What's that in acres?"

"About two thousand," the agent replied.

"I really only want about 20 to 25 acres!"

"I am showing this to you first as it has a large Georgian farmhouse with stables and out-buildings which could be converted into a large mansion, the building is not listed so within reason you could do anything with it," the agent explained.

"But what would I do with all that land? I am a venture capitalist, not a farmer!"

"That's the bonus—you could contract it out and get an income of around a million pounds a year or break it up into smaller manageable parcels as these would sell at a premium price greater than the current price of the whole property," the agent replied.

"Ben" asked the price and was told, "Twenty-three million pounds. I would guarantee you a premium of at least a thousand per acre sold, providing you commission us exclusively."

"So, what you're saying is, if I agree, I will get around two million net, my entire capital outlay back, and a Georgian farmhouse for nothing?"

"That's about it," the agent agreed.

"What's the timescale?"

"It could be done and dusted within the year," stated the agent.

They turned into the farm entrance. It was about four hundred yards from the road. "If the deal is so good, why haven't you taken it up?"

"Can't get my hands on twenty- three million; believe me I have tried, even with a consortium of friends we just cannot raise enough with the constraints our banks place on us."

"So how are you going to make money if I agree to this?"

"Fees and commission should net the business close to a million from buyer and seller," he said.

They parked in front of the farmhouse, where the red-faced owner came out to greet them and for introductions to take place before he showed them around his house. The owner asked if they would like a drink, which both declined, but he helped himself to a very large malt whiskey.

The farmhouse needed serious attention, but Geflin's real interest was the land. South-west of the farm was Assington. The furthest extent of the land was a little under a mile from the Priory, and at that point was the highest place for a radius of 20 miles, with a water tower on the peak. When Geflin spotted the tower, she saw the perfect place to launch an attack on Assington.

Back at the farmhouse, she asked about the neighbours. Nothing of interest except the southern part of his land, and the road separating it from Assington Priory. The farmer said it was now the home of the Earth Corp guy, "You must have seen him or heard about the threat we all face because of global warming. The place is like Fort Knox, the security is way over the top for this part of Essex, no merchant or professional tradesman can turn up without a timed appointment; nobody goes beyond the main entrance, tradesmen are escorted to their work and two security guards stay until the work is finished!"

Geflin was very satisfied with the deal, and the estate agent took her back to Colchester station. She didn't need to stay on to look at any other properties after all.

CHAPTER EIGHTY-FOUR

WHEN SHE ARRIVED back at Canary Wharf, she phoned the number that Alberto had given her and it was answered by Luigi Baratolli, head of the UK Mafia. Alberto had warned him to expect a call from "Ben Martin" on the encrypted phone line. A meeting was arranged at Luigi's favourite restaurant for lunchtime.

The restaurant was in Camden Town, and she took a taxi from Canary Wharf, arriving early as the journey wasn't hampered by the heavy traffic she had come to expect and to heartily dislike, unlike her apartment and the area itself.

As she approached the restaurant, the door was opened,

and she was greeted by the head waiter, "Good afternoon, sir, have you a reservation?"

She replied, "No, but I am meeting Mr Baratolli for lunch."

"Ah, you must be the guest he is expecting. Mr Baratolli uses our private dining room as the restaurant gets extremely busy at lunchtimes," she was told, looking bemused at all the empty tables as she was shown to the private dining room.

Inside, he explained that the whole building was bugged by the serious crime force, except that room, which was safe and scanned frequently, and asked, "Can I get you a drink?"

She replied, "a glass of Frascati would be nice."

Left alone in the dining room, she admired the paintings which adorned the walls. They were landscapes of various parts of Italy and well done, but she didn't recognise the name of the artist and made a point of asking the waiter when he came back with her drink.

He told her they were painted by his daughter. "She is an art student at Naples University. The restaurant buys all her work, so she has an independent income and can concentrate on her work."

"She certainly has a gift. These are really good; you almost feel that you're looking at the view and not at a painting. You can almost hear the sea lapping on the sand! Most certainly I would buy some of them if you ever ran out of room," Geflin told him.

"I'll bear that in mind. Would you like to see the menu?" he asked, but she declined, saying she would wait for

Luigi—which was not long at all, and she was still admiring the paintings when he came in.

He introduced himself, and they shook hands. "I see you are admiring my niece's work," he observed.

Geflin responded, "Yes, she is very talented."

He smiled and ushered "Ben" to the table. They both sat down and were brought the menus. They ordered a light lunch before getting down to business.

"Alberto has told me to assist you, so how can I help?" Luigi asked.

"Ben" replied, "I need a hand-held rocket launcher and three missiles, two incendiaries, one explosive, a sniper rifle with fifteen hundred metres' range, and 12 pounds of Semtex."

"What timescale are we looking at? This is a bit of a special order!" he said. "Ben" said by the end of the month would do, but sooner if possible.

"I'll see what I can do. You realise it's going to be expensive? Close to seventy-five thousand, I'd say, and cash, as it's not so traceable. I don't know who or what you're going to hit, but I imagine it will make headlines and that's going to cause a lot of flack. The least I know about it and the target the better for both of us," Luigi said.

They finished lunch, and she got a taxi back to Canary Wharf, which took three times as long as getting there.

CHAPTER EIGHTY-FIVE

AS SHE ENTERED HER APARTMENT, the telephone notified her of a message. It was from the estate agent asking her to phone him as soon as possible. She retrieved his business card and rang his mobile number. Voicemail came on and she left a message that she would be home for the next few hours.

Now she had a target, and soon the means to take out the target, so all she needed were some fall guys to take the blame for the atrocity. The attack on Assington would be a suicide mission for them. The Semtex would make suicide bomb vests which she would detonate remotely after she had fired the missiles, and all she had to do was recruit three suitable unsuspecting people.

She had considered the homeless littering the London streets at night, but the police would soon realise they had been set up. She would do better to find some anarchists or jihadists. She discounted the jihadists because of the worldwide truce, so by a process of elimination, anarchists won the dubious honour of dying for the cause of Geflin's revenge.

It was relatively easy to find information on them. The newspapers were full of stories about them protesting and being arrested. From the reports of court appearances, she got a list of names, and from the names, she found addresses, including three names with the same address.

The following day, she would take a ride out and reconnoitre, find out where they drank and try to befriend them. She needed them alive as the assault on Assington might still be a month away, she couldn't afford to have bodies hanging around for any length of time and any forensic examiner would easily discover that they were dead before they exploded if she planted them at the scene.

She rang a florist and ordered several exotic plants and flowers, which she would use to make up the drugs she might need to keep her prey fresh but oblivious to what was going on. Satisfied with her plans, she spent an hour in her gym.

The phone rang. It was the agent calling back to tell her that the farmer had received a visit from one of his neighbours, from Assington Priory. "They take their security very seriously there and believe the water tower close to their property is a real risk, so until they find a permanent solution, they want permission to place security guards there for the foreseeable future."

Geflin was seething inside but calmly said, "you told me that Anglian Water own the actual tower, and I am not interested in the land, can't you parcel it up as we discussed? And if it's that important to them, perhaps they will pay a premium to own it."

"Good idea. I'll get back to you," he replied. She hung up.

She was furious. "How do they know what I have planned?" she raged. It had to be the drone she had used which suggested an aerial attack was planned, they could trace it back to the shop, but hopefully not to her as she had paid cash and taken steps to evade the possibility of full facial recognition from the CCTV. But the farmer would have named her Ben Martin and that might be a problem.

She had two alternative identities on hand; if she ditched the Ben Martin one, she would lose a great deal of money, but the plan could still work. The water tower was just a vantage point to launch three missiles into the house, requiring a maximum of three minutes to fire. Killing the guards there would also be quick, but they would be in contact with the house security, so she would need to monitor their movements—but she could do this easily from the farmhouse at her leisure. After thinking all that through, she felt better.

CHAPTER EIGHTY-SIX

THE FOLLOWING MORNING the estate agent informed her: "They have agreed to purchase 50 acres for a million, the land they are buying is more like a corridor than a parcel, and I told them it would make selling the land either side of it difficult, but they just agreed, the money is already in our client account, so they can start building a new road to the tower from the road that runs past their property, giving them easy access to it without going through your property and Anglian Water will be able to use the same road, so you will have more privacy."

"How long will this road take to build?" Geflin wanted to know. "They say under a week, mainly it has to be levelled, as it won't be made to motorway standard, just a substantial track," he replied.

"Fine, so how soon can the farmer move out?" she asked. The agent said that it all depended on "Ben" getting his deal in place.

"Arrange a meeting for tomorrow. I'll come in my helicopter. Make sure I can land, as I understand there is a no-fly zone in place in the area," announced Geflin.

"It's only over the Priory. If you come in via Halstead, you will miss the exclusion zone," he assured her.

"Draw up a simple contract for him to sign. We will let our legal teams sort out the details at their leisure. I want to get the builders in straightaway," she told him. "See you tomorrow."

Geflin rang the bank, opened an account in the farmer's name and transferred the twenty- three million. She set up six annuities from the new account for one million each and transferred two hundred and fifty thousand pounds from each to her UK account and organised bank drafts for the same amounts to be picked up by a courier. These were to make sure his workers didn't make any trouble and the whole deal would go through with no problems. She wanted that water tower at any price.

Next, she spoke to the property developer for Canary Wharf and said that although she loved the property she just couldn't get on with the traffic and would like to put it back on the market as she had bought a property in rural Essex which suited her business plans better. The developer said he was not in the position to buy back the property as they still had several others unsold, but the property market in London was booming and he gave her the name of an estate agent specialising in London apartments. She made an appointment with the agent for that afternoon.

She filed a flight plan for the farm via Halstead and then started to break down the parts of the flowers and exotic plants to make the drugs capable of incapacitating the fall guys, potions which were thousands of years old and had been used frequently by Dark Seven.

The whole process would take several hours; then the fermenting would take even longer, settling after filtration would take a week. She would then have three types of untraceable drugs, a sleeping draft, a paralysing drug affecting the body but not cognitive ability, and a psychedelic drug to induce a sense of invulnerability. Employing these drugs, she would have complete control of her fall guys if she needed to, and when the remains of them were pieced together, no traces would be left to find.

By the time the agent arrived, everything had been cleared away. She showed him around, and the guy took pictures of the whole apartment, then he sat down and said, "It's an excellent property. How much are you looking for? Are you in a hurry?"

"Around 12 million, and no hurry," she replied.

"Ok, then what I think we will do is put it up for twelve and three quarters and see what response we get. Are you happy for us to act for you? We charge a straight fee of five thousand pounds plus 10% of anything over the 12 million. If we get the asking price, that will equate to an additional

£75,000," he said. She agreed, signed the agreement, and the agent left.

CHAPTER EIGHTY-SEVEN

IT WAS TIME TO START BEFRIENDING her victims. Now she knew where they drank. She took the tube to Whitechapel; the pub was about a two-minute walk away. As she entered, the noise was tremendous, loud music, football on the screen, and people having to shout over all the background noise.

She needed to blend in; swiftly observing what other people were drinking, she ordered a similar beer and took it to a corner table, which provided a view of the whole bar. Her victims had not arrived yet.

Unintentionally, she caught the eye of a large, drunk guy in an Arsenal football shirt who was behaving like a lout and lurching threateningly towards her. "Who you are looking at, arsehole?"

"A total plonker," she replied.

People started moving purposefully away at the prospect of a fight about to start. The drunk was about to throw the first punch, but at lightning speed, two fingers hit him in the solar plexus and all his breath was taken away as he fell to the floor. Geflin bent over the stricken figure, knelt on his windpipe and told the guy never to come into that pub again when she was in it, then recruited several people to drag him out of the pub.

She went over to the bar to apologise and asked them, "Could you ring for an ambulance? When that guy gets his breath back, he will come charging in here to try to kill me and I will have to hospitalise him."

About five minutes later, the guy had got his breath back and barged back into the pub. Geflin was 20 feet from the door as he rushed towards her; two fingers to the windpipe ruptured it and he collapsed in agony, turning blue from lack of oxygen.

Fortunately for him, the ambulance arrived at that moment. Geflin told them the guy had a ruptured windpipe and needed a tube down his throat so that he could breathe, which they set about doing before rushing him to A&E. As they were loading him into the ambulance Geflin whispered in his ear, "If I see you again, I will kill you!" It felt good to see the terror in his eyes.

She went back to her seat in the pub, greeted by smiles all around and another pint on the table. "That's on the house. That guy's been a pain in the arse and certainly will not be missed in here."

It was over an hour before his victims arrived. They soon heard about what had happened, came over to her table and asked if they could join her, to which she nodded. "It seems you've done the pub a big favour getting rid of that guy," said one of them.

"He'll be in hospital for a week. They will have to rebuild his windpipe," she replied.

"What brings you to England?" the anarchist asked. "I hate my country! Two tours of Iraq and three in Afghanistan, then they told me I was no longer required! I've only known the army. They trained me to kill, and I am bloody good at it, but nobody wants mercenaries now. I came to the UK to see if I could get a security job, but I keep failing the psychological profile test because they say I have homicidal tendencies, but I have only ever killed the bad guys or enemies. I could have killed that guy, but I didn't. I knew he would come back at me, so I taught him a painful lesson—don't fuck with me."

"What were you in the army?" one of them asked.

"I was in Delta special forces, the platoon sniper, seventy-three kills, never missed a target and they put me on the scrap heap." She could tell they were buying "his" story.

"What do you think about governments?" they asked.

"Arseholes! I blame them for pulling the plug on my platoon."

"Do you agree with capitalism?" they asked.

"It only works for the rich! The rich get richer, and the poor get poorer!" Geflin retorted.

"So, you're a communist/socialist?"

"No fucking way, I have been killing those bastards!"

"So, what do you believe in?"

"Me, I don't care about anyone or anything, look after number one that's my motto." Geflin could see that they had taken the bait and would want to draw him into their tight circle of friends.

After a few more drinks, she was invited back to their flat. The flat was large and surprisingly well equipped; it belonged to the parents of the guy called Chris Gurnal whose father was a wealthy property developer and the other two also had wealthy parents, so she couldn't understand why they had turned out to be anarchists.

All three professed to hate their parents and everything they stood for, but if they were ever successful in overthrowing the elected government, they would kill the goose that laid the golden egg, since none of them worked, and they were presumably getting an allowance - the rent on the flat would have been over five thousand a month.

She needed to plant some incriminating evidence on their computers, but that could be done later once she had a definite timetable for the attack on Assington. A couple of drinks later, she caught the tube back to Canary Wharf, having planned to see them again in a couple of days as she claimed to have a few days' work.

On the tube, Geflin had a startling revelation. Dark Seven were anarchists too! They always had been; they made a profit from the chaos they caused, undermining the political will of every country. A smile crept across her face.

CHAPTER EIGHTY-EIGHT

BACK AT THE APARTMENT, there was a message on the answer phone—an offer of £12.3 million had been made by an overseas football player who wanted to move in straightaway.

It was far too late to call the agent back, so she spent a couple of hours in the gym, sweating out any remnants of alcohol.

After a shower, she worked out a date for the hit, she would need darkness, in between the old moon and the start of the new moon would be ideal, the new moon would start in 12 days, so it depended on whether she could get everything in place for a successful hit and get away with it. Her pseudo-anarchists would be easy to manipulate, but a lot hinged on how good the new security was at the water tower. Moving into the farm would allow her to keep watch on the tower at night at her leisure. Very pleased with her achievements that day, she went to bed.

In the morning Geflin phoned Biggin Hill and told them to bring her Learjet to Cambridge where it would be based in the future. After that, she called the agent and told him to accept the offer and go ahead with the sale, the apartment would be vacant by Friday.

Next, she rang the farmer and estate agent to say everything was arranged and she would be arriving at 11:30 in his helicopter, and he should have his entire workforce attend.

She got into her leathers and rode the bike back to the Kawasaki dealer. She told him that as much as she loved the bike, it really wasn't practical. Besides that, she was moving from London to a rural location where the traffic was not a problem. The dealer sympathised and offered half the amount she had paid just eight days ago, citing all sorts of reasons for the huge reduction.

She thought of killing him on the spot but refrained, instead telling him, "If you're going to pay so little for the bike, I want it in cash." He said that was no problem and disappeared into his office, coming back with a purchase invoice and the six thousand pounds.

With that deal done, she took a cab back to Canary Wharf, where she threw a case into the helicopter, radioed air traffic control and took off for the farm, climbing to five thousand feet and keeping strictly to the flight plan.

It took just under 30 minutes. She was careful to avoid the overhead power lines during the descent to the farm and landed in what used to be a paddock. The farmer came out to greet her and take her into the house, where the agent and the workers had not yet arrived.

She asked the farmer to fire up his computer, then took over and showed him the money in his account. "You need to create your own password etc. now to adopt the account. If you draw funds from it to put into your account here, there will most certainly be tax implications. You could set up an account in the Channel Islands, or Isle of Man where your tax risk will be minimised, or keep it where is and move your funds directly from the Caymans, it's your choice," she explained to the farmer who was mesmerised by the balance in his account.

"I have set up accounts for your workers, who will get £250,000 redundancy each, which, according to the advice I sought, comes free of tax. However, the annuities I have set up will be taxed if paid into a UK bank, whereas if they leave them where they are, there will be no tax liability. They would just have to rely on debit or credit cards for transactions."

When the workers and the agent arrived, she explained it all again. One at a time, they received their envelope with the banker's draft. None of them had ever imagined having so much money and was staggered. They had expected a few thousand at best. The initial shock was absorbed, and they could now concentrate on what Geflin was about to say.

She turned to the farmer and said she needed to move

in on Thursday, then she addressed his staff telling them "Today is your last day working here, gather up and take away all your personal effects, and good luck for the future!"

To the agent, she said, "As you know, I only want the farmhouse and surrounding buildings. Please organise the auction and collection of all plants by Thursday, any crops that still need to be harvested can be sold with the land they are on, which might be an added incentive for a prospective buyer, but the land being sold must not include any right of way which affects the entrance to, or encroaches on, the buildings. I am not a recluse, but I do take my privacy very seriously, so from Friday the farmhouse will be completely oof-limits. The builders start in a fortnight and once they start, I will not return until they have finished, but I have just sold my London property and need to be here on Thursday." Nobody raised any objections to any of that and their meeting was concluded.

She took off again in the helicopter and headed for Cambridge, where her Learjet was expected in an hour. What she needed now was a reliable second-hand van.

She enquired where to find the nearest place to buy a van and was pointed to a sales centre across the road. Not really knowing anything about vans, she looked for something with a price around the amount she had in cash, found one, and went into the portacabin to talk to a salesman, who reluctantly dragged himself from his desk and brought the keys for the van Geflin was interested in.

It started the first time and sounded ok. She asked whether she could take it for a test drive. With a deep sigh and a shrug of the shoulders, he fetched the trade plates and stuck them on. She found it drove well for its ninety thousand miles, and back at the centre, she said she would buy it.

The salesman immediately sprang to life as if electrified, reeling off all the things that the company would do, service, MOT, and more, and he asked how she intended to pay for it. When she replied "cash," he said that could be a problem, to prevent money laundering on sums over two thousand. "Are you able to prove where the cash came from?"

"Yes, I just sold my motorbike for six thousand pounds. Here's the purchase invoice," she told him. He said that was fine and the van would be ready for collection on Thursday. After that, she needed to get it fixed up to look like it belonged to Anglian Water and somewhere private to get that done, a lock-up preferably.

Conveniently, Luigi phoned her just then to confirm the "merchandise" was ready for collection, so she asked him whether he had any lockups in Essex where she could conceal a van temporarily, and he promised to get back to her. She then organised the cash for him via Cayman.

Back at Cambridge Airport, she organised a deal to keep the Learjet serviced and hangered, and with that done, she flew back to London in the helicopter.

All three substances had filtered, and all she had left to do was reduce the liquid by boiling off the excess water, condensing it to produce three different, dangerous, and effective drugs. She had done this so many times before that she didn't need to test them to be sure they worked.

CHAPTER EIGHTY-NINE

THE FOLLOWING MORNING, Geflin caught the train to Whitechapel, arriving at the pub early according to old habits, so she had time to line up an escape route in case one became necessary, although she could easily take out anyone in the pub who might present a threat. With that confidence, she waited for her "team" to arrive.

They were also early and surprised to see "him". She asked them what they wanted to drink and went to the bar to order a round. Seated at the table with their drinks, she asked them what they had done in the name of their cause, and Chris told her with pride that they had taken part in riots, broken windows and punched the riot police, and had been arrested several times, the others adding their agreement.

She laughed. "Well, you're not going to overthrow a government or capitalism by throwing bricks through windows and hitting a few coppers. I thought you lot were anarchists hell-bent on causing chaos through attacks which shock the world!"

"We would if we could get the weapons and explosives," they protested.

"And what would you do with them?" she asked.

"Blow up Parliament!" they declared.

"Three budding Guy Fawkes!" she exclaimed. "You're having a laugh. You would be caught before you even started! Capitalism controls governments, take out a big player or players."

"Ok, so who would you suggest?" they demanded.

"How do I bloody know? I'm American!" she retorted.

Chris went to the bar and brought a newspaper back to the table, and they started looking through it for inspiration. Geflin pointed out a large article on Earth Corp, saying, "There you are. Who's in charge of that lot?" They all knew the answer, as it had been headline news for months. "Take him and his family out. That would make a statement around the world you could be proud of." They agreed but wondered if they could get away with it. "Not if we keep discussing it here! You don't know who might overhear. We need to go back to your flat," asserted Geflin.

Back at the flat, she set them to work on the computers, searching the web for everything to do with a potential attack on Assington Priory, unwittingly creating a trail of incriminating evidence sufficient to implicate them in the planning and carrying out of the attack.

"Inside information is what we need for a successful mission, and as I am the only person with special forces training, I will do the reconnaissance. Let's meet back here in three days to see whether it's doable. We can't leave anything to luck. It has to be planned with military precision and calculation of the risk factor. The attack must only be talked about within these walls. Carry on with your normal lives and don't do anything to attract suspicion," she instructed them before she left, satisfied that her team were fired up and engrossed in doing something she had led them to believe was meaningful for their cause.

CHAPTER NINETY

STEPHEN AND I WERE BACK at Assington. We were both wading through reports.

His were from his security team, including the news that there had been a potential drone attack on Cheltenham, just a reconnaissance drone that had collected no substantive intelligence before it had been taken out.

Using the signal to try to find the operator had indicated a general direction, but the unit had gone dead, and a team sent out to search found nothing. Likewise, the CCTV revealed nothing, although the audio had picked up sounds of a motorbike in that area. Forensic sound investigation suggested a 99% probability that it was a Kawasaki Ninja.

Of the five hundred and seventy-five thousand built,

seventy-three thousand were sold in the UK, and they were waiting for a reply from the manufacturer giving names and registration numbers, but they kept stalling, quoting the Data Protection Act. "The likelihood of getting this information is virtually zero, so there are alerts now in place across both sites for an unfriendly on two wheels," he summarised.

I said to him, "Aren't we over-reacting a bit? I bet it was the paparazzi. They are always trying to get photo scoops of what we are doing."

"Not this time," he replied.

"Remember, you control most of the media and why would the others pay for something that you give them freely at your weekly briefings? It's a gut feeling but Geflin is out for revenge and she's in the UK, so we should be very worried."

"How on earth can you come to that conclusion from a report of a reconnaissance drone?" I demanded.

"I told you, it's a gut feeling. I would say that an attack is imminent. With the funds she has, she could buy an army of mercenaries, but it's become personal. She wants us dead, and she will want to kill us herself," he said.

"But it's impossible for her to get inside here or Cheltenham to harm us," I objected.

"That's it! So, she will have to attack from the outside!" he exclaimed and summoned the helicopter pilot.

We were in the air inside for five minutes, hovering over Assington and moving gradually outwards in increasing circles. The only elevations of use to reach

Assington were the pylons and two water towers. The pylons went from east to west with the nearest to Assington about two thousand metres away, the water tower to the north of them was the closest at a thousand metres, and the other about three thousand metres.

Stephen told the pilot to get level with the tops of the towers from which we could see that the one to the north was not just closest to the Priory but also had a direct line of sight to it. From the other tower, vision was obscured by trees, and only part of the roof could be seen. The pilot could not get too close to the pylons, but while there was a clear sight of the Priory from two of them, the proximity to the high voltage line made them an unlikely choice, plus access to them would involve using a vehicle leaving tracks easy to follow by satellite across a wheat field.

Stephen wanted a closer look at the nearest tower, which was on a neighbour's farmland. He had been vetted when the initial security at Assington had been set up, and while none of the neighbours were aware of it, they all passed scrutiny.

He phoned the farmer to ask for permission to go to inspect the tower, which was owned by Anglian Water, who had the only right of way. The farmer was more than willing to show us to the tower, and we went, taking a couple of Stephen's men with us. We called at the farm to pick him up, and after introductions, continued to the tower.

I stayed in the car talking to the farmer. I had been so busy that this was the first chance I'd had to speak to any of the neighbours. I hadn't even been to the local pub.

The farmer told me he had just sold the farm to an American for 23 million and he wanted to move in by the end of the month. I said, "I didn't even know it was for sale! I might have been interested in it had I known."

"Well, I have no one to leave the farm to and I am getting too old to run it, and so are my employees, we're all past retirement age, and none of us has a pension because we never got round to it. Now I will be able to put a million into an annuity for them all and I'm not likely to run out of money. We can all have a well-deserved rest," he told me.

"I hope it all works out well for you," I replied. "Is the guy a farmer?"

"No, he's a venture capitalist," he replied.

"Farming is not very venture capitalist!" I remarked.

"Apparently, he really only wants the buildings to turn into a luxury home. The estate agent who is acting for me has put a deal together which more or less guarantees to return him 25 million within 12 months by parcelling up the land into much smaller lots, meaning he gets the house for nothing," he explained.

"Not a bad deal!" I said, "Why don't you do it yourself?"

"Capital gains tax. It would reduce the amount by half, but the buyer said he could, and would, pay the whole amount into a bank in Cayman Brac," he said.

A cold shudder went down my back and I asked him, "What's his name?"

"Ben Martin" he replied.

I saw from the car window that Stephen had made quick work of getting in and up to the top of the tower, looking directly at the Priory, where the entire house was in full view; clearly, if anyone was going to attack the place, that was an ideal place from which to do so.

When Stephen and his men got back into the vehicle, he reported that there was a clear line of sight to the house at a distance of twelve hundred metres, and I told him that the farm was about to be sold to an American called Ben Martin. The farmer added enthusiastically, "It's an amazing deal for me! I will keep most of my money, no capital gains tax to pay as he's putting the funds offshore in Cayman Brac!" I didn't need to read Stephen's mind to know he, too, had experienced a cold shudder.

Stephen phoned his New York office and ordered a full report on Ben Martin, venture capitalist, as a priority one request. He turned to the farmer and set out his concern about the water tower, its potential use to harm us at Assington, and that the threat needed to be removed.

"With your permission, I want to have my men guard the tower until a long-term solution can be found, is that ok with you?"

"I have no problem with that. Anglian Water own the tower although it's on my land, but the new owner might have some objections. I will talk to my estate agent to find out what his client thinks about it," he said.

A while later, the estate agent phoned us and said that it was not a problem for us to place guards at the tower, but the land was for sale if we wanted to secure access to it permanently.

So, a deal was done, rather expensive, but we now

owned the land, controlled the access and could put a new road in. The report on Ben Martin showed nothing unusual, and our fear subsided. If Geflin was behind the farmhouse purchase, surely she would have backed out of it when we bought the land with the tower.

CHAPTER NINETY-ONE

LUIGI CONTACTED GEFLIN and suggested lunch at the same place as their previous meeting to conclude their business. The venue needed to be free from surveillance—she couldn't risk anything going wrong now; she was so close to exacting the revenge she so badly wanted.

They exchanged identical briefcases and said nothing, which would indicate more than a regular business meeting. His car took her back to her apartment for her last night there, which she would spend erasing all evidence and forensic clues to who had lived there.

The following morning, she flew her helicopter to her new home. The farmer was still there but in the last stages of moving out. He was leaving all his furniture—which was not part of the deal—but he had nowhere to put it at such short notice and really didn't care since he wasn't coming back to Essex in the foreseeable future. Everything he wanted was already in the Range Rover, so they shook hands and he left.

She could now explore at leisure the farmhouse and outside buildings. Although there were plenty of places she could have hidden the van, she decided she would still use Luigi's safe house and keep her fellow anarchists there too if need be.

She ordered a taxi to take her to Cambridge to pick up the van and then drove to Stowmarket, to an army surplus shop on an industrial estate where she purchased camouflage jackets, boots, trousers and face paint, then went on to Sudbury to purchase four mobile phones which would be used for detonating the jackets.

Out of the briefcase, she took the address of the lock-up and tapped it into the sat-nav, which said it was 6.7 miles from Sudbury off the Bures Road.

It took about ten minutes, so many lefts and right she was totally disorientated, but eventually, it said she had reached her destination, although there was nothing to be seen from the van, so she got out to have a good look. About fifty yards away on the right, there was a padlocked gate; the key in the briefcase opened the padlock. She opened the gate, drove in and closed and padlocked the gate again behind her. The drive was quite narrow between bushes that scratched the side of the van.

About 400 yards in, there was what appeared even close

up to be a large derelict barn and a ramshackle house. The same key opened the padlock to the barn, and inside was another new garage, containing everything she needed. Not knowing where exactly she was, she looked up the postcode, and it turned out to be just 2.7 miles from the farm, which was a bonus.

She went outside the garage/barn and looked round for a high vantage point. There was a tall tree, and she climbed it like a cat, past the canopy of vegetation to about a hundred feet from where she had a full view of her surroundings. She saw the water tower and she could see her farmhouse directly west. To the north was the village pub.

She had three hours before sunset and set about covering the van with a convincing Anglian Water livery. She intended to work in natural light, avoiding using electricity and any evidence of her presence, just in case. She was determined nothing would go wrong. Now she was so close, and everything seemed to be going her way.

She finished her task, locked up and followed the sunset on foot to her farmhouse, which took longer than she thought as she followed the headland for about a mile before crossing the road and continuing to the road entrance to her farm. She collected her things from the helicopter and went indoors for a shower.

She had decided that Ben Martin, the new owner of Whitehouse Farm, should visit the local pub and introduce himself to the village. Dressed in expensive casual clothes, she set off to walk to the pub, which would have been a 35-

minute walk, but one of the farm hands in his new car stopped and asked if she wanted a lift. She ordered a pint and asked for the menu, was told about the day's specials, and ordered Shepherd's pie and veg. She really didn't know what to expect, but she was pleasantly surprised when it came.

The landlord came over to ask if everything was alright with the food, she nodded confirmation, and he asked if she was the new owner of Whitehouse Farm, she replied that she was, and he held out his hand saying, "Welcome to Assington!"

He returned to the bar where there were three burly men, sure to be security from the Priory, as they had special forces written all over them. She knew that they were monitoring her and would report back that they had seen the neighbour who had sold the land around the water tower.

After her meal, she went to the bar and ordered another drink, starting up a conversation with the landlord loud enough for the security guys to overhear, a means of drawing them into conversation, so she could feed them the information she wanted them to report back to their masters along the lines of "he's rich, no interest in the land, fed up with the traffic in London and wants rural seclusion" which would reinforce what the old owner would probably have told them.

Later on, the security team offered "him" a lift home, which "he" accepted. Tomorrow she would need to get a car and base it at the farm; the security team had a Range Rover, and she thought one of those would do nicely.

CHAPTER NINETY-TWO

IN THE MORNING, she searched eBay for Range Rovers, and there were hundreds to choose from. A Colchester used car dealer had a four-year-old Vogue five-litre petrol in black with tinted windows for thirty-five thousand pounds, so she rang the estate agent and asked him to buy it on her behalf, which he agreed to do as this client was one hell of a gravy train, from whom the agency were about to make a small fortune. He would pick her up at the farm the next day and drive her to the dealer to pick it up. After she picked up her Range Rover, she would see her anarchists and tell them the plan.

The following day, the estate agent arrived and took her

to collect the vehicle. She was quite impressed with it for its size; it handled like a car.

She put the Whitechapel address in the sat-nav and headed off to meet her team. She gave them the outline of the plan and set the date for the coming Thursday when she would come back and pick them up and go through the final details. She needed to know they were definitely up for participating, or whether she would need the drugs to kidnap them and plant their bodies at the scene.

Over the next few days, she visited the lock-up and finalised all the preparations. The camouflage jackets were now converted unobtrusively to suicide vests and would be set off by one phone call. She had made several stealth trips to the tower at night and knew the guards' routine. She would have a maximum of 14 minutes before the main house realised something was wrong, which should be plenty of time to climb to the top of the tower and fire the three missiles.

The day of the attack arrived, and she went to fetch the anarchists. She took her time in finding a car park when she got there, before choosing one in Halcrow Street. From there, it took 15 minutes to reach the pub and her anarchists were already there. She got herself a drink from the bar and took it to their table, telling them quietly, "It's on for tonight. Are you still up for it?" They were speechless, but all nodded. She continued in a low voice, "I have borrowed a Range Rover and some of the guy's clothes. He's in Spain for a month, so he won't even know it's missing. I'll put it back when we have finished with it. I want you to all leave separately and make your way to the Halcrow car park, where our car is at the rear corner furthest away from CCTV cameras, try to avoid letting any of the cameras get a clear view of your faces. Chris, you sit in the passenger seat, Rick- behind him, and Tom in the rear on the driver's side. Once we're in the car, we will be invisible from the outside, so nobody knows how many of us there are. I'm going to drive somewhere where I will explain the rest of the plan."

Twenty minutes later, they were heading north towards Epping Forest, but the traffic was shocking, and it took three quarters of an hour to get there. Without the risk of being overheard, she explained the details of the plan.

First, they would pick up some food and drink on the way to the safe lock-up. In the morning, he would go on foot to the tower and take out the three guards. "You will drive the van to this farmhouse"—pointing it out on the map—"and you will stay there until I phone you to come to the tower, use dipped headlights. We have a 14-minute time frame. I need five minutes to climb the tower and fire the missiles, so when you arrive, Chris, you bring the launcher and missiles; Tom and Rick, you will tie up the guards, and after ten minutes, we will pull out to ensure we get away. The eight hundred yards from the farmhouse should take less than two minutes. From the start, within seven minutes we will have pulled off the biggest hit on capitalism and you guys will have made a statement the world will remember for centuries, like a modern-day but successful Gunpowder Plot. We will have at least seven minutes to get away as far as possible. You will take the van at least a hundred miles away before torching it, and I will see you at the pub a week from today."

She could tell the adrenalin was flowing through their veins. The plan was quite simple, but they went over it again and again. They stopped at a Subway in Waltham Abbey and loaded up with baguettes and soft drinks.

When they arrived around 8 o'clock, she told them to wait in the car and not to get out until inside the garage. She unlocked the gate and drove through, pulling the gate closed but not locking it this time. Inside, she showed them their camouflage gear and the face paint and assured them that wearing it would render them virtually invisible. It was now a waiting game. She checked out the launcher again and adjusted the sight and range finder—one less thing to do when on top of the tower.

When they had polished off the food and drink, the clear up began. Everything they had brought in was put in black sacks; every possible surface wiped clean to remove fingerprints. There was only a hand-held Dyson, but it was remarkably powerful, and any DNA evidence left after that would only be found by a highly intense forensic examination, which was unlikely due to the cost.

It was time to go, but with a slight change of plan. Geflin accompanied them to the farmhouse to ensure they were in the right position and put her nearer the tower. Satisfied, and with her blowpipe and darts at hand, she made short work of the distance to the tower where the guards were in their normal positions. She rapidly darted all three who clutched their necks and fell to the floor, paralysed. She phoned the lads and set the timer, picked the lock and was into the tower.

The van arrived, and Chris ran across with the launcher and missiles. Geflin got to the top of the tower, loaded the first missile and fired, loaded the second and fired, then the third. All gone in 12 seconds she saw, glancing at her watch. She looked back to follow the trajectory of the missiles.

The first was about to hit its target when it disappeared and the whole area surrounding the house turned a deep orangey-red colour; the second and third followed and met the same thing. Out of this coloured haze, a beam tracked the trajectory of the missiles back to the tower where she was still holding the launcher which started to dissolve in front of her eyes.

She threw it at the beam and jumped backwards out of its path, but in doing so dropped her phone, which hit the ground close to where Chris Gurnel was standing. He picked it up. She came hurtling down the ladder, hissing urgently, "Abort! abort! See you in the pub in a week, don't forget to torch the van!"

CHAPTER NINETY-THREE

GEFLIN DISAPPEARED INTO THE WOODS, where she got out of her camouflage gear. Underneath, she had her stealth suit on and made it back to the lock-up, effected a quick change of clothes in the Range Rover then shot off to Cambridge where she checked in at the Holiday Inn, telling them she was supposed to be flying that evening but a replacement part had still not arrived so she thought she might as well get some proper kip.

She was handed the key and went to the room, lay on the bed and reflected that everything had worked like clockwork except the destruction of Assington and its inhabitants.

Even the anarchists might have blown themselves up.

Chris might well have picked up her phone after she dropped it and she had heard what sounded like an explosion while she was in the woods, making her way back to the farmhouse. That would present investigators with a forensic nightmare and if they had survived, she could still deal with them using the drugs she had prepared, when she met them the following week. No real loose ends, no way to implicate "Ben Martin" and she could still go back to Assington.

She had wasted about a hundred thousand on the hit. She started to analyse what had failed, but it was nothing she had done. The failure was down to Assington's defences. They apparently had some impenetrable force field encompassing the whole building and which she had not anticipated, let alone been able to counter.

She knew she had been off the radar for several years, but she also knew that force fields had been discovered. She got her laptop to see what she could find out but came up with nothing, which meant little as, presumably, it must be a highly classified military secret and she had no existing contacts who might help get information.

It looked as though she would have to accept that the only way to get to her enemies would be face to face, to breach the security constantly surrounding them. She recalled that every Friday in the afternoon, the top man held a press conference where there would be lots of people, a security nightmare. She needed to get a gun into the conference centre, which she could easily do the night before, then she would need a diversion, maybe like a fire alarm. She could retrieve the gun and take out both her main adversaries before making her escape all under cover of the confusion. Only bullets could stop her because her martial arts skills would outmatch anyone who wasn't a member of Dark Seven.

Confident she could escape afterwards, Geflin looked for a way into Media Headquarters. The layout of the building was available as a public record, and the conference hall media centre was on the first floor. Security would be at the entrance, so she needed was to find a toilet on the first floor where she could hide the gun. It wasn't a new building, so the toilets were all against the outside walls of the building to accommodate the waste pipes, and therefore accessible from the outside.

She needed more information, and using the co-ordinates to get a satellite view, she saw that at the rear of the building was the rubbish collection point, a couple of skips and several wheely bins. She was watching live and observed that there was still quite some activity in the early hours of the morning. She could not be sure, but the toilet windows seemed to be above the skips. The outside light was timed and came on as people entered the yard.

It all looked fairly easy, but in two hours it would be light, which meant she would have to wait for the next Friday as it would be impossible to be ready in time for later that same day. She would normally have to do a full recce of the site and have assets deployed around the hit, to create the diversion. Her hatred was clouding her judgement and spurring her on to accept no delays. She kept telling herself she could do it. What she had seen just a few hours ago was something else. The protection surrounding that man was formidable, but she was going to do this, it was becoming increasingly personal. She fell asleep.

CHAPTER NINETY-FOUR

SHE PUT THE TELEVISION NEWS ON when she woke up. The headlines were an attack and attempted assassination of the CEO of Earth Corp and his family at Assington Priory. There were fatalities as three unidentifiable bodies were found nearby, but no further details. As a result, the Earth Corp. conference for that day had been cancelled and rescheduled for the following day, Saturday.

She leapt out of bed. This was great news. She now had the chance to infiltrate the building, after all, hide the gun and the incendiary device that night, and collect and activate the device in the morning before the conference started.

She needed a press pass to get into the place. She had

several filed on her laptop with different names but all female. She got showered and dressed as Ben Martin, then took a selfie, which she used to replace the one on the ID tag.

Later that day, Geflin drove to Redbridge at the end of the M11. She had everything she needed in her rucksack and took the Tube to Marble Arch.

It was approaching midnight when she reached her target. Media Corp offices were in operation 24/7. She made her way to the rear of the building. Two cameras were facing the barrier, which meant both had blind spots, and if she kept close to the wall, no one would see her enter the delivery area.

Once inside the yard, she changed into her stealth suit and became almost invisible, especially to surveillance cameras. Using her suction pads, she climbed the wall to a first-floor window, where the quarter light was open. Reaching in, she opened the large window and climbed in.

She was exactly where she wanted to be, and amazed at how easy it was, she concealed the gun and incendiary device in the toilet cistern then left the way she came. Her confidence was boosted. This would be an easy hit, panic that would ensue after the shots were fired, and she would shout that there were suicide bombers, which would increase the confusion amidst which she would make her escape, as she had done so many times before - a piece of cake.

She put her clothes on over the stealth suit and went off to book in a room at the Hilton in order to get a few hours' sleep.

Upon arriving at Media Corps for the press conference, Geflin passed through security easily; it was very busy, and that suited her. She went up to the first floor and found the cloakroom where she had concealed her gun and the incendiary device which she activated to go off at 10:30, tucked the gun inside her trouser belt and walked into the conference hall, where she took a seat in the third row in front of the lectern. She was no more than 40 feet away and with eight shots inside two seconds, she could take out three or even four of her targets. She just had to wait for the alarm to sound and she had the advantage of knowing what time it would go off. The clock steadily ticked away.

When the alarm finally sounded, Geflin leapt up, fired two shots and almost simultaneously, several shots hit her. She was dead before she hit the floor.

CHAPTER NINETY-FIVE

THE POSTPONED WEEKLY MEETING attracted more press than normal. The attack on Assington Priory was world news, and it was only to be expected that the world's press would be there. I had lost the argument with Stephen about extra armed security. He was positive that there would be an attack on my life, and he used Tosh's men to bolster my personal security to ensure my safety.

It had been over 24 hours since the attack. The police forensics team had a terrible task of sorting through the remains of the presumed attackers, but they had managed to get fingerprints and identify all three. Scotland Yard would keep Stephen fully appraised of the investigation.

The names meant nothing to me, and my only concern was whether it was an organised attack of which they were part or just an opportunist attack planned by the three of them.

We left the Priory. Understandably, Sue was still in shock after the attack, and however much I tried to explain that we would always be safe, she still fretted. "I have to continue with my work and life must go on. I dare say this won't be the last attempt on my life, but I must carry on. We can't let those people who are against me force me to change direction. There is too much at stake," I tried to reassure her, but I knew this conversation was not over yet and would surely be continued later.

Stephen and I travelled in the verticular while my enlarged security team went the hard way, by helicopter and in vehicles. We would get a two-hour head start at Media Corps while they caught up.

Conrad was in his office putting the finishing touches to the script for the press conference as we came in. He ordered us some coffee and handed me the script, which I quickly scanned, noticing there was no mention of the attack, but before I could say anything about it, he pointed out that the question session at the end would be all about the attack, and there was information we needed to get out there as a priority before we got to that.

There had been some fantastic news. In three regions in Africa where we had purchased land, we had found water—brackish but could be filtered cheaply to make it safe for drinking—enough to support ten thousand people, according to our geologists. That would be the start to enable us to build the factories which would make the white energy units to replace the electric motors which depend on fossil-fuel-generated electricity.

Alec had some promising results from the universities, so much so that he had committed nearly a billion of his budget on the projects. I read the detailed report, but it was too much science for me to understand properly; doubtless, it would go over the heads of the press in attendance too, but if they took the press release, hopefully, their science editors could translate it into normal language. I made some changes to the script, and it was put on the autocue.

It was time to take to the stage, so we made our way to the conference centre, my newly bolstered security team surrounding me as we entered the room, and they escorted me to the lectern. Stephen and Tosh were either side of me, another man directly behind me, four more were stationed in front of the lectern, all in contact with each other via radio. They were tense and alert despite having all angles covered. The conference centre was packed as I started to speak. The script was over an hour-long as there was a lot of information to impart, and all questions would be answered at the end of the speech.

Halfway through my speech, the fire alarm sounded, causing confusion, and like lightning, someone in the ranks of the press in front of the lectern pulled out a gun and fired two shots directly at me. Stephen pushed me aside and took both bullets in his chest in the process. Almost simultaneously, Tosh had fired a couple of shots at the assassin's head, two of his men in front on the lectern had also fired, and the assassin was dead before he hit the ground.

Stephen was dying! I picked him up and rushed to the rear exit. I had to get him to a hospital and on a heart and lung machine or he would bleed to death before we could mend his heart. Tissue takes time to repair. Tears were welling up in my eyes as I burst through the fire exit knowing that the verticular would be there and could get me to a hospital in seconds.

It was there, but it was covered in a sparkling, shimmering mist. I rushed towards it and the mist enveloped me. Inside the mist was what looked like a coffin. Something told me to place him inside it. The lid came down and Stephen was totally enclosed. I soon realised this was not Utopian technology but was still familiar; of course! Infinity had come to help me. Once I had realised that, we communicated through my mind. Infinity told me that Stephen would be completely healed, but Oblivion's handiwork was about to hit the earth's crust so to be prepared. Oblivion's plan must fail for the sake of the universe. He had gone from this part of the universe to rebuild his strength elsewhere.

The lid of the "coffin" opened. Stephen looked dead, but any notion was soon dispelled as his eyes snapped open and his first word was "wow!" The "coffin" and the mist disappeared, leaving a wide-eyed Stephen prone but very much alive. With tears of joy now streaming down my face, I helped him to his feet, and we walked back into the conference hall.

We hadn't been gone over five minutes, but I expected the hall would have been cleared; however, it was still full of the press who were naturally unwilling to leave the best story in town. Security had called the police, who were now on the scene, and the assassin was in a body bag. Stephen went over to the body bag and unzipped the top to have a look at what was left of the face of the killer after several low-velocity bullets to the head. He thought he recognised him.

Stephen himself was now becoming the centre of attention, everyone could see the bullet holes and his blood-soaked shirt and suit, and how many photos were taken of him we would find out the following day when it would be the front-page news story all over the world.

I took him aside and pointed out that the press were busy speculating about him and how he was still alive; we had to come up with a convincing story, and the press weren't going anywhere soon. We went up to the apartment and found a change of clothes. He quickly showered.

In the mirror, he was stunned to find there were no signs of bullet wounds or even any scar tissue. Even the scars from previous times he had been shot had disappeared, he told me as came out of the bathroom. "Well, that's good news!" I said. "We can say that your bullet-proof vest worked, and the blood was from a nosebleed when you hit the lectern. You can open your shirt and show them your chest, so they will have to accept your explanation. No way would they believe what really happened!"

We took the lift back down to the conference centre,

where Professor Dave Mac was anxiously waiting to tell me that what he feared most had started. "I know," I replied.

THE SEVEN HOUSES OF DARK SEVEN

The Houses divide up the world into areas, with a daughter responsible for Dark Seven's influence and activity in each.

- The House of Sheflin - Daughter based in Prague - Former communist Europe
- The House of Lanlin - Daughter based in Paris - Democratic Europe
- The House of Geflin - Daughter based in New York - North and South America
- The House of Caflin - Daughter based in Sydney - Australasia
- The House of Feflin - Daughter based in Hong Kong - East Asia
- The House of Tewlin - Daughter based in Pretoria - Africa and Indian sub-continent
- The House of Deflin - Daughter based in London - UK and former colonial territories, excluding Africa, India and Australasia

Girls are born and raised in Messapth, where they stay until age seven go to Tibet to learn the special martial arts. After seven years in Tibet, at age 14, they move on to Zurich to the exclusive finishing school, and seven years later, they leave to take up their duties in their respective geographical areas. After another seven years, they return to Messapth to have daughters of their own with their studs, and so the cycle of evil continues. The only exception to the rule is Deflin, who has been allowed to marry and have a daughter in the outside world because of the usefulness of her husband.

Thanks for reading! Please leave a short review on Amazon, and let me know what you thought!

www.ingramcontent.com/pod-product-compliance
Lightning Source LLC
LaVergne TN
LVHW010307200726
843507LV00010B/1181